MY PLACE IN THE BAZAAR

BLOOMSBURY READER

Discover books by Alec Waugh published by
Bloomsbury Reader at
www.bloomsbury.com/AlecWaugh

MY PLACE IN THE BAZAAR

ALEC WAUGH

BLOOMSBURY READER

LONDON · NEW DELHI · NEW YORK · SYDNEY

This electronic edition published in 2011 by Bloomsbury Reader

Bloomsbury Reader is a division of Bloomsbury Publishing Plc,

50 Bedford Square, London WC1B 3DP

ISBN: 978 1 4482 0115 0
eISBN: 978 1 4482 0247 8

Visit www.bloomsburyreader.com to find out more about our authors and their books
You will find extracts, author interviews, author events and you can sign up for
newsletters to be the first to hear about our latest releases and special offers

Printed and bound by CPI Group (UK) Ltd, Croydon, CR0 4YY

MIX
Paper from
responsible sources
FSC
www.fsc.org   FSC® C013604

Contents

Foreword

Iwrote my first novel when I was seventeen. I am now sixty-two. In the intervening years I have published over forty books. They fill two library shelves. I sometimes survey them wistfully. They were written with high excitement and delivered to their publishers with heady hope: presented to the public in shining covers and advertised glowingly in the Sunday Press, they enjoyed, one or two of them, a brief, bright summer of approval; then one by one they went off the market. Of the books published before 1956, only three are still in print, two of them precariously. My only novel that has been consistently in circulation is the first I wrote—*The Loom of Youth*.

I do not expect that any of its 'between-the-wars' successors will be reissued. They dealt with problems that the world has solved or shelved, with situations that could not arise today, with a way of living that has vanished and with characters who were the product of those problems, those situations and that way of life. Occasionally, a sociological novel will survive as a museum piece, as a picture of a period. But I make no such claim for stories like *The Balliols* and *Kept*. I console myself with the reflection that not only many pleasant but even certain noble wines lack longevity, particularly those of Burgundy. And, in my devotion to the grape, I have always been a Burgundian rather than a Bordelais.

Yet even so a writer is reluctant to accept forty years of authorship as the pouring of so much water through a sieve. Are all those titles tombstones? Can nothing be rescued? A novel is a substantial piece of merchandise to salvage; a novel is complete in itself, it must be presented as a whole; but might there not be scattered among my twenty miscellaneous books stray passages and chapters that could be extracted and placed in a different setting? Had I not more than once filled a book with makeweight material so as to get two or three favourite pieces between covers? Might it not be possible to compress a dozen books into one or two, finding in each one something of contemporary appeal?

Rereading some of my old books with this in view, it did seem to me that the stories that have been assembled here, possess a certain undated homogeneity. The first was written in 1920, the last in 1952. They deal with different periods and places, with the First World War, with the London of the 1920s and the 1930s; with the Far East and the Caribbean, with second war counterespionage. But they have this in common: they are told in the first person singular. They are not autobiographical. Their 'I' is the observer and the recorder. But they are intimate in the sense that there is a direct contact between the author and the reader. I have always enjoyed writing in this way, feeling myself linked with the traditions of my craft, at one with the storytellers of the Orient whom I have seen in Marrakesh and Baghdad taking their place in the Bazaar, with their audience squatted round them on their haunches. That is why I chose this title for the book.

The story told in the first person obeys an established literary convention. The author tells his story as though he were recording an actual event, or series of events, of which he was the witness, but he is not giving evidence on oath in a court of law. The episode, the anecdote that he records did not necessarily happen in just that way, at just that time, in just that place and to just those people. He selects, invents and rearranges; recreating a personal experience in a special pattern. The reader recognizes this. He knows that he is being offered a piece of fiction. At the same time, he expects the self-portraiture involved in this kind of story to be exact. For that reason I have prefaced the various sections of this book with a few autobiographical details. I do not know whether the young man who wrote the first story in this book at the age of twenty-two is a very different person from the man of fifty-five who wrote the last, but I do know that the circumstances of his life were very different; I felt, therefore, that it would make the reading of these stories simpler, if I explained at various points what those circumstances were. These notes are printed in italics.

A.W.

London 1919–1926

The Loom of Youth *was published in 1917. Few novels have been the centre of more controversy. This will surprise a modern reader; the book is tame enough today; but it must be remembered that for half a century the English Public School system had been revered as one of the 'two main pillars vaulted high' that supported the British Empire. My novel was one of the first to criticize its cult of athleticism and the very first to accept as a matter of course the existence of homosexuality in the average school.* The Spectator *for ten weeks and the* Nation *for six devoted two or three pages of each issue to a correspondence debating its veracity.*

Ten days after its appearance I joined the B.E.F. in France as a second-lieutenant in a machine-gun company. Reading the reviews of my novel in the trenches, realizing that I had 'set the Thames on fire', I thought ruefully of the exciting time I should be having if I were in London. A success like this could come only once in life and I was missing all the fun of it. I felt sorry for myself. But actually I was lucky. As a junior officer responsible for men's lives in action, I could not give myself any airs. At Passchendaele and Cambrai I was a very unimportant person. Had I been in London as the lion of the season, I do not see how I could have helped having my head turned.

I was, moreover, in no position to follow up my success. Eight years went by before another book of mine sold more than twenty-five hundred copies. An abrupt and complete eclipse would have been hard to take. Those few garish weeks might have spoilt my enjoyment of the next ten years.

1

I was taken prisoner in the big retreat of March 1918, and spent the remainder of the war in captivity in Mainz. My fellow prisoners included Gerard Hopkins, Hugh Kingsmill and Milton Hayes. It was the first time that I had met on equal terms men of intelligence and education several years older than myself. Mainz was for me the equivalent of a university. I read voraciously, argued and exchanged ideas.

In the spring of 1919 I left the Army with a posting to the R.A.R.O. (Regular Army Reserve of Officers) and in the autumn joined the staff of Chapman & Hall, the venerable publishing house of which my father, Arthur Waugh, was the Managing Director.

It was a half-time employment. I spent Mondays and Fridays in the firm's offices, in Henrietta Street; the rest of the week I could devote to my own writing. I had a flat in London, but I have never been able to write in a big city. Too much is happening. I need a day-to-day eventlessness before I can concentrate upon a novel. During the winter I used to go out of London every Monday evening to a small country inn in Hertfordshire, returning on the Friday morning.

I was a keen athlete. I played Rugby football every Saturday during the winter, and cricket three or four days a week during the summer. I did my serious writing during the winter. In April, between the football and the cricket seasons, I took a holiday abroad.

Cricket and football determined the pattern of my life. They kept me not only in sound condition physically, but in touch with what are called 'ordinary people'. I was fortunate in that. It is very easy for a young writer to drift into a Bohemian set where he meets only painters, musicians, actors and other writers. Bohemians can be and usually are delightful as companions; but for the novelist they are less 'good copy' than the doctors, lawyers, accountants, businessmen whom I was meeting on the playing fields.

The 'twenties are today qualified with the adjective 'roaring'; they are presented as a period of hectic, extravagant self-indulgence. They may have been for some people; they were not for me. I was working hard. I kept early hours so as to be fit for football. I had very little money. The early 'twenties were a happy time for me, but not a wild one.

A Stranger

I was looking for a wedding present costing about three pounds and I was looking for it in a jeweller's shop in Hampstead where one often picked up bargains. I was browsing round its show cases when my attention was caught by a familiar voice. I turned to see beside the desk, a tall dark bearded man arguing with the proprietor.

'I must show you these samples. I insist. I know my firm is German. But we aren't at war with Germany any longer. I can sell you stuff at a third of the price they charge you here. A bargain is a bargain. We're businessmen not politicians.'

I stared. His back was three-quarters turned to me; the beard was thick; it covered the line of his jaw and hid his mouth, but the voice was unmistakable. It could not be any one's but Morrison's. Morrison, a man whom I should remember as long as I remembered anything.

He had joined our machine-gun company in the autumn of 1917. We had just come down from Ypres; we had been in the line eight days, had taken the remains of a village, a few kilometres of ruined land, and had lost four officers and twenty men.

We had been hurried south and were waiting to take over a quiet sector to the east of Bullecourt. We were in tents at the foot of a hill, and the fierce October rains that turned Passchendaele into a swamp were driving over us.

We sat in our leaking mess-tent, huddled round the stove, trying to be thankful that we had seen the last of the salient. Jones, who had spent most of his life in Malaya and who loathed the cold, had wrapped his sleeping-bag around his knees and was chanting a song that he had learnt from an Australian in an *estaminet* at 'Pop' the night after we had been relieved. We only knew the chorus; it went:

Cheerioh, cheeiray,
and a rolling stone gathers no moss so they say.
Cheerioh, cheeriay,
and a rolling stone gathers no moss so they say.
Cheerioh, cheeriay …

Every few minutes he would pause, take a sip at his glass, and mutter, 'I expect that poor bastard is gathering moss himself now, up in that bloody salient,' adding, 'And bloody well out of it, too.' The rest of us joined in the chorus when we felt inclined.

Then Morrison arrived. It was just before tea-time, and I can see him now as he strolled into the tent, a black figure against the night, letting in the wind and the rain. He stood there, blinking at the candle, and Jones broke off his song to growl over his shoulder, 'Who the hell is that?'

'Me, Morrison. I've just come to join you. Let's come near the fire. I'm ruddy damp.'

He was tall and burly with undistinguished features, and his uniform did not suit him. Some men look right in uniform and others don't. Morrison looked as though he had called at the Army Ordnance Stores on his way up, and asked for a stock size. He seemed to be in his later twenties.

We moved aside to make a place for him and he sat on the bench, his hands pressed forward, with the light from the open stove falling on his chest and knees, leaving his face in shadow.

'Heavens, but this is good. I had a job to get here from Bapaume,' he said. 'I don't believe I'd ever have got here at all if I hadn't bribed an A.S.C. wallah to drive me out in the town major's car. I knew he wouldn't think of moving on a day like this and it was a pity to see the old bus standing in a shed.'

It is usual for subalterns who have just joined a unit to keep quiet in the mess at first, but Morrison did not stop talking till we had heard the whole account of his journey from Grantham: how he had a row with the R.T.O. at Boulogne, how he had managed to break his journey at Amiens, and how the fool of a sergeant at Bapaume had wanted him to come up in the light railway.

'The light railway!' He laughed. 'I could see myself coming up in that damned thing. No cover to it, nothing to keep the rain off, and then I and my damned valise would have been dumped in one of these blown-up villages with no prospect of getting anywhere. I know that game!'

We thought at first he was merely the talkative ass who was anxious to make a good impression and was going the wrong way about it. We looked forward to his first turn in the line. He might not talk so much when he had to inspect his guns along a communication trench that was being shelled. It is a national heritage, that prejudice against the actor, that belief in the strong silent Englishman: we can't believe that the other sort, at its best, can be more than an amiable Falstaff. I soon learned, however,

5

that there was a good deal to Morrison.

The evening we moved up the line, my batman, Carter, came up to me with his features set in a serious expression.

'That new officer, sir, he's got too much kit. He'll have to dump some.'

Carter was the one man in the company of whom I really stood in awe. He was very respectful, but how he looked at me when he disapproved! When I first joined the section I washed inside the tent and I heard afterwards that he had gone up to my section officer and said: 'That new officer, sir, do you mind asking him not to wash inside the tent?'

It was always 'that new officer, sir'. Carter hated them: it took him a long time to get used to people, and I looked forward to seeing how he would deal with Morrison.

At that moment Morrison came in to start what threatened to be a long story about the price of cigarettes at the Expeditionary Force canteen. Carter interrupted him.

'That kit of yours, sir, there's too much of it. I can't get it all on to the limber; you'll have to dump some, sir.'

Morrison swung round impatiently.

'My kit! I need everything I've got. Now, look here, my good man, you get along and pack it up at once.'

Carter was not used to being addressed as 'my good man'. The expression of his face was respectful but obstinate.

'I'm sorry, sir, but I can't do it; you're the only officer in the company that's brought a bed out with him; I can't get it all in.'

'You can't? Then I'll have to show you. Come here.'

He opened out his valise, spread its contents on the ground, then began to pack, talking at full pace all the time. 'This hold-all goes in there, my boots there, and be very careful that my boots don't knock against my shaving glass; my collars in here, that

6

blanket there and riding breeches here, and then the bed in there, and then the bucket.'

Within five minutes he had packed the whole thing, strapped it up and, as it lay on the floor of the tent, it looked about the smallest valise I had ever seen.

'That's the way to do it. If you know how things fit in you can pack 'em away in your pocket. It's only a question of method. I've thought it out very carefully. Now unpack it again so to see if you know how it's done.'

And the great Carter dutifully unpacked the valise and packed it all again with Morrison standing there beside him talking.

'Not so bad,' he said, when Carter had finished, 'not perfect yet, not by a long chalk, but you'll get the hang of it in time; only a matter of practice.'

From that moment I respected him. He is the only man I ever saw get the upper hand of Carter.

I saw a good deal of Morrison during the next few weeks, but we never got intimate. He was a lonely man, the most lonely man I think I have ever met. His extreme volubility masked a gloomy, taciturn nature. He cared for no one. 'Friendship's not my game,' he said. I never discovered what his real game was. I don't know that he had one; he appeared to have no ambition; apart from a fierce determination to get even with some force that was, he felt, working contrary to him. Fate had loaded the dice against him, but he was not going to be beaten, he was going to see it through. In the waging of that struggle lay failure or success in life.

He had been brought up outside London in one of the northern suburbs. He had gone to a local school, thence to a local bank. He had loathed it there. 'I don't know what I shall do after the war,' he said. 'But I can't go back to that, I don't see why I

7

should; I've got no home, no one is dependent on me; it does not matter to anyone what happens to me; I don't know how I managed to stand it for so long. But one drifts into habits. I had to, while my father was alive and afterwards—well, it's hard to break a habit, and I didn't see what else I was to do; there was the club where I played bridge and billiards in the evening, there was football every Saturday in the winter and cricket in the summer; always some little thing to look forward to. I felt sure that something must turn up soon; that it could not go on like that for ever; that's the mistake we all make, waiting for something to turn up instead of going out and finding it. Some of us have good reason to be grateful to the war.'

He had, I soon found, a hard side to his nature. If he had once made up his mind he let nothing stand in his way.

Once we were taking over a piece of line from the Australians. They had had a bad time; it was a filthy night of rain and mud and the officer whom Morrison was relieving had a cold; probably trench fever coming on.

'Do you mind if my sergeant takes you round the guns? I'm feeling "dud",' he said.

Headquarters had issued strict instructions that we were to be shown round by an officer and not a sergeant, but it was a rule that no one worried about very much; as far as I remember, Morrison nearly always sent his sergeant round himself. But on this night, for some reason or other, he was determined that the officer should come round with him.

'No, I'm sorry, the captain's very strict on this. If anything went wrong there'd be the hell to pay. I'm afraid you'll have to come round with me.'

'But we never worry about that. My sergeant's been round the guns as often as I have. He knows all there is to know about them. I got shown round by a sergeant when I took over.'

'I don't care about that. I've got my orders. Come along. I can't wait here all night.'

'I'm damned if I come. The sergeant can take you.'

'All right then. Just as you like. But I shan't sign the relief paper till you do.'

They stood looking at each other. Morrison had every card in his hand.

'It's just as you like,' he said. 'Either you show me round—' For a moment I thought the Australian was going to hit him; but he turned and pulled on his steel helmet.

'Come on,' he said. All the way up the dug-out steps he coughed and choked.

Morrison included among his peculiarities a type of perverse chivalry. He always backed the losing side; in the mess he stuck up for the Sinn Feiners and Bolshevists simply because we were against them. At the Café Royal he would have been equally violent as a militarist with overwhelming arguments in favour of the knock-out blow. This was not in itself unusual. We all like to be martyrs in the abstract. But it is unusual to find anyone who puts the minority theory into practice, and Morrison did.

He was invariably courteous to German prisoners. Once we were brewing a dixie of tea, when a Prussian officer was brought along the trench. We offered him a cup, but before he had time to drink it a shell pitched on the back of the trench, scattering us with mud; the German's tea was ruined. It was a frequent tragedy of the trenches and usually an occasion for mirth. Morrison, however, had been sheltered by a traverse; without a word he handed his cup over to the prisoner. He would not have done that for one of his own men under any conditions: 'War is war,' he would have said.

On another occasion a party of prisoners were being marched through Albert and a large fat Frenchman stood in the doorway of his house shouting after them *'Les sales Boches'*. Morrison walked up to him and said quietly: 'Stop that now, we've had enough of that from you.'

The Frenchman looked at him in aggrieved amazement, then turned and shouted after the party: '*A bas les Boches, les sales Boches*'

Morrison did not say a word; he simply lifted his fist and knocked the Frenchman down.

'How would you like it if you had been taken prisoner,' 'he said' 'and some dirty civilian who hadn't been within thirty miles of the line began to jeer at you?'

I was taken prisoner during the big retreat in March, 1918, and on repatriation I was transferred to the Reserve. I presumed that I had lost touch forever with my brothers-in-arms, but under the new formation of machine-gun companies into battalions, my old company had as its adjutant a Captain Brownleigh who had been a good friend of mine at Sandhurst. He invited me to spend a week with him in Cologne before I started my London life as a civilian. 'We are living,' he said, 'in the Deutsche Ring in the private house of a German millionaire. You will be very comfortable.'

I arrived on one of those warm days that surprise us in early spring with a promise of summer; the Rhine flowed smoothly; sunshine glittered on the proud curves of the Hohenzollern Gate and the towers of the Cathedral. I felt eager, buoyant, expectant. I was delighted when I found my old friend Morrison at the bank. arguing with the cashier who had, he maintained, swindled him over the exchange.

'The limit, these German bankers,' he protested, 'absolutely the limit. I know the mark's only worth a penny, I saw it in *The Times* this morning, and here's this fellow refusing to give me more than 235 marks to the pound.'

'But, my dear sir,' the cashier explained, 'cannot you understand; today the mark is a penny, tomorrow it may be a penny farthing, things change so fast. We cannot afford to lose; we have to make our profit.'

'To hell with your profit; I want my 240 marks.'

In the end he got 238 marks and was as proud over his triumph as though he had succeeded in obtaining a reduction of his income tax.

'That's the way to treat them,' he said. 'I know how to manage the Boche.'

We found a quiet café on the Hohe Strasse. I asked him what he was going to do now the war was over.

'I don't know,' he said. 'I think I shall stay on here as long as they'll have me. It's a lazy job.'

He was, I felt, reluctant to leave a mode of life of which he had mastered the technique, in place of another of which he was ignorant.

He asked me what England was like now.

'I can't imagine it,' he said. 'I suppose it'll go back to what it was in 1913 and we shall find that everyone's forgotten all about this little interruption.'

He talked about Cologne and how the civilians had expected us to sack the place; at first they had been very servile. But things were settling down.

'They've begun to see that we don't worry about them at all; they go their way, we ours.'

He told me about the exchange and how they had raffles on it in the mess. 'Money can be made that way,' he said. 'There's a sergeant in the orderly room who invested thirty pounds in it; he gambles, buys in one day, sells out the next. He told me he made about fifteen pounds a month. He's smart, that chap. Our fellows used to chuck their ten-pfennig notes away, or else used them as pipe-lighters. What was the use of a tenth of a penny to them? But the sergeant decided to make a bank. Every man who comes into the orderly room has to turn out his pockets, and all the notes under a mark are handed over to the stores. The company has been kept in soap for the last month.'

He talked about the girls. 'They're quite different from what I expected. I thought they'd be heavy and dull. I suppose they've been keyed up by the excitement of the war and the lack of food; life seems to have flamed up in them suddenly.'

The girl at his billet was something very special. He talked a good deal about her, but I did not take what he said too seriously. It had seemed to me the usual bluff that one associated with Morrison. But Brownleigh shook his head when I mentioned it to him.

'It isn't anything to laugh about,' he said. 'One doesn't mind what a fellow does in private—after all, we're none of us perfect—and as long as he keeps quiet he can do what he likes, but Morrison's been going about all over the place with this girl, in day time too; there's bound to be a row. The General's frightfully against fraternizing and we don't know what to do. We don't want trouble and Morrison's not an easy man to tackle.'

He certainly was not. And, being one of those men who never asked intimate questions about others, he wouldn't welcome interference. I didn't envy Brownleigh his job.

But it was obviously a situation. I went to the Opera that night, and there was Morrison sitting with his girl in one of the boxes. She was a pretty flaxen-haired little creature, pale-faced, with half-closed, darkly lidded eyes. He had obviously from the conditions of his life had very little experience of women, and that little must have been confined to cheap intrigues, squalid and furtive, with shop girls and the wives of elderly businessmen. He had been swept off his feet by the refined and unabashed sensuality of this foreigner. I saw several people looking at them.

'You see what I mean,' said Brownleigh.

'I certainly do.'

'What do you make of it?'

I shrugged. 'I've seen a good deal of Morrison one way and another. We were in the same company in France, but I never got to know him. He's always been a stranger. There's a point in him beyond which one never gets. I'd let him alone if I were you.'

But Brownleigh was a conscientious creature. At Sandhurst we had used the phrase G.S.—the letters of General Service—to describe anyone who took his duties too seriously. We all liked Brownleigh, but he was definitely G.S. We were relieved when he was not made a sergeant.

'I must do something,' he said ruefully.

He did it two days later, when I was in the mess. I suppose he chose that night so that I should be there as one of the old crowd to back him up.

It happened just after we had left the table, when there were no waiters in the ante-room. Brownleigh stood up, looking extremely awkward.

'Now that we are all here, there's something that I've been thinking—that we've all been thinking—for some time past. As we are all friends, I think we ought to have it out. We've been thinking, Morrison, that you've been going about rather a lot lately—'

But Morrison was now standing too and Brownleigh checked.

Morrison looked slowly round him. His face was taut.

'I've been with you fellows for nearly two years. I've done the jobs I've had to do as well as I could. I've done my best to make things go smoothly in the mess. I've not interfered with any of you. I've gone my way and I've let you go yours. I expect you to do the same with me. My life's my own. I'm not going to discuss it. Let's cut in for bridge.'

He walked to the table and spread a pack of cards across it. Half a dozen of us followed him and cut. Scarcely a word was said that evening. Morrison won 400 marks.

Brownleigh was in a self-accusing mood next day. 'I don't know what came over me. I couldn't say a word. He looked at me and I dried up.'

'What are you going to do now?' I asked.

'I'll find a way.'

He did. Within a month Morrison was posted back to England to be demobilized.

I had given Morrison my address in London, but I had not expected to hear from him. Friendship was not his game, and it was not in terms of friendship that he wrote to me six months later. He thought I could be of use to him. 'I'm going back to Germany,' he wrote, 'to buy up curios and pictures. The old families are starving. They'll sell anything. They must have books that collectors here would care to have. You're in the trade. You could tell me the kind of book to look out for.'

We had tea together in a café off the Strand. He was not enthusiastic about his prospects, but he was glad to be leaving England. He had been offered his old post at the bank, but had refused it.

'I'm spoilt for all that,' he said. 'I've got the itch to be about

14

and doing. Can you imagine me sitting down at a desk day after day, with the other clerks grinning at me behind the backs of their hands, saying to each other, "He was an officer in the Great War; he used to order men about and have his boots cleaned by a servant, now he's adding up rows of figures at four pounds ten a week!" They are jealous, horribly jealous; and it's the same with the old men and women. They pretend to be sympathetic, they say, 'What a change it must be for you, coming back to this after the war, but I suppose you are glad, really, aren't you, to get a little quiet?' They are jealous, they grudge me the last five years, they hate me for having made a success of it, for having risen out of their class, they want to drag me back, to say "This is where you belong".'

'There's another thing too that I can't stand,' he said, 'this mad attempt to forget there was a war. People don't want to be reminded that they owe anything to us ex-soldiers. They say "Get down to work and save the nation". They're beginning to regard the ex-soldier as a fellow who has been on a holiday and is coming back to school. "You've had your fun," they say, "now you must take off your coat and roll your sleeves up." It makes me sick; before we know where we are, the country will be run by the fellows who got cushy jobs at Whitehall and the conscientious objectors who spent the last two years at Dartmoor. They had a poorish time, no doubt, those C.O.s, but they enjoyed being martyrs, and Lord help us, what about those fours years in Flanders. I'm not saying that it was the blind misery the pacifists would make people think it was. We had our good times. I was happier then than I am now and so were hundreds of others. But it was worse than Dartmoor. They want us to forget all that, they want to shove us back into drudgery, to drug us so that we shan't remind them. I can't stand it. That's why I'm going back.'

I could see his point. London was not an easy city in the autumn of 1919. I could imagine his thoughts turning nostalgically towards Cologne.

'What about that girl of yours?' I asked. 'Have you kept in touch with her?'

'In a kind of way. I'm not a letter-writer.'

That night I wrote to Brownleigh. 'I shouldn't be at all surprised,' I said, 'if he marries her out of that perverse chivalry of his. If it had been an English girl or a French one, he wouldn't worry, he'd be the cynical man of the world. "That's her look-out." But because she is a German, an enemy, he'll think that he owes her something, that he must make things right. Please keep me posted.'

A month later I got the letter I expected. Yes, Morrison had married her and taken her to live in a small house on the far side of the river.

I could picture the social embarrassments that would arise. There was Morrison, a civilian, settled in what could only be described as a conventional military society, married to a German and expecting to be treated as though he were still an officer. Some of his old friends would stick to him, but Cologne must have changed a good deal since he had left. Peace had been signed, many of the officers had their wives out, the town was full of English women.

He got his first rebuff, so the letter told me, when he walked into the Officers' Club as though he were still in uniform. The German porter told him that civilians were not allowed inside.

'You get out of my light,' said Morrison and pushed past him into the lounge.

A few minutes later the Secretary of the Club, an officer, came up to him.

'I'm very sorry, but you really can't come in here. If you care to fill in a form I'll see if you can be put up for membership, but till then you can't come unless you are introduced by a member.'

'Are any ex-officers members of the club?'

'One or two.'

'Well then, I'm going to be one and you can hurry up and get me elected.'

It was no good though; this was different from the case of the Australian officer and the relief. He had not the cards in his hand any longer, and the secretary took good care that he did not get elected.

That was a nasty blow, but if he had kept quiet it might have been all right. He could have visited the mess, his old friends would not have let him down. But he was confoundedly obstinate. It had to be a struggle with him all the time. Then he took his wife to the Opera; and that settled it.

The Opera House in Cologne is very different from an English theatre. The performance begins at half-past six and does not end till close on midnight. There are long intervals between the acts, during which one may either walk up and down the long, wide promenade that runs behind the boxes or avail oneself of the excellent supper that is served downstairs. The Opera House is the fashionable centre of the town and even those officers who did not care greatly for classical music regarded their attendance there two or three times a month as a social obligation.

And here in this delicate atmosphere of etiquette and polite properties, Morrison was inspired by some hideous folly to walk up to his old colonel, shake him by the hand and say before the embarrassed colonel realized what was happening: 'Let me introduce you to my wife.'

The colonel had his wife with him, and she had to be introduced too. When he got back to the battalion he gave the strictest instructions that, on no account, was Morrison to be allowed into the mess. 'Fellow's a disgrace to the service.'

For the next week or so Morrison must have had a poorish time.

He again took his wife to the Opera, and several fellows cut him. He went on bringing her for a little and then suddenly realized what was happening.

'My God! it makes me sick,' he said to Brownleigh. 'Here are these fellows going on the loose whenever they get the chance, and they cut me because I've had the decency to marry my girl. How many of these fellows do you think have been carrying on with German women?'

Brownleigh was the only one of his friends who kept up with him.

Brownleigh might be G.S., but he was not the man to turn against an old friend when he was down.

'I don't think he can be doing very well,' he wrote. 'I see him now and then, hanging round second-hand shops, trying to pick up bargains whenever there's an auction. He looks untidy, as often as not unshaven, his shoes unpolished, and he's begun to stoop. I went down to his place and it had the melancholy, depressing appearance of respectable poverty. A supper had been laid, a miserable meal of cold meat and some sort of pickles and cheap wine.'

I could guess from that letter at the sort of life they led, the endless friction, the embarrassment of a couple who are trying to make both ends meet. I could imagine too how love under such conditions dies out quickly, how self-respect is lost and a man and a woman begin to hate each other, remaining together through associations of the past, through a lack of the courage to own that they have failed, through a baffled sensuality. In its first stages their love had been fresh and adventurous; there had been secret meetings, the lure of the forbidden. 'Love mixed with fear is sweetest.' But it was a different thing altogether, this dreary marriage; the setting was altered, a new technique was required; and that was just what they lacked.

I could see them sitting there hostile to each other, both conscious of their own failure. I suppose she must have found things difficult. She had married an enemy, and although the fierce hatreds of the war were dying out, her family must have felt that she had been untrue to her people, that she had separated herself from them. Her old friends rarely came to see her. They did not like her husband. And, during the lonely mornings when Morrison wandered about the streets in search of bargains, she must have felt cruelly resentful.

They used to have fierce and bitter quarrels, so Brownleigh told me.

'Women can be pretty fair cats,' Morrison said once to him. 'For no reason at all they suddenly burst out and rant and curse. Eva couldn't get the soap she wanted the other day and began to abuse the English. "You are all the same," she said, "you think about nothing but yourselves. You talk big and you use fine words about the rights of little nations; and all the time you're blockading Europe, you're murdering Ireland, you're selling coal to France at a price that's ruining them. You have sent the value of the mark down to a penny, we can't get the necessities of life. Look what sort of a life I'm leading, thanks to you! Hardly enough to eat, no fun at all! No one ever comes to see me, and there you sit glowering all the time. What sort of life do you think I lead?" That's what it's like, old man. I suppose this is the sort of thing that one's got to expect at first. It's a trial though.'

A little later he told Brownleigh that she was going to have a child. It was impossible to know if he was glad or not. 'It'll keep her quiet'; that was all he said. It was another bond holding him to Cologne. But I do not think he looked ahead. He probably felt as he had in the bank before the war. 'This can't go on forever. Something is bound to happen soon.' He was tired, and he thought that when she had a child Eva would be easier to live with.

And then one morning he walked into the office of the British military police and said, 'I wish to put myself under arrest. I have killed my wife.'

They had had another fierce quarrel the night before. It was after they had gone to bed; she had a bad cold; she had not been able to get the particular medicine that she wanted and she could not sleep. She had begun to abuse the English.

'I hate the lot of you,' she had said. 'You're killing Germany, you're starving us, and you talk about internationalism, which means getting as much as you can for yourselves; and you, you're just like the rest of your nation—what sort of a life do you think I am having?'

'For God's sake, shut up,' Morrison had said.

'I shan't shut up; I'm tired of you, tired to death of you. I wish I'd never married you. I was happy before you came. I should have married one of my own people—I should—'

Morrison could stand it no longer; he took her by the shoulders and shook her, till she was quiet, then he turned round and went to sleep. In the morning he found her dead.

He was handed over to the German authorities; it was a civilian case. But the little official assured the British with great suavity that everything would be all right. *'Crime passionnel,'* he said. 'No jury would convict him. And besides—her state of health.'

The German police were anxious to keep on the right side of

the British. There was a good deal of rowdyism in Cologne. Discharged soldiers had been causing trouble; without the British it would have been hard to maintain order. In the meantime, of course, Morrison would have to go to prison. He was sent to Düsseldorf.

The affair caused naturally a good deal of excitement in a society that depended on itself for entertainment. The general impression was that Morrison would be discharged and that it was, on the whole the best thing that could have happened to him.

'After all,' said the colonel, 'what could it have led to? Think of the poor devil staying here when the armies went. There would have been no one for him to talk to. He'd have been an outcast. I doubt if his business would have paid. He could hardly have brought her back to England. She'd have hated the idea and here he'd have had to stick while his family increased, and his responsibilities along with them. It's the best way out, really. What a life he'd have had!'

Brownleigh was tempted to point out that the colonel had not done much to make Morrison's life in Cologne any easier, but it would have served no purpose and the colonel was an ordinary conventional man, who had lived by rule. It was not his fault, indeed it was no one's fault. Things had turned out that way. It looked now as though the tide had begun to turn for Morrison.

The trial was awaited confidently. A strong case for the defence had been drawn up. Numberless instances of Eva's exasperating habits were collected. A doctor was prepared to give evidence on the state of her health, and to affirm that her constitution had been weakened by the privations of war, and the lack of milk, butter and dripping. After all, *'Crime passionnel'*—that was an

21

unfailing argument and the prosecution did not want a conviction which might be presented in the English Press as another case of German injustice.

Everything, indeed, was going along smoothly, when all these plans were overthrown by the revolution in Düsseldorf. For a few days the town was in the hands of the Spartacists. The gates of the prisons were flung open and Morrison was let free.

Brownleigh thought that he would make straight for Cologne, though some believed that he would try to cross the frontier.

'After all, he can't be certain that he won't be convicted. Things go wrong. I wouldn't run any chances if I were in his place.'

The German authorities were apathetic. 'He has escaped with the rest,' they said. 'It is a little thing, that, at such a time.'

It was a fortnight before any news came through. Then the suave official appeared, bowing and scraping.

'We have heard about your friend. It is very sad. He has been found dead in Düsseldorf.'

The statement was confirmed. Morrison's body had been found in a cellar in a small side-street. The face was terribly disfigured with the jaw shot right away, but every article of clothing on the body belonged to Morrison and the pockets were full of his letters and papers; he had no money on him; from a tear on the inside of his finger, it would seem as though a signet ring had been torn off him by force.

'There is nothing to be done,' said the German. 'We are very sorry, but after all—in times like these—' He shrugged.

That was the story as Brownleigh told it me.

'It was really rather amusing,' he said, 'to see the way in which those who had before been most against him, hastened to make excuses for him now. We heard a great deal about "the rough

22

diamond", and the colonel, who had been so affronted at the Opera, insisted on giving him a military funeral.'

He told it me in person when he was home on leave. I listened in silence. Morrison was the most dramatic character I had met. I remembered how he had triumphed over Carter, how he had made the Australian officer show him round the line. I thought of the evening in the mess when Brownleigh had tried to make a fuss about his girl. He was so very vital! And even afterwards, when he had been cut at the Opera, I'm not sure that he hadn't scored. He had stuck to his self-respect. They must have been secretly ashamed of themselves, those others, as they hurried past him with eyes turned away. They must have felt uncomfortable for a long time afterwards, talking loudly to pass it off. He had been only angry. I could not realize that he was done with, finished, that his existence had been wiped out suddenly in a dark street by a chance bullet.

It was strange that I should have thought that, that I should have refused to believe that he was really dead. Perhaps mental telepathy warned me that the ending was not here. At any rate, I was not as surprised as I should have been when I heard in that jeweller's shop in Hampstead, a familiar voice voluble and insistent.

'I refuse to take no for an answer.' It was saying: 'Talk sense.

What does it matter to you how you make your profit, as long as there is a profit.'

Yes, it was Morrison all right. No one I knew had possessed to the same degree the magnetic power of making men do what he wanted.

I stood back in the shadow. I saw the old jeweller take out his magnifying glass and inspect the samples. I saw them arguing until, finally, the old man gave an order and Morrison marched out, jubilant and content, as always the master in a world of men.

I did not follow. I preferred not to find out exactly what happened in that dark side-street in a town possessed of terror. I preferred to let Morrison remain a man of mystery, to see him in my memory as I saw him first on that wet afternoon at Bullecourt, a stranger among us, standing against the sky, letting in the wind and the rain.

1920

An Unfinished Story

She paused in the doorway of the small Soho restaurant. A fur Russian-style cap fitted tightly to her head; a gloved hand, raised against her throat, kept in place the woollen scarf that was flung round her shoulders. She was barely twenty. She was not beautiful, but she had the prettiness of all young girls whose figures are slim and graceful, the charm of the green leaf and the bud.

A man rose to welcome her, very much the ex-officer, ex-Public Schoolboy type. He was tall, thin, on the edge of thirty; he had a small dark moustache and showed signs of baldness.

I could not hear how they greeted each other, but in the way in which he helped her off with her coat, I detected a slight uneasiness. 'They do not know each other very well,' I thought. I was dining alone and I foresaw that I was going to indulge my storyteller's instinct to concoct imaginary plots about the people round me. I shifted my chair so that I could watch them without turning.

The suggestion of uneasiness was repeated as he leant across the table with the menu. 'A little too eager,' I decided, 'anxious to make a success of it and overacting.' He ordered a flask of red

Chianti and drank his first glass quickly, in three gulps. Then he began to talk; amusingly, I gathered, for she smiled quite often. Once she burst out laughing; a fresh, clear laugh that, coming half-way through the meal, stressed what I had already noticed, that while he was fretted with self-consciousness, she was solely concerned with the natural enjoyment of a good dinner in pleasant company. This dinner was clearly a special occasion for him but not for her. I wondered why.

And why should he be nervous and she not? He had something on his mind.

There was no suggestion that they were lovers. They had not once looked into each other's eyes. He might be in love with her, not she with him; not yet; but that was not a cause for shyness. Surely he could not be planning a premature proposal. It is disastrous to anticipate a climax. A man of thirty must know that. Yet perhaps he was contemplating this very folly. Why?

I began to frame a story. He has been ordered abroad unexpectedly. He had gone up to Oxford after the war hoping to pass into the Home Civil, but he had failed to make up for the years he had lost during the war and passed instead into the Indian Civil. In a few days he will be sailing, leaving behind this girl with whom he has fallen suddenly in love. He has asked her out this evening resolved to bring things to a head before he sails. But of all this she is unaware, having in her inexperience mistaken his love for comradeship.

It was a situation that might be developed into what the magazines describe as a 'long-short'. It would have a topical appeal. The man's failure to pass into the Home Civil would stress the plight of the ex-officer who is passed over in favour of some one who has not seen service. He had prepared for a long slow courtship. He feels he is not the type of man to sweep a young woman off her feet. But now he has to compress into a few days the campaign of several months.

The story shaped itself in scenes: the meeting at a tennis tournament; the news of his failure in the exam; this dinner in the restaurant. I could picture them in the taxi afterwards. She is chatting casually and cheerfully. Suddenly he interrupts, leans forward, grabs her hand. She draw back, startled. As he had overacted in the restaurant, so does he now, greedily clutching her in his arms, kissing her awkwardly, stammering 'I love you'. It is a grisly failure. It might have been her first kiss and she would have her own romantic conception of what a first kiss should be. 'You've spoilt it all,' she cries, for at such moments it is the ridiculous that first occurs to us and she would speak out of her recollection of magazine heroines.

'Leave me alone! Leave me alone! Can't you see that you've spoilt everything?'

When they reached her home, she would jump out of the taxi and run straight up the steps without turning to say good-bye. And he would sit back, reflecting dismally that in three days he would sail for India; he would not see her for perhaps five years.

And then …?

But it should not be difficult to find an ending to this kind of story. While he was away he would write and ask forgiveness, protesting that he loved her, had always loved her, that he was sorry for his stupidity. When he came back, might he not hope? A trite enough letter, but if it were not trite he would be a writer of some talent, and that I did not propose to make him. No; he would write her an ordinary love-letter, and she, being an ordinary woman, would be moved by it. With the distance hiding her shyness, she would reply that she had been young and silly. He would find her more sensible when he returned. During the first year's separation they would build up letter by letter an illusion of each other out of the enchantment of things remote. When at last they met she would be faced by a prosaic Empire-builder with thinning hair, while he would find that a girl had become a woman whose prettiness had shrivelled.

Would they marry?

Probably, from a lack of the courage that looks itself in the glass and says: 'You have failed, my friend.' It should be truer to make them marry, and perhaps she might be happy in her children, while he found pleasure in the society of another woman. But, either way, a dream would have passed and that would be the object of my story; to tell simply how everything changes, how all things are in flux; not a new philosophy and one that occurred to Heraclitus, but true nevertheless.

And looking across at the couple in the corner, I thought of their fate with sympathy. They were preparing to leave; the waiter had brought the bill neatly folded upon a plate; the girl had turned toward a large photograph of the Royal Family, and was endeavouring to arrange her hair in its blurred reflection.

She was smiling and happy, ignorant of the disaster that awaited her. Within five minutes she would have been embraced clumsily, would have assured her lover that 'he had spoiled everything', and the curtain would have descended on the first act of tragedy. Could nothing be done to save her? I was indulging my pet weakness to the top of its bent when suddenly, for the first time in my life, I was the witness of a dramatic incident.

When the girl turned to arrange her hair in the blurred reflection of the sheet of glass that protected the Royal Family from dust, and, to brush a little powder from her chin, she had taken her pocket-handkerchief from her bag. The bag lay open on the table, its mouth pointing to her companion; to my amazement, I saw him lean forward, glance round the room, then quickly take from the bag a couple of pound notes; these he placed on the plate under the bill, adding another of his own.

I suppose I should have risen from my seat and called the girl's attention to the theft, but it is hard for one who has chosen for himself the role of onlooker to decide on violent and sudden action. Besides, I have learnt that interference is invariably unwise; I cannot expect others to mind their own business unless I mind mine. At any rate, whatever was the right thing to do, I did what it was natural for me to do under the circumstances; I sat where I was.

The reason for the man's embarrassment was now clear; all the evening he had been waiting an opportunity to steal his companion's money. And to think that for half an hour I had been concocting an absurd story after the manner of Turgenev, about an Indian Civil Servant and 'the girl he left behind him'! Impatiently I called for my bill, and walked out into Dean Street.

The cool air restored my confidence. It was a mistake, I told myself, that anyone might have made. We do not expect to meet thieves in actual life. And it was quite a good story that I had invented—a debt to Turgenev perhaps, but then every short story that is written today owes something to Turgenev or Maupassant or Chekov. And I had, besides, the material for another story. The young girl prattling away and the man getting more and more worried. 'Will she never powder her nose?' he asks himself, and tries to hide his anxiousness beneath a series of amusing anecdotes.

I could make them discuss the modern girl, she will say that she hates the girl who powders and paints; he will have to agree with her, seeing that her complexion is her own, although he is, for the first time in his life, hating the fresh bloom of her cheeks, wishing that she were another sort of girl. And then, at last, when all seems lost, I could make her lean forward and smell the flowers on the table, and a speck of yellow pollen would attach itself to her chin. He would, in relief, call her attention to it.

'Really?' and opening her bag she would take out her handkerchief, turn to the photograph beside them, giving him his chance.

Up to that point it would be straightforward narrative. But beyond it a lot of thought would be required. So good a motive must not be flung away, and all the way down the Charing Cross Road I turned the incident over in my mind.

Fifteen years ago I could have made him an agent in the White Slave Traffic. It was a popular theme then; every girl who came up to London looked round at Paddington Station apprehensively for the kindly old lady who would ask her if she was new to these parts. But during the last fifteen years, Villiers Street has been placarded with shilling descriptions of 'why girls go wrong', and the Bishop of London has preached a great many sermons. The White Slave Traffic had become *vieux jeu*. But even so might there not be something in the seduction motif.

Another story started to take shape.

Her brother has motored her up from Brighton. She plans to return by train. She has been invited to dinner by a friend of long standing who knew her as a child. She thinks of him as she always has, as a kind of uncle. But his feelings now that she is grown up have changed.

I pictured them at the station booking office. She fumbles in her bag, searching every pocket. She turns to him in alarm.

'I've lost my money.'

'You can't have. Look again.'

Another long, careful search, in vain.

'What am I to do?'

In her tone of voice, is the implied suggestion that he should lend her the few shillings that she needs. He shakes his head. Alas, he has not enough. But if she will come back to his flat? 'Into a taxi, quick.' But when they arrive at the flat, which would be at the top of four flights of stairs, with the flat below unoccupied, he would discover that he had no money either, that the porter had gone, and that there was no one from whom he could borrow; she would sink down on the sofa, her hands clasped before her knees, while he stood behind her wondering at what exact point …

But no. I warned myself. That would not do. What did it matter what he said next, or at what exact point she … for whatever he did, and whatever she did, the story as I had elected to tell it could only end one way—a row of dots, and a short concluding paragraph: 'Next morning, her dark hair scattered across the pillow, she woke in a strange room …'

That has been done so often. In how many novels has not that dark hair been scattered over that pillow. It was theatrical, vulgar, the sort of plot that occurs to one in the coffee-room of one's club after a heavy lunch and half a litre of red wine.

In a dejected mood I caught at Leicester Square the tube that would carry me to Earls Court. But warmth revives us and as the train rattled westwards, I began to think that though I must discard the seduction motif, there might be possibilities in the last train to Brighton. Suppose that the man had for a long time besieged the girl unsuccessfully, and that on the refusal of his third proposal he had decided that he would never secure the hand of his beloved unless he managed to compromise her honour?

That might work out. He would steal her money at the restaurant; they would reach the booking-office where the scene I have already described would be enacted. There would be the return to the flat, the discovery that the porter was out, and that he had forgotten to cash the cheque he had written out that morning.

'What am I to do?' she'd ask.

With well-simulated confusion, he would assure her that he would not mind a 'shake-down' on the sofa, and that if she would take his room …

'But I couldn't! How could I? What would my mother say?'

A little touch that would place the mother before the reader's eye—a plump, heavy woman with a small unsatisfactory husband.

A woman of strong passions, that unrelieved had focused themselves on a rigid observance of the properties.

'But what else can you do?' the young man would ask. In the end she would consent to pass the night there, and next morning they would arrive at Brighton together with the milk, to be received by the mother in a cold, melancholy room with the fire smoking dismally. Her hands would be on her hips, she would say one word, 'Well!—then listen while the young man stammered his explanations. Of course she would not believe him; he had never expected that she would, and would have been miserably disappointed if she had. He would listen to her threats and tirades, then, at the right moment, he would draw himself up to his full height.

'Madam, your accusations are untrue; the door of the room in which your daughter slept was locked all night. I slept on the sofa. But to prove my honour, and to vindicate hers, I am prepared—and shall be proud—to marry your daughter.'

A slow smile would spread across the mother's face. Honour

saved, a daughter off her hands; and at last the daughter, moved by his chilvary, might even fall in love with her knight-errant.

I considered this solution during the short walk from Earls Court station to my flat. It was original. I had never seen it done before. Such a situation is common enough in modern fiction. But the mistake is usually genuine, and that scene in the dismal parlour is the prelude to long years of married misery. Occasionally the affair is arranged by the girl, if she can trust her lover's lack of enterprise. But for a man to plan such an escapade—that would indeed be new. And I went to sleep contented, thinking that the next day would pass pleasantly in congenial work.

But a poem by a poetess, now little read, contains the lines:

> Colours seen by candlelight
> Do not look the same by day

and when the sun shone next morning through my bedroom window my plot seemed less original. It was only a conceit, after all. It said 'black' to someone else's 'white'; it turned an old coat inside out, and though it would no doubt cause some surprise if I were to walk down Kensington High Street with my coat inside out, it would be the same coat.

That is not the way to write a good story—to tack an old situation on a new one. I should have to find a different ending. But the days passed and no solution came until a friend, to whom I related the incident, made a pertinent remark.

'If the girl could see her face reflected in the photograph, why did she not see the young man take the money from her purse?'

I sat in surprised silence. Why had I not thought of that before?

'But if she saw, why didn't she say something?' I said.

'It's your job to discover that.'

And for the next few days I searched for reasons for her silence.

At last I began to see the glimmering of a tale, the fifth, that I had constructed about this romantic couple. This is what I saw: a shy young man from the provinces comes to London with an introduction to some wealthy friends. There is an attractive daughter with whom he feels that he could very easily fall in love. He suggests timidly that it would be nice if she would show him 'round the sights', for he wants to see London, and has no other friends in it. As her parents have advanced views, or perhaps because the daughter has succeeded in impressing her views upon them, his suggestion is accepted: the result is a lunch at the Criterion, a theatre, and tea afterwards. The afternoon passes so pleasantly that he suggests a dinner. He would like to see Soho.

'But I must go back and ask my mother first,' she says.

'Really?'

'Of course; it's very nice of her to let me out at all.'

He admires this sense of duty, which is probably only an excuse for a change of frock. And so she returns home to tell her mother how well everything is progressing, while he goes to the little Soho restaurant to engage a table. While he is waiting for her, he makes a horrible discovery. He has only a pound left; what is he to do? He picks up the menu and sees that it will be impossible to dine in anything like the way he wishes for less than thirty shillings. He is a stranger; the restaurant will not give him credit. There is no one to whom he can go for a loan; he cannot ask the girl on their first day together to lend him money. And so, all through the dinner there hangs over his head the menace of that piece of folded paper. What will happen? He remembers seeing once in Manchester the proprietor pitch an impecunious client headlong into the street. They could hardly

34

do that to him. He would be too big, but he will be disgraced in the girl's eyes. He has not the presence to carry off such a scene with honour. He will stammer and mumble, and try to explain and look foolish; probably in the end he will leave his watch in bail, while the girl will stand, ashamed of him and contemptuous.

He tries to make the meal last as long as possible; they have two coffees and a liqueur and many cigarettes. But the moment comes at last when she begins to collect her things. 'I must go now. It has been a lovely evening. Thank you so very much.'

He looks in misery at the piece of folded paper. Then, just as he is preparing to request an interview with the patron, the temptation comes; her bag lies open facing him; she is looking the other way. He sees money. Here is the way out; perhaps she will not notice she has lost it. She is rich. At any rate, he must run the risk. And, as she tidies her hair in the glass, she sees him take her money.

She is shocked, terribly, but it is easy to understand her silence; her curiosity is whetted, she is interested in the young man, and guesses that one day it may very well be that she will feel more than interest for him. Money is of no great concern to her.

I could see the scene clearly enough; it would provide me with excellent opportunities for dramatic dialogue; the growing uneasiness of the man with the girl's gradual appreciation of it and wonder at the cause of it, the hope, perhaps, that is the beginning of love. A good scene, but it would be impossible not to write a good scene round such an episode. But, even as I saw it, I knew that it would be useless. To what climax could it work other than the old cliché—'I knew it all along'. It would be kept as a surprise; the reader would not be told that the girl had seen the theft reflected in the looking-glass. The story would describe

35

the progress of their courtship; the heart searchings of the young man. 'If I tell her, will she despise me?' How the machinery would creak, how often it has been done before; and at last the stage would be set for the confession.

'I have something I must tell you, dear'. And she would smile and stroke his hair.

'Silly, I knew it all along!'

How trite, how banal! And the fact that it might be true would not redeem it. We are plagiarists in life as we are in books, and there are certain motives that are now impossible in a story, although they occur in life. They have been used too often. What a weariness overcomes us when we discover in a novel of matrimonial dispute that the wife is about to become a mother, so that in consequence the hero cannot run off with his secretary.

No doubt it is an affair of frequent occurrence; impending maternity frustrates an impending honeymoon. Autumn lays waste the spring. But no self-respecting novelist would allow 'the little stranger' to extricate him from a difficulty. In the same way, no self-respecting novelist would allow a heroine 'to know it all along'. It is a motif that has served its purpose. When a coin has passed through many hands the signs and figures on it are worn away; it is valueless and is returned to the mint; which is the proper place for the 'little stranger' and 'I knew it all along'.

That is one of the chief problems for the contemporary storyteller. Real events cannot necessarily be translated into fiction.

Turgenev is always obvious. He employs none of the devices of surprise and of suspended interest on which the writer of talent depends for his effects. The waters of Turgenev's narratives are so smooth, so clear, and bring the river-bed so close to us that we hardly realize how deep they are. It is not till we see the blunders which others make with the Turgenev technique that we realize to what an extent he is supreme. And it is such a simple technique. The passage of youth; the waning power of love; the recompenses of middle age; memory and regret, and a serene twilight that harmonizes and consoles. It is of these things that Turgenev speaks—simple things, and he speaks of them simply, through a technique that is miraculously adequate and sure. A man in the middle years finds under two layers of cotton a little garnet cross; three men sitting round a table talk of love; a young man, betrothed and happy, returns at night to his hotel to recapture, in a room filled with the overpowering scent of heliotrope, the buried anguish of an earlier love; a man sits in a garden, and remembers. It looks so easy; and yet, in mediocre work, how the machinery creaks. How artificial becomes the excuses for recollection. A violin playing in a certain restaurant, after many years, a tune to which the hero danced when young. A narrative that closes where it began, in the same place, on the same note, with the same sentence. What is pattern in Turgenev becomes in lesser writers a series of devices.

Now having attempted five different stories, all of them unsatisfactory, I know it is my duty to provide a conclusion that shall be unexpected and that shall ridicule my previous conjectures. I know that I ought to meet in the restaurant at a later date the hero or heroine, or both of them together, and learn the true story. There should be—I know it—a punch in the last paragraph; but that is exactly what I cannot give, for I do not know the real end of the story and have been unable to invent one.

Unsatisfactory, but intriguing too. In a world where so much is ordered by the inviolable laws of mathematics, it is pleasant to find something that is incomplete. For the first time in my life I was the witness of a dramatic episode, the sort of thing that one would not see again in a thousand years. It was a fragment in the lives of two people, and it must remain a fragment, a baffling, fascinating fragment. I am glad to have it so. Such another moment will not come to me. When the voice of the lecturer begins to fade, when the sun beats down upon the mound at Lord's and the cricket becomes slow: at all times when the mind detaches itself from its surroundings I shall return in memory to that evening at the restaurant. It will be a treasure for all time, a book in which I shall read forever without weariness. Perhaps one day I shall hit upon the meaning of it; but I hope not. I prefer to keep it an enigma, to be able to shut my eyes and watch the growing embarrassment of a young man who is planning an unnatural theft, to see a young girl stand in the doorway of a restaurant, a fur cap fitting tightly over her head, a gloved hand raised across her throat.

1921

World Tour 1926–1927

In the summer of 1924, a friend of the cricket field, A. D. Peters, set up in business as a literary agent. I was one of his first clients, and my financial position improved rapidly. In the spring of 1926 I was able to resign my desk in Henrietta Street and sail round the world.

Travel in those days was not expensive. A first-class ticket on the Messageries Maritimes, which included four months board and lodging, cost £166. My itinerary ran: Marseilles, Suez, Ceylon, Singapore, Java, Australia, the New Hebrides, Tahiti, Panama, the West Indies. I could break the journey as often as I liked within a period of two years. At that time there was no difficulty in booking a passage at the last moment. Ships were rarely crowded.

The trip began with a leisurely cruise round the Mediterranean, which provided me with the material for the story 'The Making of a Matron'.

The Making of a Matron

If anyone had told me in the spring of 1924 that I should return to London from a world tour in 1927 to find Olivia Marshall a married woman with two children and an unparalleled reputation for decorum, I should have hooted riotously and asked him what he had been drinking. For Olivia in those days was the dowager's pet example when tea-cups rattled over the failings and inadequacies of the modern woman. 'You've only got to look, my dear, at that Marshall girl, to see what all that leads to.' Nor can it be pretended that her conduct had been unlavish in its provision of opportunities for the lifted eyelid. All things considered, it would have been surprising if it had.

When the war began Olivia was sixteen years old. And during the most unsettled period that up to now an unsettled world has known, she was allowed to grow up in ways of her own choosing. She had no brothers. Her father's service was spent exclusively in the East whence leave was scanty and spasmodic. Her mother, whose diary was black with promises to attend hospital and Y.M.C.A. committee meetings, considered that she had fulfilled her maternal obligations when she had secured her daughter's enrolment at a canteen patronized by royalty. Meantime a

London that was living at the electric pressure of a perpetual ninety-six hours' leave had dispensed with chaperones. Of such circumstances the outcome could scarcely have been more than one of chance. And chance was not over-charitable to Olivia. There was an extremely pleasant subaltern in the Guards, but a machine-gun bullet at Givenchy ended that. Then there were attempts, half-hearted, somewhat desperate attempts to fill an interval; a series of experiments that terminated in a gunner major who behaved rather more than rottenly. Chance was not over-charitable; and by the time it was all over Olivia had come to feel that life was a show without a very great deal to it; nothing anyhow that it was worth making any particular song and dance about. So that when anything that seemed at all likely to be amusing came her way, she thought, 'Oh well, why shouldn't I?' an attitude in which she persisted gallantly till one day she noticed that it was more often 'I might as well, after all' that she was saying. Between which and 'Why shouldn't I?' there is a world of difference. For whereas 'Why shouldn't I?' is the defiant protestation of a faith, 'I might as well' is no more than a shrug of the shoulders, a limp acceptance. 'I suppose,' thought Olivia Marshall, 'that I'm getting bored.'

And indeed life did seem to her rather a boring business as she hurried down Queen's Gate at ten minutes past one on a bleak Sunday in mid-January. It was nice, of course, to be going to lunch with June. June was a darling and her food was admirable, and there were sure to be plenty of amusing people there to keep the conversation winding brightly and satirically down the perilous paths of personalities. She could think of no house to which she could more readily be going. But even so, she had lunched a great many times at June's during the last three years; and there were only a certain number of ways of serving sole, only a certain number of secrets one could reveal about even the most intimate of one's acquaintances, only a certain number of different types of person in the world to meet, only a certain number of opening gambits to a flirtation, only a certain number of different ways, when it came to that, of doing anything. 'And I know every one of them,' reflected Olivia mournfully as she hurried along Sumner Place, wondering whether it was for one or half-past or quarter-past she had been invited.

'One o'clock, I think it must have been,' she said, as she surveyed the number of variously graded hats that were stretched out along the wide oak table in the hall; a suspicion that was confirmed by the atmosphere of slightly constrained anticipation that she found awaiting her in the silver-walled, cerulean-ceilinged drawing-room.

'Darling Olivia,' murmured Jane, 'so punctually unpunctual.'

'But, precious, I thought you said quarter-past.'

'And how often has dear Olivia lunched here, and how often have I told her "No, not quarter-past, dear; one!" Still, let me see now, now you're here ...' And casting a many-bangled arm about Olivia's waist, June Graham lowered a sleek and unhatted head upon her shoulder and levelled a slow, vague glance upon the assembled company. 'Let me see now, you know everybody, I think.'

Olivia did not. But she knew that June, whose acquaintance was larger probably than that of any other London hostess, would find it difficult to remember at a moment's notice, the names of all her guests. So she nodded her head placidly. She had caused enough confusion already by arriving late. Besides, did names matter very much? They were only differently coloured labels for the same thing.

'You don't remember me, I see,' a languid Balliolized voice was fluting. 'But we've danced together a great many times!'

Olivia looked up incuriously. Had she? She might well have done. So many dances, so many men.

'Of course,' she responded affably, 'of course.'

The young man sighed.

'I thought you'd say that,' he said. 'I've been experimenting lately. I go up to people I've never met and they all pretend to recognize me. They think they may have and they don't want to be rude.'

'And what's the point?'

'Social research. I wanted to satisfy myself that I am not an individual, but a type. If I were an individual, people would know quite well they hadn't met me. Can you imagine, for example, anybody making that sort of mistake about Augustus John? But as for me, there are so many articles turned out to the same pattern that people can't be sure. A dismal business.'

Olivia smiled commiseratingly. 'Others,' she quoted, 'are in your plight.'

'And what, dearies,' June was saying, 'about a little lunch? Come along, Olivia.'

Her waist encircled by the be-bangled arm, Olivia wound her way into the dining-room.

'And let me see now, where is dear Olivia to sit? Ah yes, down there, next to Gerald Palmer. You know Gerald Palmer don't you?'

'My dear,' laughed Olivia, 'who doesn't?'

And that was a question to which as a matter of fact it would have been extremely interesting to obtain an answer. For Gerald Palmer was one of those people whom it is extremely difficult to place. He was tall and sparse with light brown hair that crinkled

44

backwards from his forehead. There were a few grey hairs above his ears; about his eyes there were innumerable little lines; a deep groove ran from mouth to nostril. 'Forty-one' you would say at a first glance. 'And a pretty hard-lived forty-one at that' would be your comment at a second. And you would go on thinking that till suddenly in the middle of a conversation he would become interested and his eyes would flash and his face would be lit with an enthusiasm so boyish and unpremeditated that you would mutter, 'Twenty five: he can't be a day older than twenty-five.'

Difficult to place.

Everyone knew about him, but nobody knew much. You kept on seeing him at this and the other place. But it was hard to recall where you had seen him first. He had no intimate friends apparently, nor any family. He seemed to be well off. It was said of him vaguely that he did something remuneratively in the City. 'Gerald Palmer, who doesn't know him?' It would have been interesting to know where the ramifications of his interests ended.

'I suppose that I shall be seeing you,' said Olivia, 'at the Cranberrys' on the twentieth?' For Gerald Palmer was the sort of person with whom you opened a conversation in that way.

Gerald Palmer shook his head.

'The twentieth? Ah no, on the twentieth, where shall I be? Why yes, in a world of minarets.'

'Egypt?'

'Constantinople.'

Olivia sighed. 'I would rather see Constantinople than any city in the world,' she said.

'Then why don't you come with me? I shall be alone.'

And that was how it started. For although Olivia had been deciding twenty minutes earlier that she knew such few different ways as there were of doing such few different things as existed beneath the sun; although she was familiar with the opening gambits of that for which flirtation is a kindly label; although she knew that while some will protest wildly that flight to China is the only alternative to suicide upon a doorstep, others will remark casually that February is a miserable month in London, and that there are worse things than the sunlight of the Côte d'Azur; and knowing it, had learnt that between that ardour and that torpor is a difference only of technique, that each amounted in the end to precisely the same thing; although she was convinced that life had not left a single surprise in store for her, there was in his off-hand invitation a quality of such indifference, that it would be a pity, she thought, to leave its true nature unexplored.

'Oh, well,' she mused, 'why shouldn't I?'

Three days later a rolling, rattling P.L.M. express was sweeping them out of a frost-held country.

'And did you sleep well?' Gerald was inquiring.

'I had the place to myself, and I don't think I turned over twice the whole night through.'

'I was less fortunate. I shared my sleeper with a Bavarian, and we found it impossible to reach any compromise on questions of ventilation. At the present moment, however, life might be a good deal worse.'

It was a little hard indeed, Olivia reflected, to see how it could have been much better. Bright and gay across the breakfast-car a warm Mediterranean sun was streaming; through the open window stretched on all sides of them the ochre-brown, green-studded Provençal fields. It was good in that sun-soaked atmosphere to recall the winter-bound rain-swept Paris of yesternight.

With a clatter of brakes and a series of diminishingly excruciating jolts the train drew up beside a platform.

'Avignon,' said Gerald Palmer. 'What a pity we haven't time to stop.'

And in his slow, musically modulated voice he began to speak of the ruined relics, the pomp and pageantry of that medieval city.

With an amused, interested smile, Olivia listened.

Really, but he was a curious man. As a prelude to a honeymoon—and experience of life had not suggested to her any other reason for which men invite women to accompany them on Mediterranean cruises—this in a not uncrowded life was the most astounding episode. It was twenty-four hours now since his car had called for her in Pitt Street, and in the course of those twenty-four hours in not one word or gesture or intonation had there been offered the slightest hint that there were attached any romantic possibilities to the expedition. That the preliminaries to such possibilities could be scarcely easy she would have been the readiest to admit. A circumstance which had indeed more than a little peppered the flavour of her anticipation. She had come prepared, during the early stages at any rate, for a nervous and diffident companion. Nothing, however, had been further from Gerald's behaviour than embarrassment. There he sat, chattering happily away about papal history as though it were the most normal thing to squire unchaperoned girls you scarcely knew about the Orient.

'So you've never seen Athens,' he was continuing. 'I regard it as the greatest of privileges to be allowed to show you the Acropolis for the first time.'

And as she sat there listening patiently: 'I wonder when he'll lift the mask,' she thought.

The boat was due to sail at noon, and the train did not reach Marseilles till shortly before eleven. 'Straight to the ship,' he said, proceeding with such efficiency to grapple with porters, cab-drivers and *douaniers,* that it seemed only two minutes later that he was saying, 'And now I expect you'd like to unpack your things'; that a *maître d'hôtel* was being requisitioned; that there was a consulting of yellow charts; that half the stewards on the ship, it seemed to Olivia, were competing to conduct her to the most spacious stateroom on that not unspacious steamship, the *Paul Verlaine.* She opened her eyes wide as she came into it. 'At any rate,' she thought, 'he knows how to do one well.'

For it was in truth, that stateroom, as complete an experiment in luxury as the company of the *Messageries Maritimes* has undertaken. There were thick pile carpets on the floor and brocaded curtains across the porthole, and the beds were wide and the lights silk-shaded. There was a little gleaming walnut writing-desk, and an agreeable maid to unpack her trunks and arrange her frocks on the endless series of hangers in the inlaid wardrobe, and turn on the shining taps in the white-tiled bathroom, and scatter Houbigant bath-salts into the churned and steaming water, so that by the time Olivia came on deck to feel cool on her cheeks a breeze that blew softly over the palest of pale blue waters, the world seemed to her a singularly well-ordered place; and when Gerald came up to ask her about the cabin, 'It's a dream,' she murmured gratefully, 'a dream.'

'Splendid,' he said. 'Mine's quite decent, too.'

'What!' she gasped. 'Yours?'

'Yes, quite a jolly one. On the port side. Nice fellow sharing it with me, too. James Wellaway. I've arranged for him to sit at our table. He's just gone into the saloon to order cocktails. Let's join him.'

For the next five minutes, till she had recovered from her astonishment, Olivia talked with incredible rapidity, not so much at James Wellaway as through him. As well, indeed, she might, for her first impression of the tall, fair-haired, clean-shaven, modishly unkempt young man whom Gerald introduced to her, was one of complete transparence. 'Don't tell me anything,' she felt like shouting. 'I know all that there is to be known about you: your upbringing, your school, your college, your ideas on every subject, your attitude to every situation. Not a word, I beg of you.' And so her chatter rattled on till she had recovered her composure, and could look steadily again at Gerald Palmer.

When she did, there was that in her eyes which not many men had seen before. For Gerald Palmer had done that for her which very few people, least of all herself, had bothered to do of late: he had respected her reputation. And she felt for him the same sort of pathetic gratitude that a child feels when it is presented with an elaborate toy for which it is several years too old. 'He's a perfect dear,' she thought, 'if a rather silly one'

That night Olivia tried on many frocks before she decided on the one which best became her, and she spent long minutes before her mirror, smoothing the cool, creamed surface of her cheeks, pencilling the darkened eyelashes, heightening the gloss and shimmer of her nails, and afterwards when she danced with Gerald Palmer, she drew close to him, and her eyes were dilated and very tender.

'I'm so happy here,' she sighed, 'so very happy'.

A confession that drew from her companion the liveliest expression of delight. 'I so hoped,' he said, 'you would. The Mediterranean is incomparable in the variety of its associations.' And when she suggested later that it would be cool and quiet on the upper deck, he told her all about the early Phoenician traders till ten o'clock when he apologized for feeling sleepy.

'That Bavarian fellow,' he explained, 'kept me awake practically all night.'

Explained in a voice so incontestably assured that she realized with a surprise, that luckily the darkness hid from him, that here was no opening move of any gambit but the quite genuine resolve to sleep.

'Like anything to drink before I go?' he asked.

She shook her head.

'No thanks,' she replied briefly. 'I'm tired too.'

'Ah well, till tomorrow then.'

Tomorrow. It was one of those days whose memory, if one were to live for a thousand years, would remain unblurred. The sea was blue, as blue as turquoise and as clear; and calm, so calm that you expected to hear the sound of tearing silk as the ship slid through it. And like a tent the mantle of the rich sun's gold was over you. And across the sky's pale blue here and there small dove-coloured clouds were drifting. On the horizon faint and shadowy was the outline of the coast: of the coast or perhaps of islands; you could not tell, they were so dim and distant; and as the slow hours passed you came to think of them, those vague shapes, not as real places that one day you might chance to visit; they seemed to belong rather to those unmapped kingdoms for which the spirit always is a little homesick, those countries of the imagination where life is as one would will it, where are the people, the things, the places, one will never see.

And all through that long day's enchantment Gerald and Olivia sat side by side in long wicker chairs while Gerald talked in his slow, musical voice of the history that had been mirrored in those calm waters, the peoples that had settled, the civilizations that had flowered there; all that long conflict of ideas and arms; a history to which, to her intense surprise, Olivia found herself listening with absorbed attention. 'This is,' she thought, 'the most interesting as well as the most odd creature I have ever met.'

And sometimes as he talked his eyes would glow and his face would light with that eager boyish expression that made him seem a young man in the early twenties, breaking his first lance with life.

'It would be rather marvellous,' thought Olivia, 'to make him look like that about one!'

Early next morning they arrived at Naples. And in an ill-sprung car along a road which sets a standard of irregularity unapproached in Europe, they drove out with a band of other tourists to survey Pompeii, under the direction of a melancholy Ethiopian whose nature seemed to have found a congenial setting in that site of abandoned pleasures. 'Two thousand years ago.' With those words he began and ended every comment. He swung like a censer, their valedictory refrain about him.

'What about that secret museum?' murmured someone.

It was quite clearly the chief object of curiosity among the more sincerely self-confessed members of the party and there was a fine to-do when it was announced on their arrival that entrance was only accessible to men.

'But art,' protested a fierce-eyed Scandinavian, 'is above morals.'

'I know, I know,' murmured the lugubrious Ethiopian. 'We live in an age of prudes. They were more honest people two thousand years ago.'

To Olivia, however, the faces of the men as they came out were far more entertaining than anything there could have been for her to see inside. James Wellaway, as she had anticipated, emerged into the daylight with a sheepish smirk: a large, thick-shouldered, much-whiskered Parisian smiled roguishly. 'Not calculated,' he muttered, 'to increase one's self-esteem.' But on Gerald Palmer's face there was no sign of consciousness that the incident might have been the occasioning of the least embarrassment.

'Most interesting,' he told Olivia, 'most interesting. I wish you could have come. I'm not sure that it isn't the most significant clue to the period one has. It reveals their attitude to those things so completely; that they should have been able to fresco their rooms like that.'

Olivia blinked twice quickly. Surely an astounding man. 'I wonder,' she thought, 'if he's the sort of man for whom women simply don't exist. Somehow I don't think it's that.'

She was more than certain that it wasn't three hours later, when he stopped suddenly before a shop in Naples.

'By Jove,' he said, 'your dress!' It was a very elaborate affair that he was pointing at: a background of gold tissue, draped opulently with brocade and velvet.

'Ah, no,' she said. 'You'd want a big-featured woman to carry off a thing like that. I'd be submerged by it.'

'I'm not so sure, we'll see.'

Olivia was certain, though. She was small-boned, and she dressed always so that her frocks might be a setting and no more. She was not striking enough to wear striking dresses. 'It'll never do,' she said.

The girl in the shop was inclined to agree with her.

'But I am sure, Madam,' she said, 'that we shall be able to find something else that will. I will show Madam afterwards. This is, of course, a very lovely frock, but as François said when he designed it, it is not everybody's dress. If Madam will just lift it so. Yes, like that. Yes, oh, but … after all, Madam, I am not certain.'

Not certain! Ah, but Olivia was. With a little gasp she realized that this dress which never under any circumstances would she have looked at twice, was the one flamboyant dress in the whole world that it would be possible for her to wear without loss of personality.

And Gerald had been the one to spot it.

'You're right,' she said, as she walked out of the dressing-room, and for the first time in connexion with anything that directly concerned herself she saw the boyish glint of enthusiasm in Gerald's eyes.

'I thought I wasn't wrong. And this dress,' he added to the assistant, 'has got to be on the *Paul Verlaine* without fail in two hours' time.'

As Olivia sat that evening before her glass, the fingers that were pencilling her eyebrows nearly trembled. For the first time for seven years she was badly floundering. She was out of her depth and knew it. She did not understand this man. She did not begin to understand him. And the situation was getting on her nerves. 'He's got,' she decided, 'to lift that mask.' But though she devoted more attention that evening to her complexion than she could remember ever to have done before, though fifty heads were turned breathlessly in her direction as she strode resplendent in her new frock into the dining-room, though rarely as she danced had the light in her eyes been softer or more languishing, it was of Attic culture that they talked, she and Gerald, in the cool quiet of the upper deck, and punctually at ten o'clock he remarked that it was extraordinary how sleepy the sea air made one.

'This,' thought Olivia, 'is getting desperate.'

It had grown more than desperate by the time the *Paul Verlaine* had sailed out from the Piraeus and the Acropolis had grown indistinguishable against the red-brown background of its hills. Twelve hours of Doric columns had left Olivia's nerves a rag of tatters. The situation had grown too much for her. There was something more than exasperating about a man whose face would be filled with the most thrilling rapture by a piece of masonry, and who would desert the company of an admittedly attractive girl every evening at ten o'clock.

'I can't stand it,' Olivia muttered, 'I can't stand it.' Her chin was firm and her fists clenched resolutely. 'Somehow or other, I don't care how, and I don't care upon what terms, but somehow or other I'm going to make this man make love to me.'

There is a wind blowing in your face as you draw near the Bosporus, a wind that has been chilled and whetted by the Russian snows, and as Olivia leant shivering against the taffrail of the *Paul Verlaine* looking out at the white line of coast that was Stamboul, 'I wonder,' she asked, 'if it's worthwhile staying up on deck for.'

'I'd give it another five minutes,' said Gerald Palmer, 'if I were you.'

By the time those five minutes were at an end, there had ceased to be any question of worthwhile.

For it is a miracle, that first sight of Constantinople. One has been so often disappointed; there are so many places of which one has been led by pictures and photographs to expect too much, that one has grown disillusioned about the accepted beauties of the world. It is down the side streets of history that one looks now for the rare, the unpremeditated moment. And so, as that low line of mosques and minarets becomes distinct, you smile. 'Ah, but this,' you say, 'is merely an effect of light and distance; in a minute or two the mean ugly little houses will grow plain, as they did at Rome and Athens, and we shall see antiquity drossed by its setting of modernity. It will pass, this moment, for it is illusory.' The ship draws closer and the outline of domes and turrets grows more clear; but there are no mean houses, only green lawns and gardens running down to the city wall. And slowly the boat swings round into the harbour and high on your right is Galata, and before you, beyond the shipping through a faint lilac mist, the exquisite low-lying crescent of Stamboul; and with a gasp you realize that it is, in fact, the city that was loved of Loti, all that has been ever said in praise of it.

'So this,' said Olivia, 'is the thing you've come for. Are you disappointed?'

'Disappointed! It's so much lovelier than anything I expected that I shan't have the heart to go on shore. I couldn't run the risk of being disillusioned.'

'I trust, however,' a voice at his elbow murmured, 'that that will not prevent Miss Marshall from making a tour of it.'

'My dear Wellaway, I was about to suggest that it would be a kind thought if you would squire her.'

Olivia blinked at them. A whole day in that boob's company. Still, even for boobs there were uses in the world. For Olivia was an ardent student of the cinema, and had been instructed by films innumerable that if a man affected to ignore a woman she had only to display interest in another, to rouse the sluggard's ardour. Than which, in point of fact, there are policies far less effective.

'I need hardly say,' she cooed, 'how grateful I should be to Mr. Wellaway if he would.'

And in her eyes there was a look that made the boob draw breath extremely quickly. For though Gerald might have her guessing, she was on firm ground where Wellaway was concerned.

'Fair game,' that's how he had summed her up. 'One of those bachelor girls one heard so much about. One wouldn't get such a bit of luck coming one's way twice.' That was his attitude to her, and she knew it.

So on the next morning it was with Wellaway that she drove through the winding, irregular, dog-infested streets; and very winding and very irregular they were, and the car was not well sprung, and every few yards they would find themselves jolted against each other, so that their shoulders were touching half the time, and their hands kept brushing and 'I wonder,' thought Olivia, 'if men realize how we make use of them.' And there was a smile fluttering on her lips as she lay back in the car, listening while James Wellaway said each in turn the things she had expected of him.

She wore that night the dress that had been bought for her at Naples, and all through dinner she cast about Wellaway's enchanted neck the wreaths of her wit and elegance; without apparently, however, disturbing her host's composure. He was so glad, he said, that they had had a jolly day. He had just sat on deck watching the city under its aureole of changing lights.

'He doesn't believe I'm serious,' thought Olivia.

So it was with Wellaway that she danced the first three fox-trots, and it was beside Wellaway that she sat afterwards in a quiet but not too quiet part of the lower deck. And 'It's marvellous, too marvellous,' he said to her; 'never met any girl like you before, been looking for one like you all my life. Moment I saw you I knew. One always does, I think, don't you? First sight and all that?'

And Olivia nodded her head and waited patiently till she heard along the deck a voice that she recognized as Gerald's. Then she raised her voice.

'Do come here, Gerald,' she called out. 'It's so exciting. James has just asked me to marry him.'

'And that,' she added to herself, 'leaves it up to Gerald.' For Wellaway would, she knew quite well, be inadequate to the situation. And if this didn't make Gerald give himself away, she did not quite see what would.

If he had, however, anything beyond general amiability to give away, he most emphatically did not give it.

'Why, how idyllic!' he cried. 'I've no need, I'm sure, to ask you if you've said "Yes".'

Eight stressful years had taught Olivia to take her cues up quickly.

'I wanted you, Gerald dear,' she said, 'to be the first person to wish us luck.'

And as James Wellaway, the fingers of his left hand fluttering awkwardly at his tie, muttered inaudible acceptances of Gerald's congratulations: 'I suppose I've got to marry the creature now,' Olivia thought.

Not that she had not one or two cards left to play. Nor, indeed, that she regarded marriage, should the worst arrive, as a necessary deterrent to her resolution. All the same it would be as well for Gerald to realize all that he was missing.

So the next day it was not Etrurian statuary but the duties of a wife that Olivia discussed with him.

'The trouble about the modern wife,' she explained to him, 'is that she forgets that her first job is to make a home. That's what a man marries for, a home. He expects it and should be given it.'

And she explained how she proposed to make James Wellaway's house a model of domestic efficiency. To all of which Gerald Palmer agreed most heartily. 'There's nothing like a home,' he said. And when they reached Smyrna he spent half a day ransacking that city of dust and ruins till he unearthed a dinner service that should be worthy of so noble a decision. And Olivia thanked him prettily and decided to play another card. 'I'll show him all he's giving up.'

So the next day she explained to him that the mistake most good housewives made was that they forgot that an effort was needed if they were to retain their husband's love. It was no good letting the ashes cool. Did not Balzac say that the ideal wife was always a mistress to her husband. And so that Gerald should have no doubt about what she meant, that evening when he was standing in a conveniently adjacent shadow she embraced her fiancé in such a way as to convince that young person that he was standing on the brink of a most shattering experience.

'The strain of an engagement,' she said to Gerald, 'is terrible … when one loves … as I do.'

He nodded his head sympathetically. Yes, it was terrible, a long engagement and the propinquity of a ship. 'Perhaps,' he said, 'I might be able to do something for you.'

And that was the last night that Olivia spent alone in the luxurious stateroom. For early on the following morning they reached Alexandria, a city in which Gerald Palmer was not without influence and position, and with influence and position it is possible to obtain even special licences in an incredibly short time.

'So that's that,' thought Olivia, as she watched the cabin boy dispose of her husband's trunks.

Olivia's worst enemy could scarcely accuse her of the weakness of self-pity. From the start she had stood up to life and made the best of more than one bad job. Not, she realized as the *Paul Verlaine* steamed into Marseilles, that this was such a particularly bad one. Wellaway's yearly income had transpired to be a five-figure one. Four days of marriage had converted her restive prey into a docile and adoring slave. Nor did she feel quite so uncertain now of Gerald Palmer. She had begun to make her mind up about him. He was afraid, like so many other men, of the responsibility of paying court to an unattached young woman. That was it. He had been afraid. Now, however, that she was married … For it must be remembered that Olivia Wellaway was in those days an extremely cynical young person over whose conduct eyebrows were lifted and tea-cups rattled. And she had not been many days in London before she rang up Gerald to suggest that she should come and see his library. 'I was so interested,' she said, 'in all you told me about Tuscan statuary.'

She bought a new frock the day before her visit. And the greater part of the afternoon she spent in one of those small establishments in Duke Street where they smooth your skin, and manicure your nails, and do things to your hair which have the effect, so its promoters say, of imparting gloss. And when she arrived at Gerald's flat she said that her hat was too tight and flung it on a chair, and displayed so lively an interest in Etrurian pottery that she spent two hours in Gerald's library, peering over his shoulder at volume after volume with the glossed and scented hair as near as hair well can be to a cheek; an interest so keen, in fact, that Gerald insisted when she left on lending her an immense volume on the subject which nearly broke her arm during the five minutes she spent looking for a taxi. 'I wonder,' she thought, as she sank sadly but gratefully back into its cushions, 'if my looks are going off.'

When she got back she sat for a long while anxiously before the mirror. 'No,' she decided at length, 'it can't be that.'

And when her husband returned from golf and murmured

something about getting some letters written before dinner, she drew close to him and placed her hands upon his shoulders and her eyes were languishing and he forgot all about his letters. 'No! it can't be that,' she said, as she sat rearranging her hair afterwards.

Still, it must be something.

And then suddenly she understood. Why, of course, but how ridiculous of her, that she should not have thought of it before. What else could it be? He thought she was too easy. He was one of those men who were only attracted by what was difficult. Thought she was too easy, did he? Ah, very well, but she would show him …

And that very evening at Mrs. Parchment's dance she smacked loudly, so that every one who could not see might hear, the face of a young man who had every reason for believing that the display of a little fervour would be encouraged. And at Mabel Gillett's she kept her face stonily calm when Archie Malcolm told a story that was only relatively advanced. And a friend who had become involved not over-creditably in a divorce suit had a vaguely general invitation 'for any day next month' declined in the third person. So that long before the time came for the readers of the *Morning Post* to be informed of Marjorie Wellaway's arrival in the world, it had become universally understood that you had to be pretty careful what you said or did when Olivia Wellaway was about. And by the time Marjorie's life had come to be gladdened by a brother, her mother's rigid regard for the proprieties had become so accepted as to have ceased to be an occasion for limericks.

But Gerald Palmer has not noticed. And nothing is less likely than that he ever will. For we live in an age of amateur psychologists who dig deep for what lies upon the surface. And what it all amounted to was this: that Gerald Palmer, curious though it may sound, did not happen to be attracted to Olivia in what Edwardian heroines described as 'just that way'. And having learnt in a stern school the amount of patience and ingenuity that was required to overcome the reluctance of those ladies by whom he was, he had never imagined that he could, as Wellaway would have put it, ignite where he was not ignited. He simply had not thought about Olivia like that.

And so that is how the matter stands. And in the meantime Mrs. James Wellaway is growing hourly more unapproachable. The conventions have no more staunch defender. And the decades will pass. In twenty years' time she will be the terror of her nieces, and I am rather sorry for the young men who want to escort Marjorie to dances. And I can hear nephews cautioning each other: 'For heaven's sake don't let Aunt Olivia know!' and their parents whispering, 'What will Olivia say if she finds out!' And I can see a hard black pencil striking out the undesirable names upon a calling list …

And by that time every one will have forgotten that she was once Olivia Marshall.

And I daresay that it always has been more or less like that.

1926

The Last Chukka

I had no intention of visiting Siam when I started my world tour. It was one of those unexpected things that happen easily and quickly in the unhurrying East. I mentioned in the Penang Club that I had sponsored at Chapman & Hall's a novel about the Siamese teak forests called *Brown Wife or White*. 'In that case you ought to see the country,' my host said. 'A friend of mine is Forestry Adviser there. He's starting on a jungle trip next month. Why don't you join him?' A telegram was despatched, and two weeks later I was trudging in an elephant train with a cohort of coolies through the heat and mud and rain of the forest areas that lie north of Chiengmai.

In those days the teak trade was highly prosperous; it was organized almost exclusively by the British with the co-operation of the Danes, whose links with the country have been always close—the Siamese have been called 'The Danes of Asia'—and the atmosphere at Chiengmai, the H.Q. of the teak trade, was like that of a British Colony. I felt, after spending a month in the Federated Malay States, that I was still in the British Raj.

My jungle trip lasted for three weeks; we marched twelve to fourteen miles a day, striking camp at dawn, arriving at our next point early in the afternoon, an hour or so ahead of the elephants; to sleep sometimes under canvas, sometimes in one of the company's compounds. The path led through rocky mountain paths and flooded rice-fields. I learnt then under what tough conditions the early pioneers had developed the areas where their companies had concessions.

I spent a night in the compound of a young manager who seemed, in his health and cheerfulness, his efficiency, his sense of duty and responsibility, his friendly but firm treatment of his staff, to typify all that was most admirable in the type of Briton who went overseas. On my return a week later, I found him pale, sweating, shivering, stretched out on a long chair under blankets, struck down by malaria.

From the veranda of his bungalow I could see across the brown waters of the Menam down which the logs were drifting on their slow five years' journey towards Bangkok, the towering splendour of the jungle. There it stood, lovely and cool and green in the October sunlight. It was so beautiful. You could not believe that anything so beautiful could be so full of poison, that those green recesses concealed not peace and quiet but disease and misery and decay; that the very depths of that luxuriant greenery betrayed the malice of its heart, that the measure of its beauty was the measure of its hate, that the very creepers that festooned the trees, heightening their grandeur, making them lovelier than any trees in the West could be, were in fact slowly crushing them to death, eating away their strength, replenished with it, as the fever that fed upon this young man's strength.

In recent months I have often wished that rather more of the busy bureaucrats whom I have watched in Bangkok and Singapore, bustling about with their brief-cases repairing the ravages of 'colonial exploitation', had experienced the realities of 'the bad old days' before the age of antibiotics and air-conditioning.

After my trip on my return to Chiengmai I was taken round the leper hospital by the Senior Padre.

We went first to the men's part; and to that part of it which had been set out as the plan on which ultimately the rest of the hospital was to be rebuilt. It had been arranged like a garden suburb, in a series of small crescents; with neat, brightly painted bungalows each with its carefully ordered plot of ground in front. The gravel paths were trim and closely weeded. In the centre of each crescent blazed gorgeously an immense bed of flowers, and on the steps and on the verandas of the bungalows the patients lounged lazily in the heavy sunlight, gossiping and chewing betel-nut. It was very home-like.

'To begin with we used to let them marry,' the Padre told me. 'Leprosy is not the contagious thing it was once taken for. With proper precautions there is no reason why the children of lepers should be infected. But we found it involved us in too many complications. To carry on at all it was essential to separate the men and women.'

We were crossing, as we talked, the waste part of ground dividing the men's quarters from the women's, which a collection of patients, in whose systems the disease had made inconsiderable progress, were converting into a further series of paths and gardens.

Midway between the two sections was the chapel. And as we drew close to it, the Padre's pace slackened. It had been built only a couple of years back, and he could never pass it without a feeling of profound thankfulness that life should have been granted him long enough to see the completion of it. He was an old man, past sixty, weakened by fever and overwork. To build such a chapel had been one of his life's ambitions.

For thirty-seven years he had had to wait.

When he had come to Siam as a young man from Washington, there had been nothing at Chiengmai—nothing: no mission, no school, no hospital. There had not even been a railway beyond Bangkok, and with funds scanty and supplies five weeks away, he had realized that till the schools and hospital were established, every consideration but those of the most bare necessities must be denied. He had waited for thirty-seven years, till the time had come when he could build according to his dreams. There it stood now, a high, white building, very bare and open, as was inevitable from the conditions of the place, but possessed of genuine beauty in its austere dignity of naked line.

'We have two services a week,' he said, 'and though there is no compulsion, there are very few of the patients who do not attend. They are all Christians; within a week of their joining us, they come of their own accord to be baptized. It is only natural after all. They were brought up as Buddhists, but Buddhism, for all its beauties, is not a religion that holds its hand out to the pariah. When the Buddha saw a leper, he was filled with disgust and turned away; the Buddhists have allowed their lepers to lie unwanted about their streets. But Jesus, when He saw a leper, was moved, stretched out His hand and told His disciples that they should have care for lepers, so that the leper, who all his life has held himself to be an outcast, discovers that after all there is a God who cares for him. He turns naturally to the God whose heart is so great that it has room in it even for the poor leper.'

Beyond the chapel were the women's quarters. They had been arranged for the most part in long dormitories divided off into deep but narrow rooms, with seven to ten mattresses in each.

'It seems to work better this way with women,' explained the Padre. 'We once tried putting them in bungalows like the men, but the moment they get in couples they start quarrelling.'

And turning to the bunch of women who were seated in the shady corner of the veranda, he began to joke with one of them about the bamboo basket she was plaiting. He pretended that she was a saleswoman and he a customer.

'I will give you thirty satangs for your basket.'

And she, in the true Lao spirit, began to bargain with him.

'Oh no, master. It is worth eighty at the very least.'

'Perhaps then I might give you forty.'

'But I would not take less than sixty-five.'

As they haggled the other women joined merrily in, with laughter, relishing this travesty of a scene that had been so familiar in the life they had abandoned. They looked happy, but it was hard to look without revulsion at a woman in whom the disease was reaching its last stages. Her nose, as though the heel of a fist had been pressed ruthlessly upon it, was flattened back upon her face. The hands with which she was preparing her dish of curry were almost fingerless; while her feet, one of which was wrapped round with bandages, were no more than slabs of flesh marked here and there with certain irregular projections.

'You've got to have a strong stomach to stand that,' I said.

The Padre shrugged his shoulders.

'One gets used to it, and besides, one knows that they're not unhappy really. They're all in the same boat. It makes a big difference, that.'

'But you must have trouble with them sometimes?'

'How do you mean?'

'With the young ones, with those who are only affected slightly. That rule about marriage must weigh on them pretty heavily.'

'They're at liberty to go.'

'And do they often?'

'Occasionally.'

'Do they come back?'

'More often than not.'

I could understand their going. There was something pathetic about those little bungalows that had all the appearance but none of the reality of a home.

'It must be lonely,' I said.

'That's the way Butterman talked,' he answered.

I caught the reference.

I knew well enough the story he referred to. It was a story that everyone who was in Malaya about that time had heard.

I had heard it from so many sources that I am able to tell it now in straightforward narrative, without needing to explain where and how I learnt each separate detail; indeed I should find it impossible to remember how I came to put the jigsaw puzzle together piece by piece. I see it as a single story—the story of the white man's battle with the jungle.

Butterman had been a familiar figure in Penang and Ipoh and K.L. For fifteen years he had worked in the Moulmin-Madras Timber Company, and he had often been down to the E. and O. He had once even stayed over there for a week or so of his leave. He was a popular enough fellow; good at games, generous with his money; though too reserved, too inexpansive, as a result, it was said, of his lonely stretches in the jungle, to make close friendships. He was an ambitious and conscientious worker; steady, trust-worthy, unemotional, keeping his temper and his head. Everyone respected him. 'He's the sort of man you can feel safe with. He'll never do anything unexpected,' it was said of him.

No one was more surprised than the Padre when Butterman arrived in the station unheralded and for no very obvious reason, to request, his first evening at the club, that he should be shown round the leper hospital.

It was the first time during his fifteen years in Chiengmai that he had displayed any interest in the mission's work. His behaviour was as curious as his request. He asked a number of questions with a startlingly unexpected interest and intensity. He demanded to know the symptoms of leprosy. When he was told where the first signs were to be seen, he repeated slowly over and over again, 'The hands and feet; yes, yes, the hands and feet.' He asked about marriage; of the probability of a leper's child being infected. He maintained with a curious fierceness that it was unfair to deny them marriage. He did not apparently listen to anything that the Padre said. Then suddenly without warning he held out his hand.

'It's been very good of you,' he said. 'It's been most interesting. It's a magnificent work … no idea that it was anything like this. Well, good-bye, Padre, good-bye.'

The sudden change of tone was as curious as it was embarrassing.

'We needn't surely say good-bye,' the Padre said. 'I shall be seeing you at the club tonight.'

'Afraid not. Going back to the jungle this afternoon.'

'What! After only two days here!' It was a surprising announcement, for Butterman's camp was a good week's march distant.

'Yes, only just came to have a look round. Good-bye, many thanks, and—' he hesitated, then drawing close to the Padre he touched him on the shoulder, lowering his voice to the tone which one employs for the communication of a shady confidence— 'about that other business,' he said, 'you're quite right, you know, quite right. There are some people who aren't fit to marry.'

It was a leave-taking as astonishing as it was abrupt.

All day long the disturbing impression of that odd interview remained with the Padre, so that when he happened to find himself alone for a moment beside Arnold, Butterman's manager, at the large round table on which after sundown drinks and glasses were set out, he returned instantly to the subject.

'I'm a little worried about one of your fellows,' he said. 'Do you mind if I talk to you about him?'

Arnold looked up quickly. Heavily built, with a small imperial and moustache that scarcely concealed the thickening and sagging of his chin-line, he was in point of years little more than youthfully middle-aged, but the tropics had begun to take their toll of him. One thought of him as old.

'One of my fellows? Who?'

'Butterman.'

'Butterman?' He echoed the name incredulously. 'But there's nothing wrong with him. He was fit enough a few hours ago when I saw him off!'

The Padre didn't reply directly.

'Wasn't his coming all the way down from Behang-Kong for a two days' visit rather curious?'

Arnold shrugged.

'I don't know. I give my lads a pretty free hand in the way of breathers. One has to. The jungle's a curious place. For month after month you'll be working along quite happily, everything seems all right, then suddenly one morning something snaps, your nerves are gone, and you know that if you stay another hour there, you'll be off your head. A queer place, the jungle.

69

The size of it, the loneliness, the never seeing a white man for weeks on end; the bouts of fever, and all that hidden life of the jungle crowding so closely round you. Sometimes it's like a hand throttling you.'

And sitting back in the calm of his last weeks, he mused on the number of men that he had known of whom the jungle in one way or another had got the better. The loneliness, the fever, the privation, the autumn rains, and the summer heat; one by one they had gone down before them, with broken health or broken nerves.

'I don't think there's much wrong with Butterman,' he said. 'He merely felt that it was time he had a rest.'

The Padre was unconvinced, however.

'He behaved very curiously at my place this morning. I was wondering if there might not be something worrying him. I don't want to interfere, but he hasn't got himself mixed up with any girl here, has he?'

Arnold laughed: a rather coarse, brutal laugh.

'I'm afraid, as far as a sleeping dictionary's concerned, Butterman's Lao is going to remain as inadequate as it's always been.

He's never had any use for that sort of thing.'

'Exactly. And it was just because of that that I was wondering whether he mightn't have started now. Wasn't there some talk about his getting married during his last leave?'

'There was talk, but when it came to the point he decided that it wasn't fair to bring out a white woman to a place like this. I dare say he was right: it's no place to bring up children, what with the heat and the monotony. It's a dog's life for a young girl. There's only one woman in a hundred that could manage it. He didn't say much to me about it; muttered something as far as I

70

can remember about some fellows being not fit to marry.'

The Padre started. It was the same oddly arresting phrase that Butterman had applied to the celibate lepers at the hospital. Not fit to marry …

'I wish,' he said, 'that you'd have a rather careful look at him next time you're in the jungle. I can't help being worried about him. I'm not at all sure that he doesn't want more than a three days' rest.'

'What'll you have, a gin and bitters?'

'No, thanks. I'll stick to *stengahs.*'

'Right. Will you mix your own?'

It was the hour when life for the teak-wallah is at its sweetest, the hour just after sundown, when the air is cooling after the long day's heat, when the body, after the long day's work, is refreshed by the evening's bath, and by the afternoon's 'lie off', when *pahits* and *stengahs* are set out on the small camp table, and tired limbs lie slackly along the deep canvas chairs. It is the hour that consoles and cancels everything that the day has known of thirst and exposure and fatigue. And Arnold sipped at his whisky, tranquillized by the profound content of physical exhaustion, while Butterman with minute care set himself about the preparation of a *pahit.*

It had been a long hard day. They had been up at five while it was still dark and, sending their carriers ahead of them, had marched two hours before breakfast. There had been no rain for several weeks and in consequence the paths across the paddy-fields were dry, but even so the going had been extremely hard; they had marched seventeen kilometres; the greater part of it had been over rugged hilly passes, and they had come into camp a full three hours ahead of the elephants. A hard day. But it was worth it now. At no other price could you purchase this exquisite sensation of utter languor.

Out of the corner of his eye Arnold watched Butterman sip critically, then appreciatively, at his gin and bitters. They had been together for three days now, and as far as he could see there was nothing wrong with the chap. His accounts and his reports were in perfect order. His comments on the working of the teak had been extremely lucid, extremely practical. He was right enough. There had been nothing but a momentary touch of nerves that Padre Martin had magnified out of all proportion. A touch of nerves, and who should know better than he how common that was, after twenty-five years of it out here.

Twenty-five years: a long chunk out of a man's life. Not that he was regretting it. At the beginning he had been resentful. That morning when his father had taken him into his study to explain. Yes, that had been bitter-enough-tasting medicine. 'I'm very sorry, my boy,' his father had said to him, 'but things have not been going too well with me of late. And I cannot afford to send both you and your brother up to Oxford. You are the elder and you have the right to the first consideration. At the same time to a man such as your brother who's an intellectual pure and simple, whose career will probably be one of scholarship, a university education is a far more important thing than it can ever be for you. It seems to me indeed essential to his future. Whereas I feel that while you would be handicapped you would not be crippled by its absence. If you insist, of course, on what is after all your right, I will never refer to the matter again. I must say I hope though …'

Yes, it had been bitter medicine, but he had swallowed it. And here he was now going back to London in the middle forties, retiring on a capital of forty thousand and a pension, which was more than that brother of his would be able to do if he lived to eighty. He had swallowed the medicine to the last drop. He had played the game through to the last chukka. All down the course he had kept his head. He had not flung his money about on expensive leaves. He had not married his Lao woman like those others had, and when he had come back to Chiengmai as station master he had not allowed himself to become fettered by those bonds of propinquity and habit which others had found hard to break when it came to the last. He had built Cheam a little bungalow beside the river, and when the children had grown up he had sent them to be educated in Malaya. He would play the game by them, he would leave enough when he went away for them to have a start in life. They should have their bread and butter, and if they wanted the jam to spread on it, well, they must find that for themselves. And as for Cheam, she would be happy enough with her bungalow and a paddy-field or two. She would not feel she had been ill-treated. She was unwesternized. She believed, as all Laos did believe, that the mere fact of a man and woman living together constituted marriage, and that marriage meant simply the observances of certain practical obligations. He had observed those obligations. He would leave a clean record here. He was getting the best of both worlds, getting it both ways.

His last jungle trip. In a few weeks now Butterman would be coming down to Chiengmai, to take over. A good fellow, Butterman: sound, steady, practical. It had been ridiculous of Padre Martin to imagine that there was anything wrong with him. He was getting old, the Padre, old and fanciful and fussy. A good fellow, but getting old; had seemed old even in those distant days when himself had been a junior assistant.

And as he lay back in the long comfort of his chair, living over the days of stress and struggle, his eyes began to close, and hi.

mouth to sag. A hard life, a good life, and now London at the end of it. The best of both worlds, he had had the thing both ways.

A good life, a hard life. His head began to nod … In another minute he would have been asleep had not a shriek at his elbow abruptly disturbed his reverie: a wild, uncanny shriek it was; like that of an animal maddened by fear and anger. 'Heavens!' was his first thought, 'a tiger.' But before he had had time to blink his eyes, he had realized that this was no occasion for alarm.

'Good heavens, man,' Butterman was shrieking. 'What on earth are you doing with those socks?'

He had risen to his feet: his whole body, for all that he was trying to support himself against the table, was shivering as though with ague; nor could he keep steady the arm with which he was pointing at the astonished 'boy', who was gaping in the doorway of the tent, a pair of white socks dangling from his hand.

'What are you doing?' Butterman shrieked. 'Who told you that you could touch them?'

The boy was so frightened that he could scarcely speak.

'The socks master wear today,' he stammered, 'they dirty. I go wash.'

'And who told you that you could wash them?' Butterman bellowed. 'How dare you touch my things without permission? I'll tell you when I want things washed. You put them back.'

The boy hesitated.

'They dirty, master,' he explained. 'Master no can wear.'

For answer Butterman beat madly with his fists upon the flimsy table, making the glasses and the bottles shake on their tin tray.

'You put them down,' he shrieked. 'You put them down.' And as the boy hurried back into the hut, he sank into his chair with

74

a slow gasp. His eyes were blazing and his cheeks were pale, his lips trembled and there was a circlet of sweat along his forehead. He lay back breathing heavily as though he had completed an immense effort, as though he had been preserved from an immense danger.

'They spy on one,' he said. And he pronounced each word separately and distinctly, as a child does when it repeats a lesson. 'You can't trust them. All the time you have to be on your guard against them. Spies. Every one of them. Spies!'

Arnold made no reply. He nodded his head and sipped slowly at his emptying glass. But he knew in that instant that it was over no fancy that the Padre was worrying.

'I was wondering,' he said some ninety minutes later, as the boy was clearing away the dinner, 'whether it wouldn't be a good idea for you to come back to Chiengmai with me tomorrow. You'll be taking over in a month or so, and it wouldn't be a bad idea if we were to work side by side for a little, so that you can see how things fit in.'

Butterman, who since his recovery from the outburst had been exchanging in a perfectly normal manner the mixture of personalities and business that are the basis of conversation, eagerly welcomed the suggestion.

'I'd be very grateful if I might. There are one or two things that I'm not too sure about.' And he began to discuss certain points of routine and policy in a fashion so lucid that Arnold began to wonder whether after all he and the Padre were not simply imagining things.

There couldn't be anything wrong with a man whose brain was as clear and collected as this.

Before the night had passed, however, there had occurred another slight, but following on what had occurred previously, strangely disquieting incident.

For some reason or another, Arnold had found that he could not sleep. To compose his thoughts he had decided to read for a few moments. He had been unable, however, to find the matches and walking to the opening of his tent was just about to call his boy when he saw that Butterman had a light burning still. To avoid disturbing the camp he walked across the few yeards of ground that divided the two tents.

'Sleepless too?' he began, 'I was wondering …' then stopped abruptly before the unexpected sight that confronted him.

Cross-legged upon his haunches, Butterman was seated on the small rubber ground-sheet beside the bed, with the wide black silk Chinese trousers in which it is the fashion for Europeans in Siam to sleep, rolled back over his knees and with a large heavy-powered electric torch he was examining his naked feet.

'Good Lord,' said Arnold, 'what's the matter? Have you got mud-sores or something?'

Butterman had given a start at the first sound of his friend's voice, but the expression of surprise changed quickly to one that Arnold found impossible to diagnose. It was a mixture of know-ingness, and suspicion, and furtive cunning; a look that was at the same time a shield against detection and an invitation to share in a conspiracy. There was triumph in it, and fear, hatred and distrust and friendship. And when Butterman spoke his voice had a peculiar intonation that should have been the key to the mystery, but was at the same time an added veil across it.

'Not yet,' he said, 'not yet. Nothing that you can see as yet.'

And Arnold as he heard it shuddered as though he had been brought face to face with something that was uncanny and unhealthy, something that was outside the experience of practi-cal mortality.

There was an odd smell of burning about the house. For a week ever since their return from the jungle, it had clung fugitive and intermittent to the wide-windowed, wide-verandaed bungalow. For half a day or so you would think it had disappeared, and then suddenly as you came into a room or went on to a veranda you would meet it, vague, sinister, repellent. And for hours, although it was so slight that a stranger coming into the house would not have noticed it, the smell would follow you. You would taste it in your food and in your wine. It would be upon the soap with which you washed your face and in the flowers which were upon your table. You waited for it, sought for it, in the same way that during a sleepless night you will listen with a straining ear for the faint rattle of a window pane in a distant corridor.

'For God's sake,' muttered Arnold irritably to his boy, 'can't you find where that smell comes from? It must be something that the boys are doing in the kitchen.'

But the boy lifted his clasped hands before his face.

'No, no, master,' he pleaded. 'Boys worried by it as much as master. No can find, master, no can find!'

It was in the liveliest of ill-tempers that Arnold went in to breakfast.

In the doorway of the room he paused.

Butterman as usual was down already. He was seated in a wicker chair on the veranda manicuring his nails. It was a habit to which he was becoming increasingly addicted. The hours of idleness that most men devote to pipes and cigarettes he would spend drawing a long steel file slowly round the oval of his nails, lifting his fingers to the light to examine his handiwork; then once again remitting the supple metal to its task. A testy comment rose to Arnold's lips, but he bit it back; the fellow was his guest here after all. And walking over to the table he took his seat at it.

The laundry account had been placed on a slip of paper beside his plate, and as the meal had not yet been served, he picked the thing up and glanced at it. It had been arranged in two columns; down one side of it was a list of the various articles: shirts, collars, singlets, handkerchiefs. And against each article was set in the first column the number of pieces that he had sent, in the second those that had been sent by Butterman. He amused himself for a moment by a comparison of the number. Shirts, collars, hand-kerchiefs; the same number identically. Then suddenly he gave a whistle.

'Good lord! man,' he said. 'You're pretty economical in socks.'

Butterman looked up quickly.

'Economical? Socks? What do you mean?'

'Do you know that you haven't sent a single pair to be washed this week?'

Butterman did not answer. Instead he rose to his feet and walking to the table, leant forward over it.

'Don't you think,' he said, and he spoke slowly, articulating each word carefully. 'Don't you think it would be better if I were to go back to my own house now? It was extremely kind of you to offer me the hospitality of yours. But I must not trespass on it too long. The alterations that were being made to mine are prac-tically completed. Don't you think it would be better if I were to go?'

Arnold watched him closely. There was nothing unusual or unexpected in Butterman's suggestion. A man preferred to be among his own things. But behind the intonation of the words, 'Don't you think it would be better,' it was almost as though he had heard a threat. It was absurd, of course. Butterman and he were old and proven friends. It was absurd, utterly absurd. He would have to watch himself. A man was in a bad way when he began to imagine things.

'Oh, don't you worry about that, my dear fellow,' he said. 'It's only for another day or two. It's so jolly having you. Life gets a little lonely sometimes for an old bachelor like myself.'

'Old bachelor,' he repeated, and the pitch of Butterman's voice rose suddenly to a laugh. 'Why didn't you marry then? What was to stop you marrying? And now you are finding yourself lonely!'

'Well, sometimes, naturally.'

Again Butterman laughed, a high-pitched laugh, that was a cackle almost.

'Lonely! Those homes that are not homes, that have all the appearance, but none of the reality, none of the sweetness of a home! Lonely, yes, I think I'd better be going, Arnold.'

'It's as you choose, of course. But if you go I shall be extremely sorry. It's nice having you.'

'Nice having me? But why, why should you like having me?' He did not wait, however, for a reply. 'Well, if you want me, I suppose I might as well. Here, or another place, it comes to the same thing.'

And pulling back a chair he sat down hurriedly at the table. At that moment the boy arrived with breakfast.

It was the usual two-course meal. Eggs and bacon, preceded by a sardine fish-cake. But though Arnold doused his plate in tomato ketchup, and stirred three lumps of sugar into his tea, through every mouthful that he took he was conscious of that acrid, persistent taste of burning. No wonder they got nervy with this smell about the place.

'By the way,' he said, 'Padre Martin will be dropping in today for tiffin.'

79

Butterman grunted.

'Good fellow, Martin,' Arnold added.

Butterman made no comment. He finished his fish-cake, helped himself to three of the four eggs upon the dish and consumed them resolutely. 'Whatever else there may be wrong with him, the fellow's appetite's all right,' thought Arnold. It was not till he had finished his fourth piece of toast and marmalade that Butterman spoke again.

'Do you often,' he asked, 'have Martin here to tiffin?'

'Not too often; now and again.'

'Once every four months or so, for example?'

'About that.'

'And when did you ask him last?'

'I forget, some while back at least. It seemed about time to be asking him again.'

Butterman grunted.

'Tiffin isn't a very usual meal to be asked to. It isn't like dinner, is it? One doesn't usually,' he went on, 'ask a man to tiffin unless it's for some special reason. I wonder why you asked Martin here today.'

'My dear fellow …'

But Butterman, once he had set the question, appeared to have lost all interest in the subject.

'Here, or another place,' he said cryptically, 'it comes to the same thing.'

And rising from the table he walked over to the wicker chair by the veranda, drew from his pocket the long steel file and set himself once again to smooth the curved surface of his nails.

Arnold drew a perplexed hand across his forehead. Where was he? What was happening to him? Was this the friendly, familiar world in which he had lived so long? As he walked out of his bungalow, he felt himself to be escaping from the poisoned atmosphere of some prison house.

He had left the house earlier than usual, but the car was already waiting for him.

'Straight to the office, master?' asked the Syce.

Arnold shook his head. He had need before the day's work started of a few moments of fresh air, and the arrival of the laundry account had reminded him that there were several articles of which he stood in need.

'Drive to Yem-Sing's,' he said.

It was nine o'clock: the heat of the day was still some hours distant, and the main street of Chiengmai was crowded with men and women hurrying by in their brightly-coloured singlets: many of them carrying slung across their shoulders deep tins of water and baskets of fruits and vegetables. They drove slowly, for the motorcar was as new a visitant as the railway to North Siam, and neither had the Laos acquired the habit of avoiding danger, nor had the drivers learnt to resist the thrill of speed; incapacities so regrettable in their consequences that the authorities had marked at either end of the main street a series of artificial bumps in the centre of the roadway to enforce a slackening of pace. At a speed of little more than five miles an hour Arnold's car drew up before a Chinese store.

'I want quite a lot of things, Yem-Sing,' he said.

The merchant passed his hands across each other; and his lips parted gratefully over teeth blackened by many passages of lime-tinged betel-nut, as Arnold hurried through his list.

'Six shirts,' he repeated, 'six singlets, two dozen handkerchiefs, a dozen pair of socks, white socks. Ah, but that is the one thing I cannot manage. I have not in my shop a single pair of white socks left.'

'What!'

'I am sorry, master, extremely sorry.' And in the Lao fashion he lifted his clasped hands before his face. 'But only a week back the *naï* Butterman came in here and bought every pair of white socks I had.'

'The *naï* Butterman!'

'Yes, master, truthfully. "How many pairs have you of white socks?" he asks. Forty or fifty pairs, I tell him. "Very well," he answers, "I will take the lot." '

'Forty or fifty pairs!'

'To be exact there were forty-seven.'

For the second time that day Arnold rested a perplexed hand upon his forehead. Forty-seven pairs, and not one pair sent to the laundry; and in the jungle that curious outburst against his servant; and that strangely intonated phrase: 'Wouldn't it be better if I went?' Those questions about Martin; the odd expression of his eyes when he had come that evening into his tent. Where was it, what had happened to it, that friendly, that familiar world?

As he came out into the sun-drenched street he noticed Martin's car passing on the other side of it.

'You're coming to tiffin today, aren't you?' he called out.

For answer the Padre drew his car up beside the pavement.

'Tell me, how is Butterman?'

Arnold shook his head helplessly. 'It's something I don't understand. Something I don't begin to understand. At times he seems perfectly all right, so perfectly all right that I begin to wonder whether it isn't just myself imagining things. It's a hopeless situation.'

'I know, I know. And we're so far here from everything. If we could only get him down to Singapore or Bangkok even. If only a specialist in these things could look at him. It's outside my scope.

I can only guess at things. Ah well, at any rate, we shall have some common ground to compare notes on after tiffin.'

It was a tiffin of which Arnold was able subsequently to remember little. He could not recall what they ate or what they drank, or of what they spoke. There remained only the recollection of vague constraint: of himself talking loudly and incessantly on topics that were of no interest to him: of Martin's thin, high-pitched voice breaking in with an occasional comment: of Butterman taciturn and glowering, eating prodigiously of every dish: a vague impression. Everything that was said and thought during the early stages of the meal was muffled and obliterated by the one unforgettable moment of dramatic action. The rest was dim. He could not even remember how that moment had come about. Suddenly it had been there upon them. One minute it had not been, the next it was. One minute he had been talking in quick, querulous, excited sentences, the next for some obscure reason unknown to him he had ceased; had realized suddenly that Butterman in a trance almost of detachment was leaning on his elbows across the table, the hands lifted before his face, examining his fingers with the minutest care; had realized that the Padre in a trance also was gazing at them as in moments of hypnotic influence the subject will gaze at some bright object, a shilling, a crystal, a metal disc; found himself as his voice trickled into silence, gazing in his own turn, fascinated, spellbound, at those thin, tapered fingers that slowly one by one Butterman was revolving under his inspection.

Of how long they sat there Arnold had no idea. It was one of those instants that belonging as they do to eternity are timeless. There was the dateless interval of silent gazing, then the sudden shattering of that instant; the lifted head, Butterman's glance passing from one to the other, and the coming into his face as he realized he was being watched of an incredibly sinister expression.

'Ah!' he said. 'Ah!' And he laughed, leaning farther forward across the table, so that his hands were held almost beneath their faces. 'Look at them, look closely—they're interesting hands. They're firm, strong hands; feel the bones, how strong they are. Such strong hands, it wouldn't be difficult for them to kill a man. They'd go round his throat so quietly: they'd just tighten, tighten, tighten, so firm and strong: such firm strong fingers, right to the finger-tips, to the very extremities: the extreme extremities.'

Coldly, regularly, inexorably, like the chill, persistent rain of a northern twilight, the words followed one another. Then suddenly with a laugh, he flung himself back in his chair.

'By the way, Padre,' he said jovially, 'I know what I wanted to ask you: you're the very man to help me. I wonder if you could find a new boy for me?'

The change of attitude was so startling that the Padre could do no more than stammer feebly:

'New boy? But what's wrong with the one you've got?'

'What's wrong?' and into the voice had returned the note of menace. 'He spies, that's what's wrong with him, he spies. And I've no use for people who spy on me. I should remember that, Padre, if I were you. I get rid of them … one way or another. You'll get me a new boy, won't you?

'By the way, Arnold,' he went on. 'I've thought of rather a good scheme for stabilizing the value of the tical round Be-koy.' And for the next twenty minutes he discussed that very real problem of jungle life, the fluctuating value of exchange, with admirable clearness.

'I can't make it out,' said Arnold afterwards. 'There are times when he seems the sanest man I've ever come across. At others … well, you saw what he was like … and one can't place it, that's the trouble. One doesn't know what one's up against.'

It was at that moment that the boy who had been moving for some seconds at Arnold's side, came forward. On his face was a peculiar smile of triumph.

'I have found out, master,' he announced, 'whence comes that smell.'

'Ah!'

'It is the *naï* Butterman.'

'What!'

'Yes, master, the sweeper discovered it. Every morning the *naï* Butterman burns in his bathroom the pair of socks that he has worn the day before.'

Although there had been no creak of a lifted latch, no sound of a footfall in the passage, Arnold was conscious as he bent forward among the papers on his desk that someone was standing beside him in the room; someone who stood watching him with intent, malicious eyes. And for a moment he felt so terrified that he did not dare to move, did not dare to disturb that silent watching, did not dare to face the menace that was waiting him. Then with a quick jerk of resolution he looked up.

'Well, Butterman,' he said, 'and what is it I can do for you?'

By an effort of will he kept his voice natural and level-toned. But he felt the palms of his hands go moist as he met that glazed, uncannily bright stare.

'I'm rather busy at the moment,' he went on, 'but if you'd care to sit down and wait a little …'

Butterman laughed. He was not wearing a topee, and the hair

that fell dankly along his forehead was dishevelled. There was no collar-stud at his throat and the silk tie that held his shirt was knotted loosely. His sleeves were rolled above his elbow. In his eyes there was that same expression of hunted and desperate cunning with which he had leant forward an hour back across the tiffin table, and his laugh had that false unnatural note which one associates with the villains of melodrama. In his hand he was holding a heavy Colt revolver.

'Wait,' he cried. 'Oh, I don't mind waiting for a little. I'm in no hurry. Padre Martin will be at the hospital another two hours yet.'

'So you're going to see Padre Martin?'

'Yes, when I've done with you,' and stepping forward he seated himself on the edge of the table, without lowering for an instant the revolver that he had levelled at Arnold's head. 'So you thought you could spy on me,' he said; 'that you could bring me down from the jungle, and keep me in your house and spy on me; that you could have Padre Martin to tiffin with you, watching and watching till the moment came. You thought you were very clever, didn't you, that I shouldn't see through you as easily as I saw through that boy of mine. You weren't quite clever enough, though, were you?'

'Now, my dear fellow, do be sensible. What on earth is there that we could be spying on you for?'

'Spying on me, what for? Ah, but my good fellow, there's no need for me to pretend things any longer. We know well enough, we three, you and Martin and I. My boy may suspect, but he doesn't know. There's just we three, and there's no need for us to hide things from each other. We can be open now, can't we? It's so easy to be open now. Nothing's any longer at stake. It doesn't matter what we say or what we reveal; because in such a little while now there'll be only one of us who'll know. Only one left by … well … shall we say by three o'clock?'

And as he leant back laughing heartily, with the revolver held unwaveringly before him, the nature of his plan grew plain to Arnold.

'So you're going to shoot me first; then you're going up to the hospital to shoot Martin.'

Butterman nodded.

'At the same time I don't quite see how you'll manage to get both of us.'

'No?'

'How could you hope to, my dear fellow? Think! A revolver's a noisy thing. You'll have no difficulty in doing me in, we'll admit that, but how will you ever get out of here when you have? There's only one way out of this room, the way you've come, through the main office, and there are three clerks there, to say nothing of a porter at the gate. What'll you do when you've finished me?'

'I shall walk straight out through your office to the car that is waiting for me in the porch.'

'With all those clerks there?'

'They won't stop me. They'll be too astonished. People always are when something unusual happens. They'll be stunned into inaction. Suppose, for instance, you were to stand up on a table in the Ritz, shout "Silence" and then recite at the top of your voice an indecent limerick. What, do you imagine, would happen? That you'd be flung out? Nothing of the sort. People would just sit and gape at you, the waiters, the band, the diners, and you'd get down from the table, walk straight out of the room, and no one would say a word to you. Which is exactly what I shall do when I've shot you. I shall fire twice to make quite certain; then I shall walk out and no one will say a word to me. Long before the hue and cry has started I'll have settled my account with Martin.'

He spoke calmly, quietly, with the acute, clear sanity, that during the last days had characterized his discussion of every topic. It was as though by some law of compensation, the sickness that had warped one side of his intelligence, had intensified his perceptions in every other. And as Arnold sat back in his chair a sensation of utter helplessness possessed him. Through the window of his office he could hear the hooting of a car. In the office beyond two of his clerks were softly chattering together. Above his head the punkah was flapping lazily; the boy who worked it, the string of it tied round his toe, was rocking, half asleep, with a slow, measured rhythm, only six feet away behind that partition of thin match-board. All round him was the friendly, familiar world, pursuing its friendly, familiar course. And here he was trapped and weaponless.

'I should doubt,' continued Butterman, 'whether it was worth while prolonging the discussion.'

And on the butt of the revolver his finger tightened.

Arnold braced himself. He was not the man to meet death un-protestingly. His desk, which was flanked with two narrow sets of drawers, was cut away in the centre to ease his legs; and he wondered whether he might not be able by slipping downwards suddenly, and pushing upwards to overturn the desk and Butterman simultaneously. Anyhow it was worth trying. Even if he did not save his own life, he might create sufficient disturbance or delay to rescue Martin. Slackening the muscles of his legs and gripping tightly the seat of his chair so as to ensure strong leverage, he steadied himself to dive. ONE—TWO—he began to count, but just as he was about to spring, he noticed a sudden change in his assistant. A perplexed look had come into his face, the muzzle of the revolver had begun to waver; he lifted his left hand towards his head, his lips quivered. He staggered to his feet, to stand swaying stupidly. His fingers loosened their hold on the revolver, letting it fall clattering upon the floor. 'My head,' he sobbed, 'my head.' And his face pressed tightly into his hands, he began to sway like a drunken man across the room.

'Sunstroke!' gasped Arnold. 'Sunstroke! He had no topee!'

And leaping to his feet, he caught the reeling body into his arms.

An hour later in the small hospital ward that is reserved for American and European patients, Arnold and the Padre were standing at the foot of Butterman's bed. He was less restless now, packed as he was in ice, but he still tossed occasionally from side to side, and from his lips fell ceaselessly a delirious muttering.

'Those little painted bungalows up there …' that was the gist of his tortured rambling. 'Shut away up there by oneself, all the sweetness of one's life denied one: the softness of a woman's arms, the softness of a woman's smile, not fit for them, not fit … too great a danger … the hands and feet … the bones eaten away, perishing … the scorn, the helplessness … not fit … not fit … they take one and they shut one away up there. They spy on you and watch you, wait till they are quite certain, then they take you … take you … and shut you away in a little bungalow … leave you there to rot and perish … fingerless, toeless, featureless, they wait and watch and wait for you.…'

That was the gist of what he said.

'So he thought,' murmured Arnold, 'that he was a leper, that we were spying on him. But he hasn't a symptom, has he, of leprosy?'

'Not a symptom.'

89

'Then in heaven's name ...'

But the Padre lifted his hand. 'Wait a moment,' he said, 'I think I see.'

And as they stood there listening, gradually, through the labyrinth of repetitions and inaudibilities, the meaning of his trouble wound its way into the daylight, so that they came to see through what association of ideas the fever of an uneased longing had worked through that distracted brain till its owner had come to believe himself the victim of that dread disease.

'Not fit to marry,' the voice went on; 'the loneliness and the monotony and the fever; for eight months of the year living by herself ... no dancing, no theatres, the treachery of the climate ... and if she were to go out to the jungle, the squalor of a narrow tent ... not fit to marry ... the fellow who would dare to ask a woman to share that life ... not fit to marry ... You're right, Padre, not to let them marry ... to shut them away in those little painted houses ... danger's too great ... the softness and sweetness of a woman, the way she smiles, the way she speaks, the way she opens her arms to you ... the swooning sweetness of a woman ... no, no, Padre, you're quite right ... they'd only degrade it, spoil it, tarnish it, out in the jungle ... too squalid, too narrow ... lights and music and laughter ... must give it them ... they must have it ... not fit to marry ... shut them away in those bungalows ... leave them to rot there in their sickness ... not fit to marry, Padre ... you're quite right ... shut us away, the lot of us ... not fit to marry, not fit ...'

So the voice babbled on, and across that bed of suffering, Arnold's eyes met the Padre's in a look that absolved them of any need of words. They understood. There was nothing further to be said.

Another white man had been beaten by the jungle.

They got him back.

A fellow in the Sarawak Company had his leave hastened by several weeks, and Butterman, his suspicions momentarily stifled by the weakness that followed his recovery, allowed himself to be persuaded by one of the junior assistants to accompany him. He would never come back, of course. Letters had been sent ahead to the London Office. The facts had been set out. Arrangements would be made for the proper medical treatment on the ship. There would be a pension waiting, and efforts would be made to find him a suitable job at home. In eighteen months probably he would be all right. Siam was finished though. Never again would he see the steaming, luxuriant greenery of the jungle, nor the little attap huts beside the river, nor watch the grey logs swing slowly on their long road south to Bangkok.

Another white man beaten.

It was wistfully, with a heavy heart, that Arnold walked down to the Chiengmai Club on the evening of the day on which they said good-bye to Butterman. One less among them, and how few there were left now of his contemporaries. Martin and the Consul and Atkinson who ran the Sarawak Company. New faces otherwise, new faces that came and went: fellows that came out for a year on trial and flung their hands in after seven months; fellows who signed on as permanents, whom every one liked and trusted, for whom every one prophesied quick promotion, and of whom the jungle sooner or later got the better, who were brought in as Farquharson had been on a stretcher, broken by malaria; or were sent back on a liner, their nerves gone, like Butterman. A hard life, too hard possibly for the white man. Not many came through as he had done to the last chukka. And in a few weeks he'd be going.

Only a few weeks now. And for the first time in the course of those twenty-five years, those seven chukkas, he experienced a feeling of regret, almost of nostalgia at the thought of saying good bye to these familiar scenes. Twenty-five years. A large chunk out of a man's life. His youth and his early manhood, his first grey hairs; and he began to wonder whether he would find life in London so good a thing as he had expected. What would there be after all for him to do? His contemporaries would be strangers to him now, and it was not easy to start making friends at forty-five. His father was dead; his brother settled down in Chichester. There were no open doors waiting for him. And he remembered with misgiving the life that is led in London by the majority of pensioned Englishmen: the aimless empty days, the hanging about the Sports Club, the waiting for some fellow to drop in with whom you may exchange gossip of the far places you will not see again. Long empty days, and the drab, furtive romances with which one endeavoured to enliven them.

He hardly spoke during his game of golf. And afterwards when the sun had set, and the brief tropic twilight had darkened into night, he did not join the others at the large round table where the bottles and glasses were set out. Instead he walked slowly home wards at Martin's side, and as they turned through the gate of the Club, for the first time in his life he passed his arm beneath the Padre's. For a little way they walked in silence: in a silence that was, however, peculiarly intimate. The Butterman incident had drawn them very close together.

'We shall miss you,' the Padre said at length. 'I sometimes wonder what we shall do without you. It isn't so much that we shall be losing a friend, though that will be bad enough; for we've become accustomed to the loss of friends. It's, if you'll forgive my saying so, what you've stood for here. Life isn't easy, in a small society like ours. There are many temptations, many difficulties.

I don't think we shall realize till you've gone, how much you've meant in … well … the keeping of things clean and straight.'

It was the first time that the Padre had ever spoken intimately to Arnold, but there was no sign of embarrassment in his speech.

'We shall miss you,' he said, 'more than I can say.'

'Yet I've not been what you'd call a good man, Padre.'

The Padre hesitated a moment before he answered. Not out of any embarrassment, but because he was searching for the exact words with which to convey his meaning. He knew well enough to what Arnold was referring: the small bungalow beside the river, and the unbaptized children who were growing into manhood in Malaya.

'A good man,' he echoed. 'I suppose by our Western ideas you wouldn't be. And I don't mind admitting that when I left America, I came here in the belief that there would be two main evils for me to fight against. Alcohol was one, and the second and greater one, the white man's attitude to the brown women. But that's forty years ago. And in the course of forty years one's view-point alters. I don't mean that I think right the things I once thought wrong; it isn't that, but that those things which I once looked on as mortal sins, seem now, well, how shall I put it, just rather a pity. There are other things that are very much more important than a standard of chastity that can never be more than relative. Courage, forbearance, kindliness; above all things kindliness; those seem to me now the most truly Christian qualities. We are so few here and so far. It is so terribly important that we should be patient with one another. We shall miss you more than I can say.'

They had reached the bridge over the river, the point where their road separated, and there were tears in Arnold's eyes as he said good night to Martin, and it was slowly that he strolled on in the warm darkness, under the tropic stars, watching the muddy waters of the Be-kang swirl past him. Twenty-five years. And it was a strange world that awaited him, a world where he would have no certain habitat, where no one needed him, where no one perhaps would miss him when he went. He had talked of getting things both ways, but might it be that it was to end in his getting them in neither? Something like a sob rose in his throat as he faced the prospect of his uprooting. He was loved after all and needed here. For a long while he lingered, beside the river, and when finally he hastened his pace it was not in the direction of his own house, but in that of the small bungalow where he had spent increasingly little time of late.

To his surprise he found Cheam alone. She was dressed, for he had never made any attempt to Westernize her, in a short blue silk jacket that fell shapelily over a gold and scarlet sinn; her feet were bare; her hair, that was bright with coconut-oil, was drawn back tightly into the clutch of a high tortoiseshell and enamel comb. Her teeth, for from the betel habit he had discouraged her, were unfashionably clean. But from the corner of her mouth she was puffing slowly at a large white cheroot. As he came into the room she lifted her head in the calm, unemotional manner that had from the first characterized their meetings. There had never been at any time between them what Europe would have admitted as passionate relations.

She looked at him steadily and incuriously. But as their eyes met he was conscious on this evening of self-discovery, of a curious sense of kinship with her. They were in the same boat after all, exiles both of them; exiles from their youth and their ambitions. This life of theirs together had not been by any means the thing they had dreamed of for themselves. It was something quite other that they had planned. He had had his dream of Oxford, of English life and English shires and she, no doubt, of such a mating and such a life as had their roots in the dateless annals of her race. But for each of them fate had intervened; on each had been laid the duty of obligation to a family. He had come here that his brother might go to Oxford, and she in her turn had come to him because her parents could not afford to refuse the three hundred rupees that were her purchase. They were both in the same boat. And that same curious sense of belonging to this woman and to this country of his exile, that earlier in the evening had made him forsake the round table and the laughter and the drinks, returned with redoubled force upon him. England had grown a foreign country to him. He had taken root here, by Babel's waters.

Softly across the night came the tinkle of a temple bell: the symbol of that Eastern doctrine which preaches subservience to one's fate: the acceptance unprotestingly of one's *dharma*.

'I shall be retiring, you know, Cheam,' he said, 'in a few weeks from now.'

She bent her head slowly forward and he knew well enough what was passing behind that inscrutable masked face. How much of paddy-field was he to offer her and how many ticals.

'Very likely,' he said, 'I shall be staying on in Chiengmai. I am thinking of building myself a house across the river. It would be easier probably if you were to leave this bungalow and come and live there with me.'

Again she bent her head. Her face showed neither pleasure nor surprise. Child of Buddha, she was subservient to her *dharma;* to her fate, as to his ardour, passive and irresponsive.

'In which case,' he went on, 'it would probably be simpler if we were to be married according to English law.'

'It is as the *Naï* wishes,' she replied.

1927

'Tahiti Waits'

I shall never forget my first sight of Tahiti.

For months I had been planning to go there. For weeks I had been dreaming of going there. But on the eve of my arrival I craved for one thing only: a magic carpet that would carry me to London. I had been travelling for seven months and I was very tired: tired of new places and new settings. My ears were confused with strange accents and my eyes with changing landscapes. To begin with there had been the Mediterranean. Naples, Athens, Constantinople. A few hours in each. A hurried rushing to the sights: then the parched seaboard of the Levant. Smyrna with its broken streets, and hidden among its ruins the oasis now and then of a shaded square where you can drink thick black coffee beside fat Syrians who puff lazily at immense glass-bowled pipes. Smyrna and Jaffa and Beyrouth. An island or two. The climbing streets of Rhodes, the barren ramparts of Famagusta. Then Egypt and the mud houses. And the tall sails drifting down the Nile. Then Suez and the torment of the Red Sea when the heat is so intense that perversely you long to be burnt more and at lunch eat the hottest of hot pickles neat, till the inside of your mouth is raw: a torment that lapses suddenly into the cool of the Indian Ocean.

There had been Ceylon. The Temple of the Tooth at Kandy, with its scarlet and yellow Buddhas so garish and yet so oddly moving, as though there had passed into those pensive features something of the brooding faith of the hands that chiselled them; and the lake at Kandy after dusk, when the fireflies are thick about the trees; and the streets of Kandy on the night of the Perihera, when gilt-shod elephants lumber in the wake of guttering torches.

And afterwards there had been Siam. Bangkok with its innumerable bright-tiled temples and the sluggish waterways that no hand has mapped; those dark mysterious canals, their edges crowded with huddled shacks, their surface ruffled by the cool, slow-moving barges in which whole families are born, grow up, see love and life and die. Siam and the jungles of the north through which I trekked day after day slithering through muddied paddy-fields, climbing the narrow bullock tracks that cross the mountains. There had been Malaya, green and steaming when the light lies level on the rice-fields; and Penang where I had lingered, held by the ease and friendliness of that friendly island, cancelling passage after passage till finally I had had no alternative but to cancel the visit I had planned to Borneo.

'I'll spend a month in Sydney,' I had thought. 'Then I'll push on to the Pacific.' But I had been away five months before I left Singapore, and each place that I had been to had meant the forming of new contacts and relationships, the adapting of myself to new conditions. And as the *Marella* swung into Sydney Harbour and I saw lined up on Circular Quay a smiling-faced crowd of relatives and friends, that sudden sensation of nostalgia which is familiar to most travellers overcame me. England was at the other side of the world. I was lonely and among strangers. That very afternoon I was enquiring at the Messageries about

97

the next sailing for Noumea. And as a month later the *Louqsor* rolled its way eastwards through the New Hebrides, I lay back in my hammock chair upon the deck, a novel fallen forward upon my knees, dreaming not of the green island to which each day the flag on the map drew close, but of the London that was waiting a couple of months away.

And then I saw Tahiti.

But how at this late day is one to describe the haunting appeal of that island which so many pens, so many brushes have depicted? The South Seas are terribly *vieux jeu*. They have been so written about and painted. Long before you get to them you know precisely what you are to find. There have been Maugham and Loti and Stevenson and Brooke. There is no need now to travel ten thousand miles to know how the grass runs down to the lagoon and the green and scarlet tent of the flamboyants shadows the road along the harbour; nor how the jagged peaks of the Diadem tower above the lazy township of Papeete; and beyond the reef, across ten miles of water, the miracle that is Moorea changes hour by hour its aureole of lights. And there has been Gauguin; so that when you drive out into the districts past Papara through that long sequence of haphazard gardens where the bougainvillaea and the hibiscus drift lazily over the wooden bungalows, and you see laid out along their mats on the veranda the dark-skinned brooding women of Taravao, their black hair falling down to their knees over the white and red of *the pareo* that is about their hips, you cry with a gasp of recognition, 'But this is Gauguin. Before ever I came I knew all this.' Everything about the islands is *vieux jeu*. And yet all the same they get you.

For that is the miracle of Tahiti, as it is the miracle of love— for though you have had every symptom of love catalogued and described, love when it comes has the effect on you of something that has never happened in the world before—that the first sight of those jagged mountains should even now touch in Stevenson's phrase 'a virginity of sense'.

As the ship swung slowly through the gap in the reef I could see the children bathing in the harbour. There was a canoe drifting lazily in the lagoon. The quay was crowded with half the population of Papeete. They were laughing and chattering and they waved their hands. As the ship was moored against the wharf and the gangway was let down, a score or so of girls in bright print dresses, with wreaths of flowers about their necks, some quarter-white, some full Tahitian, scrambled up the narrow stairway to welcome their old friends among the crew. The deck that had been for a fortnight the bleak barrack of an asylum became suddenly a summered garden. The spirit of Polynesia was about it, the spirit of unreflecting happiness that makes the girls wear flowers behind their ears, and the young people smile at you as you pass them by, and the children run into the roadway to shake your hand.

That evening I walked slowly and alone along the water-front. The air was heavy with the scent of jasmine. A car drove by; a rackety old Ford packed full on every seat, so that the half-dozen or so men and women in it were sitting anyhow on each other's laps, their arms flung about each other's shoulders. In their hair was the starred white of the tiare. One of them was strumming on a banjo; their voices were raised, their rich soft voices, in a Hawaiian tune. Here, indeed, seemed the Eden of heart's longing. Here was happiness as I had never seen it and friendliness as I had never seen it. Here was a fellowship that was uncalculating and love that was unpossessive, that was a giving, not a bargaining. I wondered how I should ever find the heart to leave.

Which is how most of us feel on our first evening in Tahiti, and yet, one by one, we wave farewell to the green island in the sure knowledge that in all human probability we have said good-bye to it for ever.

One of the advantages of being over sixty is that one can talk without embarrassment about the peccadilloes of one's youth. But when I first wrote about Tahiti, I was too young and too near to actual events, to set down a faithful record of my stay there. Instead I wove out of my experiences and impressions the story of a young Englishman, whom I called Simmonds, a man of my own age and background who had decided to spend nine months in travel before taking up the partnership that his father's death had left open for him in a motor business. His story was in large part mine.

Like me and like so many others when he saw the peaks of the Diadem towering about the lazy township of Papeete, he ordered his trunk up out of the hold. New Zealand and Samoa could wait. He had four months more to spend. He could spend them here.

That evening from his hotel balcony, he watched the sun set behind Moorea. Beside him was Demster, a fellow tourist of a month's standing whom all the afternoon, he had been cross-examining with eager curiosity.

'I wonder what you'll make of it,' the older man was saying.

'I suppose it'll end in your taking a house in the country some-where; that'll mean an island marriage. It's the only way, I'm told, of getting a girl to cook for you. No one bothers about money here.

And a girl would consider herself insulted if a bachelor asked her to work for him without living with him. They're simple folk. Frocks and motor-rides and love. That's their whole life. I don't suppose that if you took a house you'd be allowed to remain long in it alone.'

'That's what they tell me,' Simmonds said.

The velvet of the night was soft and scented; down the lamp-lit avenue under the tent of the flamboyants, arm in arm the flower haired girls were strolling. The air was fragrant with a sense of love, sensual and tender love, such as the acuter and bitter passions of the north are alien to.

'I expect,' he said, 'I shall leave life to decide that for me.'

That evening as the two men were walking along the water-front a voice hailed them, and two young women who had been riding towards them jumped off their bicycles.

'What, still here and still alone, and on a Tahitian evening?'

It was the elder who spoke, an American, gay-eyed and mischievous, married for ten years to a French official; much wooed by the younger Frenchmen and by none of them, rumour had it, with success, she was held to be the most attractive woman in Papeete. But it was the younger that Simmonds noticed. Never had he seen anyone to whom the trite simile of flower-like could be more appropriate. She was small and slight, with pale yellowish hair and cornflower-blue eyes. Her body in its pale green sheath of muslin seemed in truth to sway like a stem beneath the weight of the blossom that was her face.

Introductions followed.

'Mr. Simmonds arrived this morning,' Demster said. 'He fell in love with Tahiti so much that he's decided to stay on.'

The American raised her eyebrows meaningly.

'In love, why, sure, but with an island!'

They laughed together.

'I can't think how I shall find the heart to leave,' said Simmonds.

'That's what you all say at the beginning,' said the younger woman.

'And do they all go away?'

She shrugged her shoulders.

'Some stay, of course; most go. To most people Papeete is a port of call. They're the tourists who stop for a month or two, and the officials who've come for three or four years, sometimes for half a lifetime. And the naval officers who are stationed on and off for a couple of years. Then there are a few Americans who spend their summers here. But in the end they go, nearly all of them. If you live here, you have rather a sad feeling of being— oh, how shall I put it?—like a station through which trains are passing. People come into your life and go out of it. It's like living in an hotel rather than in a home.'

'But you're happy here?'

She pouted.

'It grows monotonous, you know.'

'To me it seems like the Garden of Eden.'

Again the cornflower-blue eyes smiled softly.

'I wonder if you'll be saying that in four months' time. You know what they say about Tahiti? That a year's too little a time to stay here and a month too long. They may be right. But when I was a child I always used to wonder whether Adam and Eve were really sorry to be cast out of Eden. I always wondered what they found to do there; didn't you, sometimes?'

She spoke half whimsically, half wistfully, in a voice that was lightly cadenced and with that particular purity of accent that is to be found only in those to whom English has come as a 'taught language', a purity that seemed in its peculiar way symbolic of her charm.

'Perhaps,' Simmonds answered her. 'But I'm very sure that I shall be heart-broken when the time comes for me to go.'

The American interrupted him.

'Perhaps it won't be you who'll be heart-broken.'

Again there was a general laugh.

'At any rate,' she concluded, 'I hope you won't get too domesticated to come and see us sometimes.'

The invitation was made friendlily and genuinely enough, but it was of her companion that he was thinking as he accepted it, and it was about Colette that he sought information of Demster the moment they were alone.

'Who is that girl?' he asked. 'You haven't met her before, I gather?'

Demster shook his head.

'I know all about her, though. It's rather a sad story. Her father was a Canadian who came over here to direct a store; her mother was a young French girl who fell in love with him and married him. Four years later, when the time came for the man to return to Montreal, he calmly informed her that he had a wife in America; that if she wished to have him arrested as a bigamist she could; but that if she did, his income and means of supporting her would cease; that the best thing would be for her to say nothing and to accept the allowance he would continue to send her, provided she made no attempt to leave the island. For Colette's sake she decided to accept. But everyone knows, of course, as everyone knows everything in Papeete. It's a sad story.'

Simmonds nodded. He could understand now the wistful expression of those pale cornflower-blue eyes; he could understand why she had spoken wistfully of the station through which trains hurried, and he could imagine with what weight even in this free-est of free countries the knowledge of her parentage must press on her. 'She must always feel,' he thought, 'apart from others. Never able to mix wholeheartedly among them.' Yet in spite of it all her nature had not soured. 'I hope,' he thought, 'that that isn't the last I'm going to see of her.'

Four times a week there is a cinema performance in Papeete, and on those evenings the streets and cafés of the town are empty. Two weeks later to Simmonds standing on the steps of the long tin building during the ten minutes' interval, it seemed that there were clustered in the street below, round the naphtha-lighted stalls where the little Chinese proprietors were making busy trade with ices and coconuts and water melons, every single person with whom he had been brought in contact during his stay in the hotel.

There was Tania, one of the last direct descendants of the old royal family of the Pomaris, her black hair dressed high upon her head, a rose silk Spanish shawl about her shoulders, chattering to the half-dozen or so girls, with whom he would idle most after-noons away over ice-creams in the Mariposa Café. There was the Australian trader with whom he would discuss the relative merits of Woodfull and Macartney. A couple of French officials he had met at the *Cercle Coloniale* and others whom he knew by sight, the girls from the post office, the assistants from the three big stores, the skipper of the *Saint Antoine;* all that numerous crowd that he had watched from the balcony of his hotel, stroll-ing lazily along the harbourside. He had learnt to recognize most of the people in the town by sight during that three weeks' stay.

And he had done most of the things that one does do in Tahiti during one's first fortnight there. He had driven out round the island, through Mataiea, past the short wooden pier on which during the last spring of the world's peace a doomed poet wrote lines for Mamua. He had spanned the narrow isthmus of Taravao; he had lunched at Keane's off a sweet shrimp curry; he had bathed on the dark sands at Arue, and in the cool waters of the Papeno River. He had chartered a glass-bottomed boat and, sailing out towards the reef, had watched the fish swimming in and out of the many-coloured coral. And day after day the sun had shone out of a blue sky ceaselessly and night after night moonshine and starlight had brooded over the scented darkness, and Simmonds was beginning to feel a little bored.

Maybe that girl had been right, he thought, about a year being too little a time and a month too long.

And gazing a little despondently at the thronged roadway, he wondered how he should employ the fourteen or so weeks that must pass before the sailing of the *Louqsor*, the French cargo boat, by which he had planned to return to Europe.

'Well,' a voice was asking at his elbow, 'and is it still the Eden that you expected?'

The question was so appropriate to his mood that he could not resist laughing as he turned to meet the smiling flower-like features of Colette Garonne.

'At that precise moment,' he said, 'I was just wondering whether you weren't right about Adam and Eve finding it a little dull in Eden.'

'You too, then, and so soon.'

'I was just feeling …' But she was so divinely pretty, even under the harsh glare of the electric lights, that he could not retain his temper of despondency. 'I was just feeling,' he said instead, 'what an enormous pity it was that we couldn't go on to supper and a cabaret after this, as we would if we were in London.'

'So you've come all this way to regret London.'

'To regret that there's nothing to do after eleven; for there isn't, is there?'

'Not in the way of cabarets.'

'In any way, then?'

She pouted.

'The Bright Young People drive out in cars.'

'Where?'

'Anywhere. To bathe, or out to Keane's, or just to sing. That's the island idea of cabaret.'

'In that case …' He hesitated. Often as he had sat before going to bed on the hotel veranda he had envied the crowded cars that had driven singing through the night below him. It had seemed so carefree and lighthearted with a lightheartedness with which he was not in tune. But he had felt always shy of suggesting such an expedition to any of his friends. On this occasion, however, the impelling influence of cerulean eyes emboldened him. 'Why don't we have a cabaret this evening?'

It was her turn to hesitate. 'Well,' she said, pausing doubtfully.

He could tell what was passing in her mind. Though he had seen her often enough, smiling greetings at her, they had not talked together since the night when Demster had introduced them. And she was uncertain, he could guess that, as to the types of companion that he would be selecting for her. He made no effort, however, to persuade her. He had the intuition to realize that at such moments it is the wiser plan not to urge the reluctant to say 'Yes', but to make it difficult for them to say 'No'. Less than a yard away Tania was chattering noisily in the centre of a crowd of friends, and stretching out his hand, Simmonds touched her on the arm.

'We were thinking of driving out somewhere after the show. What's your idea of it?'

'Sweetheart, that it would be heavenly.'

'Who else'll come?'

Tania glanced round her slowly.

'There's you, and I, and Colette, and Marie; and we'd better have Paul to amuse Tepia.'

In a minute or two it had been arranged.

'Then we'll meet outside Oscar's the moment the show's over.'

It was one of those nights that are not to be found elsewhere than in Tahiti. It was October and the night was calm. From the mountains a breeze was blowing, swaying gently the white-flowered shrubs along the road, ruffling the languid palms. Westwards over the Pacific, a long street of silver to the jagged outline of Moorea, was a waxing moon; clouds moved lazily between the stars. The air was mild, sweet-scented with the tiare, a sweetness that lay soft upon their cheeks as the car swayed and shook and rattled eastwards. The hood of the car was up, for in Tahiti there is always a possibility of rain: and for the islanders the landscape is too familiar to be attractive in itself. It is for the sensation of speed that motoring is so highly valued an entertainment. And as the car swayed over the uneven road, they laughed and sang, beating their hands in time with the accordion.

For an hour and a half they drove on, singing under the stars.

'Where are we going?' he asked at length. 'Isn't it time we were thinking about a bathe?'

'Not yet, sweetheart,' laughed Tania. 'Let's see if Keane's up still.'

'At this hour?'

'One never knows.'

For there are no such things as regular hours in the islands. One is up certainly with the sun, and usually by nine o'clock in the evening one is thinking about bed; but there is always a possibility that friends will come: that a car will stop outside your bungalow: that a voice will cry, 'What about driving to Papeno?' And you will forget that you are sleepy, a rum punch will be prepared, and there will be a banjo and an accordion, there will be singing and Hula-Hulas, and hours later you will remember that a car is in the road outside, that you were planning to bathe in the Papeno River; laughing and chattering, you will stumble out of the bungalow, pack yourselves anyhow into a pre-war Ford and, still laughing and singing, you will drive away into the night, to wrap *pareos* around you and splash till you are a-weary in a cool, fresh mountain stream. It is an island saying that no night has ended till the dawn has broken, and at Keane's there is always a chance of finding merriment long after the streets are silent in Papeete. And sure enough, 'Look, what did I say?' Tania was crying a few moments later. Through the thick tangle of trees a light was glimmering; there was the sound of a gramophone and clapping hands.

There were some dozen people on the veranda when they arrived; a planter from Taravao had stopped on his way back from Papeete for a rum-punch; there had been a new record to try on the gramophone, some boys on their return from fishing had seen lights and had heard singing, one of Keane's daughters had taken down her banjo and a grand-daughter of Keane's had danced Hula-Hulas, while beakers of rum-punch had been filled and emptied; twenty minutes had become five hours and no one had thought of bed. It was after midnight, though, and probably, without the arrival of any fresh incentive, in another half-hour the party would have broken up. As it was, a cry of eager welcome was sent up as Simmonds' car drove up, and another half-dozen glasses were bustled out, another beaker of rum-punch brewed, and Tania, seated cross-legged upon the floor, her banjo across her knees, was singing that softest and sweetest of Polynesian songs,

Ave, Ave, te vahini upipi
E patia tona, a pareo repo

that haunting air that will linger for ever in the ears of those that hear it; that across the miles and across the years will wake an irresistible nostalgia for the long star-drenched nights of Polynesia, for the soft breezes, and the bending palm trees, the white bloom of the hibiscus, and the murmur of the Pacific rollers on the reef; for the sights and sounds and scents, for the flower-haired, dark-skinned people of Polynesia. And as Tania sang and the girls danced, and the men beat their hands in time, the magic and beauty of the night filled overbrimrriingly, as thriftlessly poured wine a beaker, the Western mind and spirit of the young English tourist.

'There's nothiing like it,' he murmured. 'Not in this world, certainly.'

'Nor probably,' quoted Colette, 'in the next.'

And he remembered how a few hours earlier, in a mood of boredom, he had thought of Tahiti as a frame without a picture. He could understand now why he had felt like that. He had been looking at it from the outside. One had to surrender to Tahiti to let oneself be absorbed by it.

'It's no good looking at Tahiti from outside,' he said.

Colette sighed. 'Outside. But that's what so many of us have to be.'

He looked down at her in surprise.

'Outside! You!'

'It's not always so easy to surrender. You've got to surrender so much else as well.' She paused, looked at him, questioningly, then seeing that his eyes were kind, continued: 'For me to be absorbed in it, for me to be inside this life, it would mean living the same life as all these other girls, and, well, you know what that is. I couldn't; it's not that I'm a prude, but you know what my life's been; my mother's had a bad time. I'm all she's got. It would break her if anything were to happen to me.'

'If you were to marry, though.'

She laughed, ruefully. 'Who's to marry me? Who, at least, that I'd care to marry. There aren't so many white men here. It's not for marriage that the tourist comes. The English and the Americans who settle here as often as not have left wives behind them. At any rate they've come because they've tired of civilization. They're not the type that makes a conventional marriage. And though the French may be broad-minded about liaisons, they're very particular about marriages. As far as they're concerned I'm damaged goods. It's not even as though I had any money. And I must stay on here. I can't leave my mother. I'm not complaining. Please don't think that. I'm happy enough. But I've never felt, I don't suppose I ever shall feel, as though I really belonged here.'

She spoke softly, her voice sinking to a whisper; and as he listened. pity overcame him. She was so sweet, so pretty; it was cruel that life should have been harsh to her, here of all places, in Tahiti. It was true, though, what she had said. What they had both said about belonging here. One had to surrender to Tahiti, to take it on its own terms. Otherwise for all time there would be an angel before this Eden, with the drawn sword that was the knowledge of good and evil. He had talked a few minutes since of being himself inside it, but he was a tourist like any other, with his life and interests ten thousand miles away. He had a few weeks to spend here: a few weeks in which to gather as many impressions as he could. And perhaps because he loved the place so well, something of its mystery would be laid on him. But it was not thus and to such as he that Tahiti would lay bare her secrets. You had to come empty-handed to that altar; you had to surrender utterly; you could not be of Tahiti and of Europe. You would have to cut away from that other life, those other interests. Your whole life must be bounded by Tahiti; you must take root here by the palm-fringed lagoons, and then, little by little, you would absorb that magic. The spirit of Tahiti would whisper its secrets into your ear. You must surrender or remain outside. Wistfully he looked out over the veranda.

It was so lovely, the garden with its tangled masses of fruits and flowers. The dark sand, with the faint line of white where the water rippled among the oyster beds; and the long line of coast, swerving outwards to a hidden headland, with beyond it, above the bending heads of the coconut palms, the dark shadow that was the mountains of Taravao; and over it all was the silver moonlight and the music of the breakers on the reef; and here at his feet, one with the magic of the night, were the dark-skinned, laughing people to whose ears alone the spirit of Tahiti whispered the syllables of its magic.

And as he leant back against the veranda there came to him such thoughts as have come to all of us under the moonlight on Tahitian nights. He thought of the turmoil and the conflict that was Europe: the hurry and the malice and the greed: the ceaseless battle for self-protection: the ceaseless exploitation of advantage: the long battle that wearies and hardens and

111

embitters: that brings you ultimately to see all men as your enemies, since all men are in competition with you, since your success can only be purchased at the price of another's failure. He thought of what his life would be for the next forty years; he contrasted it with the gentleness and sweetness and simplicity of this island life, where there is no hatred since there is no need for hatred; where there is no rivalry since life is easy, since the sun shines and the rain is soft, and *feis* grow wild along the valleys, and livelihood lies ready to man's hand. Where there is no reason why you should not trust your neighbour, since in a world where there are no possessions there is nothing that he can rob you of; where you can believe in the softness of a glance, since in a world where there are no social ladders there is nothing that a woman can gain from love-making but love. Such thoughts as we all have on Tahitian nights. And thinking them, he told himself that were he to sell now his share in his father's business there would be a sum that would purchase litde enough in Europe, where everytli-ing had a market price, but that would mean for him in Tahiti a bungalow on the edge of a lagoon, wide and clear and open to the moonlight, and there would be enough work to keep idleness from fretting him; and there would be a companion in the bunga-low, and children—smiling, happy children, who would grow to manhood in a country where there is no need to arm yourself from childhood for the fight for livelihood.

And at his elbow there was Colette, exquisite and frail and gentle. 'Why run for shadows when the prize is here?' England seemed very distant, and very unsubstantial the rewards that England had for offering, and along the veranda railing his hand edged slowly to Colette's; his little finger closed over hers; her eyes through the half-twilight smiled up at him. They said nothing; but that which is more than words, that of which words are the channels only, had passed between them. And on the next morning when he was strolling down the water-front along with the half of Papeete, to welcome the American courier, he blushed awkwardly when he heard himself hailed by the gay-toned American voice. 'Hullo, hullo,' she called. 'And it's a whole week since we said good-bye to Mr. Demster, and you're still living virtuously at Oscar's!' He blushed, for Colette was at her side, and her eyes were smiling into his, and between them the thought was passing that the time was over for him to make an island marriage.

'I've got three months left,' he laughed. But it had ceased, he knew, to be a question of weeks and months. But of whether or not he was to make his home here in Tahiti. The magic of the island and the softness of Colette had cast the meshes of their net about him: the net that in one way or another is cast on all of us who watch from the harbour-side our ship sail off without us. Of the many thousands who have loitered in these green ways there cannot be one who has not wondered, if only for an instant, whether he would be wise to abandon the incessant struggle that lies eastward in America and Europe. Not one out of all those thousands.

Yet it is no longer true that those who come to the islands rarely leave them. Sydney and San Francisco are very close. The story of most loiterers in Papeete is the story of their attempt not to commit themselves too far, to leave open a loophole for escape. Time passes slowly in the islands, and usually before they have become too enmeshed something has happened to force on them the wisdom of delay.

For Simmonds it was the arrival on the *Manganui* of the liveliest thing in Australian salesmen that he had ever met. It happened shortly before ten o'clock. Like a whirlwind a short, plump, perspiring, serge-suited figure hustled its way into the Mariposa Café, tossed its felt hat across a table, and leaning back in a chair had begun to fan its face with a vast brown silk handkerchief.

'My oath, but this is the hottest place I've struck! My oath, but a gin sling would be right down bonza!'

The two waitresses who were leaning against the bar gazed blankly at him.

'My word, but you aren't going to tell me that you've got no ice!'

He spoke rapidly, with a marked Australian accent, and the girls, who could only understand English when it was spoken extremely slowly, did not understand him. They looked at one another, then looked at the stranger, then looked again at one another and burst into laughter. It was time, Simmonds felt, that he came to the rescue of his compatriot.

'Suppose,' he suggested, 'that I were to interpret. These girls don't understand much beyond French.'

'Now that would be really kind. And it would be kinder still if you were to order yourself whatever you like and join me with it. You will? Good-oh! That's bonza. You staying here? Well, I pity you. Myself? My oath, sir, no! When that boat sails for dear old Sydney I'll be on it. No place like Sydney in the world. Manly and Bondi and the beaches. Nothing like them. Dinky-die. New York can't touch it. Just come from there. Been travelling in wool. Did I sell much? My oath, sir, I did not. But I've learnt the way to sell. Those Yanks know how to advertise. Personal touch. Always gets you there. Straight at the consumer. Me addressing you, that's the way. The only way. Now look here,' and lifting his eyes he began to glance round the room in search of some advertisement that would illustrate his point. "J'irai loin pour un camel," he slowly mispronounced; 'don't know enough French to tell if that's good or not. Let's see. Ah, look now,' and jumping to his feet he pointed to a large cardboard notice that had been hung above the bar:

ASK OSCAR

He KNOWS.

'That's it,' he exclaimed. 'Couldn't be better. No long sentences. Nothing about our being anxious to give any information that tourists may require. Nothing impersonal or official. Nothing to terrify anyone. Just the impression of a friendly fellow who'll give you a friendly hand. The very impression you want to give. My oath it is!'

He began to enlarge his theme. He began to discuss American publicity, international trade and the different conditions in America and Australia; and Simmonds, as he sat there listening, found himself more interested than he had been for weeks. He had been so long away from business. And when you got down to brass tacks was there a thing in the world half as thrilling? It was a game, the most exciting, and the highest prized. Your wits against the other man's.

And as he sat there listening, he felt an itch to be back in that eager competitive society. He had always found that he did his best thinking when he was listening. Something said suggested a train of thought, and as the Australian's conversation rattled on an idea came suddenly to him for the launching of the new model his firm had been designing for the autumn. The exact note of publicity to get. He saw it; he knew it. Get a good artist to illustrate it, and for a few months anyhow they'd have everyone upon the market beat. His blood began to pound hotly through his veins.

And then, suddenly, he remembered: that there was going to be no return to London; there was going to be a selling of shares and the building of a bungalow: a succession of quiet days spent quietly; and an immense depression came on him, such a depression as one feels on waking from a pleasant dream: a depression that was followed by such a sensation of relief as one feels on waking from a nightmare. 'It wasn't true. None of it had happened yet.'

While the Australian chattered on, Simmonds leant forward across the table, his head upon his hands. What did he want, to go or to stay? To go or stay? For he realized that he must make a choice, that it must be either England or Tahiti: that the one was precluded by the other. And was it really, he asked himself, that he was weary of the strife of London, that the secret of Polynesia was worth the surrender of all that until now he had held to make life worth living? Was it anything more than a mood, the bewitching effect of moonlight and still water and a pretty girl that was luring him to this Pacific Eden?

'I must think,' he thought. 'I mustn't decide hurriedly. Whatever happens, I must give myself time to think.'

Even as he decided that, he saw on the other side of the street beside the schooners the trim figure of Colette. She was carrying a parasol: her head was bared, he saw all the daintiness of that shingled hair, and he caught his breath at the thought of saying 'Good-bye' to so much charm and gentleness. 'I'm not in love with her,' he thought. 'But in two days if I were to see more of her I should be. And if I were to fall in love with her, it would be in a way, I believe, that I'm never likely to again. I shall be saying good-bye to a good deal if I catch the *Louqsor!*

That catching of his breath, however, had warned him that it must not be in Papeete that his decision must be come to. If he were to stay on at Oscar's with the certainty of seeing Colette again in a day or two he knew only too well that he would commit himself irremediably.

'Whatever happens,' he said, 'I must get away for a week and think.'

It is about forty miles from Papeete to Tautira, and every afternoon Oscar's truck, a vast van of a Buick, lined with seats, made the rocking three hours' journey there along the uneven island road. It is an uncomfortable, but by no means unpleasant journey. As the car jolted on past Paiea towards Papiieri a feeling of assuagement descended on the turmoil of Simmonds's heart. He had need of the rest and quiet of the districts. He was carrying a letter of introduction to the chief, who would find room for him somewhere in his bungalow, and there would be long lazy mornings reading on the veranda, bathing in the lagoon, with tranquil evenings in the cool of the grass-grown pathways.

It was very warm inside the truck. Every seat was occupied, and since all the gossip had been exchanged and it: was too hot for the effort of conversation, one of the drivers had taken out his accordion and was playing softly. Already they had left behind them the more formal districts; Papara and Paia and Mataiea. They had passed the narrow isthmus of Taravao; the scenery was growing wilder. There had been little attempt made here to keep the gardens tended. Bungalows had been set down apparently at hazard, among the tangle of fruit and flowers; the women who were stretched out on mats on the verandas no longer wore the European costume. It was over the white and red of the *pareo* that their black hair fell. In some such Tahiti as this it was that Loti loved. But it was vaguely that Simmonds was conscious of the landscape. His eyelids had grown heavy; tired by bright colours. His head began to nod.

He woke with a start and to the sound of laughter. 'I make nice pillow?' a voice was asking him. And blinking, he realized that his head had sunk sideways on the shoulders of the girl who was beside him. She was tall and handsome, a typical Tahitian, with fine eyes and hair, and a laughing mouth.

'I'm so sorry,' he began.

She only laughed, called out something in Tahitian to the driver, and taking Simmonds by the wrist, drew him back towards her.

'Bye-bye, baby,' she said.

But he was now wide awake: vividly conscious of the girl beside him. Her coloured cotton dress was bare above the elbow, and through the thin silk of his coat he could feel the full, firm texture of her skin. She was strong and healthy with the glow and strength of native blood. Beneath her wide-brimmed, flower-wreathed straw hat she was laughing merrily, and as he leant a little more heavily against her arm she giggled and again called out in Tahitian to the driver. There was a ripple of laughter through the truck. He flushed uncomfortably, drawing away; but the girl smiled friendlily and pulled him back.

'No, no, you tired, you sleep.'

There was no sleep, though, now for him. But lest the excuse for nearness would be taken from him, he half closed his eyes and leant sideways against the soft, strong shoulder, conscious with a mingling, half of excitement, half of fear, that each minute was bringing them nearer to Tautira, that he and this girl would be close neighbours. It was not till they were within two hundred yards of the chief's house that she jerked her knee sideways against his.

'Wake up now,' she cried. 'My house here.'

118

She stretched out her hand to him and as he took it, her fingers closing over his, pressed lightly for a moment. Her fine bright eyes were glowing, her full, wide mouth was parted in a smile. He hesitated, wondering whether to let the incident close. He decided to. They were in the same village, after all. They were bound to be seeing each other again. As the car rolled on along the road he leant out of the window to look back at her. She, too, had turned and, standing in the garden before her bungalow, waved her hand at him.

If all Tahiti is a garden then is Tautira Tahiti's garden. The roads are overgrown with grass. There are no fences and no boundary lines. Hens and pigs wander about the gardens and paths and houses as they choose. They will find their way home at evening. There is no one who could be troubled to steal. And since the meat market of Papeete is many miles away, the natives still live upon the produce of their hands: the fish they catch and spear and the bread-fruit that they bake.

The chief, a large, strong-hewn figure, clad only in a *pareo*, although he had not received a white visitor for several months, received Simmonds with no excitement or surprise, with a simple unaffected welcome.

It would be quite easy, he said, to prepare a room for him; and there would be some dinner ready in about an hour. He would not, he feared, be able to join him at it, for he had to supervise the evening's haul of fish. But they would have a long talk next day at lunch-time. He had served in the French Army during the war, winning the Médaille Militaire; they would doubtless have experiences to exchange. And with extreme courtesy he had left him.

It was cool and quiet in the house. But for all that the air was soft and the sunset a glow of lavender behind the palms, there was no peace for the spirit of Simmonds. He was restless and ill-at-ease; his mind was busy with thoughts of the tall, bright-eyed girl, and after dinner, as he walked out along the beach, the memory of that firm, soft shoulder was very actual to him.

Should he be seeing her, he wondered; the chief had explained to him where the nets were being hauled ashore. As likely as not the greater part of the village would be assembled there. But probably she would have some other man with her. He had been a fool not to have spoken to her on the truck. That had been his chance and he had let it slip. That is, if he had wished to be availed of it. And did he? He did not know. There were so many rival influences at work. He knew the speed of coconut wireless, how quickly gossip spread. Days before he had left Tautira Colette would have heard of his adventure. He could not return to her after it. It would mean the end for ever of any thought of staying permanently on the island. For he knew that between himself and a girl such as the one he had sat next in the truck there could be no permanent relationship. There could be no question of love between them, on his side, anyhow. Very speed-ily he would have exhausted the slender resources of her interest. Nor, indeed, would she herself expect anything but a Tahitian idyll. Tahitians were used to the coming and going upon ships. She would weep when he went away, but though there is tear-shedding there is no grief upon the islands. She would console herself soon enough. If he were to yield to the enchantment of time and place he would have in the yielding answered that problem which had perplexed him. But did he want to? He did not know. Against the heady hour's magic was set the fear of loss: the loss of Colette, and also insidiously but painfully the loss of health. What did he know, after all, about this girl? And in that moment of indecision, in the forces that went to the framing of that indecision, he appreciated to the full in what manner and in what measure the corning of the white man had destroyed the simple beauty he had found. Even here one had to be cautious, to weigh the consequences of one's acts. And as he strolled beneath the palm trees to where he could see dark groups of clustered figures, he pictured that vanished beauty; pictured on such an island on such a night, some proud pirate schooner drawing towards the beach; pictured the dark-skinned people running down to welcome them, the innocence and friendliness of that hospitality; pictured the singing and the dancing, the large group breaking away gradually into couples, the slow linked strolling beneath the palms, the kissing and the laughter; the returning to the clean, fresh bungalows; the loving while loving pleased. And that was finished. Gone, irrecapturable, never to be found again upon this earth; never, never.

Still undecided, he walked on to take his place among the crowd gathered upon the beach.

It was a homely scene; the long row of men hauling at the nets, shouting and encouraging each other, and the women seated upon the sand, clapping their hands with pleasure as the fish were poured, a leaping, throbbing mass, into the large, flat-bottomed boats. He had not been standing there long before a hand had been laid upon his arms and a laughing voice was asking him: 'Well, you not sleepy now?'

She had seemed attractive enough to him on the truck, but now hatless, with her dark hair flung wide about her shoulders, there was added a compelling softness to her power. And as he looked into her eyes, bright and shining through the dusk, her lips parted in a smile over the shining whiteness of her teeth, he felt that already the problem and his perplexity had been taken from him: that life had found his answer.

121

They sat side by side together on the bottom of an upturned boat: very close so that her shoulder touched him: so that it seemed natural for him to pass his arm about her waist, for his fingers to stroke gently the firm, soft flesh of her upper arm. Afterwards, when the nets had been hauled in and the division of the fish arranged, they strolled arm in arm along the beach. From the centre of the village there came a sound of singing. In front of a Chinese store Oscar's truck had been arranged as a form of orchestral stand, the drivers had brought out their banjos, and on the wooden veranda of the store a number of young natives were dancing. They would sing and shout and clap their hands, then a couple would slither out into the centre and standing opposite each other would begin to dance. They would never dance more than a few steps, however. In less than a minute they had burst into a paroxysm of laughter, would cover their faces with their hands and run round to the back of the circling crowd.

'Come,' said the girl, and taking him by the hand, she led him up into the truck. It was a low seat and they were in the shadow; the moment they were seated, without affectation, she turned her face to his, expressing in a kiss, as such sentiments were meant to be expressed, the peace and happiness of a Tahitian evening. And the moon rose above the palm trees, lighting grotesquely the jagged peaks of the hills across the bay. The breeze from the lagoon blew quietly. Through the sound of the singing voices he could hear the undertone of the Pacific on the reef. Slowly, wooingly, the sights and scents and sounds that have for centuries in this fringe of Eden stripped the doubter of all thoughts of consequences, lulled his doubts to rest. For a long while they sat there in the shadow of the car; her chin resting against his shoulder, his fingers caressing gently the soft surface of her cheek and arm.

'Tired?' she asked, at length.

He nodded. 'A little.'

'Then we go. You come with me?'

The question was put without any artifice or coquetry, as though it were only natural that thus should such an evening end.

His heart was thudding fiercely as they walked, quickly now, and in silence, down the path between low hedges towards her home. When they reached the veranda she lifted her finger to her lips. 'Sh!' she said. 'Wait.'

There was a rustle, and a sound of whispers; the turning of a handle, the noise of something soft being pulled along the floor, then a whispered 'Come,' and a hand held out to him.

It was very dark. From the veranda beyond came the sound of movement. As he stepped into the room his toe caught on something, so that but for her hand he would have fallen. He stumbled forward on to the broad, deep mattress. For a moment he felt an acute revulsion of feeling. But two arms, cool and bare, had been flung about his neck, dark masses of hair scented faintly with coconut were beneath his cheek; against his mouth, soft and tender were her lips. His arm tightened about the firm, full shoulders, the tenderness of his kisses deepened, grew deep and fierce.

That people is happy which has no history. There are no details to a Tahitian idyll.

There was a bungalow, half-way towards Ventura. It was small enough, two rooms and a veranda, with little furniture; a table, a few chairs, a long, low mattress-bed, but there was a stream running just below it from the mountains; cool and sweet.

Here at any hour of the day you could bathe at will. And there was green grass running down towards the sand; from the veranda you looked towards Moorea, over the roof was twined and intertwined the purple of the bougainvillaea, and the red and white and orange of the hibiscus; across the door were the gold and scarlet of the flamboyant, and when you have those things, you do not need furniture or pictures or large houses.

During the three months that he lived there, Simmonds went but rarely into Papeete, and during them he came as near as perhaps any sojourner can to understanding the spirit of Tahiti. It was a lazy life he led. When he was not bathing, he would lie out reading on the veranda; he ate little but what came from within a mile of his own house. Bread and butter came certainly from the town, but that was all. Once or twice a week he and Pepire would go up the valleys to collect enough lemons and bread-fruit and bananas to last for days. And her brother and cousin would always be coming from Papeete or Tautira, so that it was rare for him to wake in the morning without finding some visitors stretched out asleep on the veranda. They were profitable guests, however, for in the evening they would sail towards the reef and spear fish by torchlight or else they would go shrimping up the valleys, and afterwards, while Pepire would prepare the food, they would sit round with their banjos, singing.

And he was happy; happier than he had ever been. Had he not known that he was leaving in three months he would have probably looked forward with apprehension to the time when Pepire would have begun to weary him. As it was, he could accept without fear of consequences the day's good triings. As Europe understands love he did not love her. He cared for her in the same way that he might have cared for some animal. And indeed, as she strode bare-footed about the house and garden

124

she reminded him in many ways of a cumbersome Newfoundland puppy. Her behaviour when she had transgressed authority was extraordinarily like that of a dog that has filched the cutlets. On one occasion she went into Papeete with a hundred-franc note to buy some twenty-five francs' worth of stores. When he came in from his bathe, he found her standing with her hands behind her back gazing shamefacedly at the pile of groceries on the table beside which she had laid a ten-franc note.

'Well, what's that?' he asked.

'The change.'

'But how much did all that cost?'

'Twenty-seven francs.'

'And ten makes thirty-seven, and fifteen for the truck, that's fifty-two. What's happened to the other forty-eight?'

She made no reply, but sheepishly and reluctantly she drew her hands from behind her back and produced the four metres of coloured prints with which she proposed to make a frock.

She was always surprising him in delightful ways. There was the occasion when he returned from Papeete with a rather pleasant Indian shawl. She surveyed it with rapture, but before she had thanked him she asked the price. And whenever any visitor came the first thing she would do would be to run and fetch the shawl and display it proudly with the words: 'Look. He gave me. Five hundred francs!'

'I wonder,' he thought, 'whether the only difference between an English and a native girl is that what an English girl thinks a Tahitian says, and what an English girl says a Tahitian does?'

It was only on occasions that he would wonder that. In the deeper things he realized how profound was the difference between brown and white. Had they been English lovers, loving under the shadow of separation, their love-making would have

125

been greedy, fierce and passionate. But passion is a thing that the Islanders do not know. The Tahitians are not passionate. They are sensual and they are tender, but they are not passionate. Passion, though it may not be tragic, is at least potential tragedy, and tragedy is the twin child of sophistication. For Pepire, kisses were something simple and joyous and sincere. And yet during the long nights when she lay beside him he would wonder whether he would ever know in life anything sweeter than this love, so uncomplicated and direct. Intenser moments certainly awaited him, but sweeter …? He did not know.

Once only during those weeks did he see Colette. A brief, pathetic little meeting. He had gone into the library at Papeete to change a book, and as he stood before the shelves, turning the pages of a novel, she came into the shop. It would have been impossible for them not to see each other.

'What ages since we met!' she said, and she, as well as he, was blushing.

'I don't come in often now,' he said. 'I'm living in the country.' 'I know.'

In those two syllables were conveyed all that his living in the districts meant.

'You're still going by the *Louqsor?*

And in that question was implied that other question. How seriously was he taking his new establishment?

'Oh, yes, in another three weeks now.'

'Then I'll see you then if not before.'

With a bright smile she turned away; that, and no more than that.

And so the days went by.

Wistfully for him now and then.

For the closer that he grew to the Tahitian life, the wider, he realized, was the chasm between him and it. He would never find the key to Tahiti's magic. And soon there would be no mystery left to find. A few years and Tahiti would be a second Honolulu. She was self-condemned. Somehow she had not had the strength to withstand the invader. And, looking back, it seemed to him symbolic that it should have been by the spirit of Tahiti that his determination to settle in Tahiti had been foiled. For it was the spirit of Tahiti expressed momentarily in Pepire that had entrapped him into the weakness that had made a permanent settlement there impossible. The fatal gift of beauty. It was by her own loveliness, her own sweetness, her own gentleness, that Tahiti had been betrayed. And yet it was back to the sweetness that it had destroyed, that ultimately the course of progress must return.

The monthly arrival of the American courier is the big event in the island life.

But, for all that, it is only on the departure of those rare visitants, the *Louqsor* and the *Antinous,* that you get the spirit of an island leave-taking. For Tahiti is a French possession, and it is from the taffrail of the Messageries Maritimes boats that the French, who are the real Tahitians, who by long sojourning have identified themselves with the island life, wave their farewells to the nestling waterside.

For beauty and pathos there is little comparable with those last minutes of leave-taking. When the greater liners sail from Sydney the passengers fling paper streamers to the waving crowds upon the wharf; but in Papeete there is no such attempt to prolong to the last instant the sundering tie. For those that were your friends upon the island have hung upon your neck the white wreath of the tiare and the stiff yellow petal of the pandanus, so that your nostrils may for all time retain the sweet perfume of Tahiti; and over your shoulders they have hung long strings of shells, so that you will retain for ever the soft murmur of the breakers on the reef, and it is not till you have forgotten those that you will forget Tahiti.

No ship has looked more like a garden than did the *Louqsor* in the January of 1927. There were many old friends to wave farewell from its crowded decks, some who were saying good-bye for ever, if anyone can ever be said to say good-bye for ever, since for all time the memory of that green island will linger green. There were others who were going to France on leave for a few months. The Governor of the Island was returning to Paris for promotion. There were a number of officials; three or four naval officers; and on the lower decks a large group of sailors from the *Casiope* returning to Marseilles. It was a gay sight. A squad of soldiers had lined up to salute the Governor, a band was playing, the sailors were singing farewell to their five-days' sweethearts:

Ave, Ave, te vahini upipi
E patia tona, e pareo repo.

A few yards from Simmonds, Colette, frail and dainty, was smiling wistfully at him from beneath the shadow of her parasol. As he saw her he turned away from the crowd with whom he was gossiping—Pepire, Tania, and the rest—and came across to her.

She received him with a smile.

'Do you remember saying four months ago that you'd be heart broken when the time came for you to leave?'

'I remember.'

'And are you?'

He hesitated, for as he looked down into the flower-like face he knew the measure of his loss, knew what he had missed, what there had been for finding; knew also how impossible it would have been to find it, since certain things precluded other things, since that which he had been looking for bore no relation to the practical ordering of life. When he answered, though it was in terms of Tahiti that he spoke, it was of himself and her that he was speaking.

'As long as I live I shall remember,' he said, and his voice was faltering. 'And there'll be a great many times, I know, when I shall regret bitterly that I ever came away. But I shall know, too, that it would have been madness for me to have stayed. I came at the wrong time. If I'd come as a boy of twenty, before I'd begun European life, I could have stayed. Or I might have stayed if I'd come as a middle-aged man, a man of fifty, who'd outgrown ambition. But I came at the half-way stage. I've taken root over there. I've identified myself with too many things. I've got to work to the end of them.'

She nodded her head slowly. 'I understand,' she said. 'I think I always did understand.' Then, after a pause and with eyes that narrowed, and in a voice that trembled:

'Tahiti waits.'

But from the deck a bell was ringing. The friends of the passengers were crowding down the ladder; from the taffrail those who were leaving were slowly waving their farewells; the band was playing, the squad of soldiers were presenting arms, the sailors on the lower deck were singing. Slowly, yard by yard, the *Louqsor* drew out into the lagoon, the crowd was drifting from the quay, the tables in the Mariposa Café were filling up, officials were bicycling back to their offices, there was a lazy loitering along the waterside under the gold and scarlet of the flamboyants. A canoe was being launched, some children were bathing in front of

Johnnie's. Papeete was returning to its routine. Some friends had come. Some friends had gone. A new day had started.

With a full heart Simmonds leant over the taffrail. The strong winds of the Pacific were on his cheeks. He thought of London and his friends; of a life of action; the thrill of business; the stir of ideas and interest. Oh, yes, he would be glad enough to get back to it. But though his blood was beating quicker at the thought, the wreaths of pandanus and tiare were about his neck, and the sweet, rich scents were in his nostrils; and before his eyes, in the soft shadow of a parasol, was a flower-like face, with eyes that narrowed; and in his ears was the sound of a voice that trembled: 'Tahiti waits.'

1927

England 1932–1939

In the summer of 1927 I paid a second visit to Tahiti. Sailing from Marseilles towards Panama, I paused in the French West Indies and thus began a long association with the Caribbean that produced two novels; No Truce with Time *and* Island in the Sun, *and a number of sketches and short stories that were collected in 1958 in a volume called* The Sugar Islands.

In 1930 a travel book of mine Hot Countries *was a Literary Guild selection in the U.S.A. It introduced me to New York which soon became a second home for me.*

In 1932 I married and my life till the outbreak of war was based on England, with annual visits to New York. My wife bought a Queen Anne house in Silchester on the edge of the Roman city of Calleva. I maintained in London a small one-room pied-à-terre *flat. During this period I wrote three chronicle novels in the Galsworthian manner about English professional life and a number of short stories, most of which appeared in* Nash's. *Two of them were told in the first person.*

A Pretty Case for Freud

I noticed him in the first place because he was the only other person in the pavilion wearing a silk hat. I had the excuse of having come on there from a wedding. But I should have gone back and changed had I known how conspicuous I should be. It was ten years since I had been to the Varsity Match at Lord's; and I was astonished by the change: by the empty stands, the absence of smart frocks, the lounge-suited atmosphere of the enclosures. A social occasion, for whose sake in remote rectories mothballs had been once shaken out of braided coats and wide-brimmed 'toppers' stripped of their tissue wrappings, was now a very ordinary cricket match in which the general public took little interest. As I walked in my sponge-bag trousers and shining hat through the long, high, many-windowed morning-room, I felt as antediluvian as the curved bats and pastoral portraits that adorn its walls: so antediluvian that as I took my seat beside the one other Edwardian survival, a hackneyed Latin tag—the tongue that it is a solecism now to quote—actually seemed appropriate to the occasion. I thought of Lord's as the pre-war pages of *Punch* present it; of Lord's as I had known it in the early 'twenties; the tight-packed mounds; the coaches by the Tavern;

the parade of parasols between the innings; colour, excitement, glamour; and now this: Homburgs and bowler hats in the pavilion, long terraces of white beside the screen … *Nos duo turba sumus,* I thought, as I leant sideways towards my fellow relic.

'I wonder,' I asked, 'if I might see your scorecard?'

He turned; and I immediately forgot that it was a need for sartorial kinship that had decided my choice of seat.

He was one of the most striking-looking men that I have ever seen.

He was young: in the latish twenties; and handsome in a clear skinned way. But it was not merely his good looks that startled me. The impression that he made is not to be explained by any cataloguing of separate features; high forehead, grey-blue eyes, full mouth, long pointed nose. I was no more conscious of those separate features than one is of the pattern on a transparent lampshade. Just as there are two kinds of lampshade, the one whose object it is to transmit a softened light and the other that is a decoration, simply, a self-sufficient ornament requiring, like a stained-glass window, a light within it to reveal the intricacies of its design—it is a question of which matters, the lampshade or the light—so are there certain types of face, the one in which the personality is subservient to the featured mask of lip, brow, cheek, to which it gives mobility and meaning, the other in which you are so exclusively conscious of the personality behind that mask that you sometimes find yourself unable to describe the physical appearance of someone with the very texture of whose thought you are familiar.

It was like that now. I was conscious not of a handsome face, but of a new person; of someone who was masterful but unworldly; practical but inexperienced; masculine but with that look of anticipation, of waiting to be fulfilled that you expect to find in a young girl; a combination of characteristics so self-contradictory that the obvious corollary to their catalogue would be: 'What a mass of complexes. A pretty case for Freud.' That was what you would have expected.

He wasn't though. He was of a piece, without self-consciousness; the kind of man who does not know what the word shyness means.

I was curious, alert, excited. 'I've got to find out who you are,' I thought.

In the lazy atmosphere of a cricket match it is easy to start a conversation. Only a small amount of perseverance is required to maintain it. The cricket was slow, desultory, undramatic. In a little while we were more interested in our talk than in the match. At any rate, I was. His talk had the same contradictory characteristics as his appearance. It was boyishly eager, yet at the same time authoritative. It was the talk of one who stood on the brink of experience, yet was accustomed to the exercise of authority. More baffling still, though his voice had a slightly mannered intonation, it had no trace of the drawl that you would expect to find in a fashionably dressed young man. He was a puzzle, right enough: a puzzle that I meant to solve.

The hands of the turret clock pointed to five o'clock. Stumps would not be drawn till half-past six. In an hour and half I ought to be able to find out something about him, with any luck.

Luck came my way.

An exchange of ideas became an argument, a point at issue which could only be settled by the consultation of a particular book of reference. I had fancied the book was in the Pavilion library. It did not prove to be; or anyhow, we could not find it. I happened to have a copy at my flat.

'It's not five minutes' walk away,' I said. 'Let's go back there afterwards and have a sherry.'

'Let's go back now. This cricket bores me.'

An answer that combined his boyishness and his authority; his readiness to accept new suggestions with his assumption that no wish of his would be contradicted. It did not occur to him that I might want to stay on and watch the cricket. Like a schoolboy on his way to a party he chattered without stopping till we reached the large, barrack-shaped apartment-house on whose highest floor I have a one-room flat where I keep clothes and papers, that I use as a kind of office *pied-à-terre* when I am alone in London.

'Is this where you live?' he asked.

I nodded.

He looked up inquisitively at its straight sheer surface, as though he were seeing this particular kind of building for the first time; as though he were a foreigner obtaining the material for a mono-graph 'How London Lives'. As I opened the cocktail cabinet and set about the preparation of an 'old-fashioned', he deployed none of the diplomatically assumed indifference with which it is custom-ary to take stock of a new room without letting it appear that you are conscious of being in one. With an unabashed curiosity he took a mental inventory of the room: its lighting, its shelves, its chairs, its pictures, the jumble of knick-knacks along the mantel-piece; then started on a tour of investigation, taking up a book, peering into an etching, lifting a cigarette-box; without comment, as though he were visiting an exhibition, till suddenly, with a note of real interest in his voice, 'What's that doing here?' he asked.

He was pointing to the framed original of a jacket design for one of my novels.

'That? Oh, I'm responsible for that.'

'You drew the picture?'

'No—wrote the book.'

'What, you, the author!'

There was a surprised excitement in his voice that I should have found extremely flattering had not experience counselled me against a readiness to believe that here, at last, I was about to meet that perfect, that dream reader whom every novelist is convinced must exist somewhere, the one reader who has not only read everything that he has written, but read between the lines; for whose sake he has left 'i's' undotted and 't's' uncrossed in the calm confidence that 'anyway, *he'll* know what I'm about'. I have learnt to distrust that sudden glow in the voice, that quick light in the eyes. A case of mistaken identity, I tell myself. The tribute of sudden interest is in fact intended for the Chairman of Chapman & Hall, or the author of *Vile Bodies*, or more probably for the horse-trainer at Newmarket. On those rare occasions when I really am the target at which enthusiasm is directed, it is usually to receive some such testimonial as: 'I've been wanting to meet you for so long. There's a mistake in that last book but one of yours that I've been longing to point out. On page thirty-seven you talk about Mildred's gas fire, and in the last chapter you have coals falling through a grate. Now I wonder if anyone else has spotted that?'

Previous experience did not encourage me to expect from my guest's excitement a long, sympathetic, interpretive analysis of my short stories. I should have been disappointed if I had.

'There's something I've always wanted to ask you. Was Julia Thirleigh really the model for your heroine?'

'Well …'

It is the kind of question that usually a novelist resents; resents because it is impossible to reply honestly. The answer is always

'Yes and no'. No full-length character is ever a direct portrait; yet no character that is alive has not been drawn in part from life. A trick of speech has been borrowed here, a gesture there. The process of creation must start somewhere; must have some solid foundation in experience. But by the time the story is quarter finished, the novelist has forgotten his model altogether; his character has developed a temperament and destiny of its own, is a separate entity, has become, that is to say, created.

Usually, at least, that is the way it happens. In the case of Julia Thirleigh it had been admittedly rather different; possibly because I had 'put' her into the kind of novel that is less a story than an argument, that requires distinct types to contrast different points of view. I needed a character to typify the débutante of the late nine-teen-twenties, the second edition of the Bright Young People, the London of the slump. And it was just because Julia is herself less a person than a type that, when I had finished the book, I was astonished to find how closely my finished character resembled the model which I had meant to employ merely as a first sketch: so closely that I did not see how a great many people could fail to recognize her. In such a connexion Julia was the very first name that would come to any moderately well-informed person's mind. Through a decade when young women not only claimed, but asserted, their right to the same independence as their brothers, Julia was the most discussed of those Londoners whose activities are photographed week by week in the *Tatler*, *Bystander* and *Sketch*. She was not so much famous as notorious. She had avoided, it is true, any open scandal. She had not shot an unfaithful suitor, been convicted as a drug addict or cited in the divorce courts. To that extent she had been discreet. At the same time, she had been subpoenaed in a slander suit that had been heard *in camera*. It was at one of her bottle-parties in a top-storey studio that a free fight with gate-crashers had ended in a crumpled figure on the pavement and a comment from the coroner that only her most loyal friends held to be unjustified. There had been no open scandal. But the clothes she had worn, the company she had kept, the places she had frequented, her manner, her habits, her whole way of living had given her the kind of label that made her current coin in any argument. 'Well now, take somebody like Julia ...' and when people said that, no one had any doubt of what was meant.

Prudence as well as friendship counselled me to show my manuscript to Julia before I delivered it to my publisher.

She returned it with a very typical remark.

'I don't use Blue-grass.'

'Is that your only comment?'

'My only criticism.'

'There's nothing there that you object to?'

'Why should there be?'

'Well ...'

She smiled.

'Is there anything in your book that people haven't said about me and believed about me?'

'There's a difference between gossip and a thing said in print.'

'If your publishers are afraid of libel I'll write them a letter of absolution.'

I could scarcely deny, in the face of that, that I had used Julia as a model, yet I was reluctant to admit that my character was a photograph. I hedged.

'In a kind of way,' I said.

'You did? I'd always heard you did, but I wasn't certain. You must know her, then?'

'I was lunching with her yesterday.'

'Yesterday!'

He regarded me with a strange veneration, as though I were haloed in such a light as had transfigured Moses on his descent from Sinai.

'Yesterday! I can hardly believe it. I've heard so much about her, read so much about her. It's strange to be meeting somebody who really knows her. Is she as beautiful as her photographs? She must be. They are all so different. Yet they are all beautiful. I suppose there are hundreds of people in love with her. There must be. Is she in love, herself? Do you think she ever has been in love, really? I suppose she must have been. At the beginning. But, I don't think she can be, now. She must be waiting for the big thing; filling an interval; decorating an interval; that's what you suggested in your novel.'

I hadn't. But I let that pass. The bubbling Niagara poured on. Was she happy? Was she lonely? Was she one of those who had faced the Gorgon and whose tears had dried? He used various similes. I barely listened to his questions. I was too occupied with my relief at having found a way of continuing and enlarging my acquaintance with this very astonishing young man.

'If you're so interested in Julia, why not come here on Friday at cocktail time? She's coming.'

'What ... Julia Thirleigh ... here! ...'

His great eyes grew wide with incredulous astonishment, like a four-year-old darkie's when you offer it a silver coin.

'She said she'd come but I'll ask her to make a special point of it. I'll need to know your name, though, if I'm to introduce you.'

He looked surprised at that. But in a different way: as a school-master might when a pupil makes an elementary mistake.

'You don't know? I'm Bishopsbourne.'

Then I knew. Then I understood.

140

During a decade when the careers of the blue-blooded classes have followed unpredictably erratic courses, few members of the aristocracy have been subjected to more unexpected somersaults of circumstance than the present and tenth Lord Bishopsbourne.

When, in the April of 1914, he celebrated his ninth birthday as the Hon. Martin Forest he had an elder brother, a six-months-old nephew, three unmarried sisters, and a grandmother. His father, the seventh Lord Bishopsbourne, was one of the most amply endowed landowners in Kent. Martin was destined, that is to say, for the comfortably obscure existence of a second son. Within four and a half years, however, the accidents of war had deprived him of his father and his brother, the 1918 epidemic of influenza had proved too virulent for his nephew, and his grandmother had summoned the family solicitor to her presence.

'Martin is now the tenth Lord Bishopsbourne,' she said. 'Death duties have been paid three times in as many years. I imagine the estate is almost bankrupt. But I want figures—the precise figures, please.'

She was angular, thin-lipped, tight-stayed, her throat held high by whalebone. Her eyes were bright, and her voice was sharp.

The family solicitor hesitated. He had prepared, during the quarter of an hour he had been kept waiting, a concise and persuasive little speech. The situation was bad, he would explain. Mortgages would have to be raised. It would be many years before the estate would be able to maintain its former standard. He would very strongly recommend that the estate should be placed upon the market. There were a number of war profiteers who would leap at the opportunity of obtaining a house with such traditions and associations. A very good price should be obtained. A smaller property could then be purchased, and a comfortable way of life assured. The arguments had been neatly tabulated in his mind. He hesitated, however, as those small bright eyes fixed themselves on his and the sharp voice snapped: 'Figures—I want the precise figures, please.'

A great many other men had hesitated in that presence. Lady Bishopsbourne was a survival of those Victorian potentates of the hearth who, at a time when women possessed no political or legal status, had controlled their families with the unquestioned authority of a medieval monarch. 'You may take away my property at marriage. You may deny me a vote and the right to plead in court; but'—the voice snapped and the keen eyes flashed—'I will admit no contradiction, no interference in the conduct of my domestic interests.' There were many such women in Victorian England. There are very few in our ampler Georgian day. Lady Bishopsbourne was one of them.

The solicitor, hesitated, cleared his throat, began his argument. She cut him short.

'Nonsense,' said Lady Bishopsbourne. 'A man's duty is to his family, to the traditions of his family. Martin will accept those responsibilities. The sooner he starts the better. He will leave Eton at Christmas. Latin and Greek will be of small use to him now. He must learn his job.'

And so, at the age of thirteen, Martin was taken away from school to be placed under the guidance of an agent. Instead of memorizing Greek verbs, he pondered the problems of tithes, of soil, of crops and grazing. He exchanged the wide landscape of scholarship for the narrow compound of agriculture. He was living through the most dramatic epoch of modern history, but his interests were as blinkered as those of any medieval Trappist. He met no one of his own age and class. His days were spent with farmers, tenants, grooms, shepherds, with the middle-men through whom he sold his hops. In the life of what is called the 'county', his grandmother forbade him to take any part.

'We cannot afford to entertain,' she told him.

No Cinderella could have been more cut off from life.

It had gone on like that for fifteen years; fifteen years during which, while other families had depleted their resources with extravagance, he repaired his with industry and economy. On his twenty-sixth birthday he was as rich as his grandfather had been. On his twenty-ninth birthday his grandmother had summoned him to her presence.

'The time has come for you to find a wife. You will take a flat in London. I will arrange suitable introductions.'

So much of his life was common gossip ...

It was easy now to unravel this mass of contradiction. What other result could have been produced by such a combination of training and heredity. He had inherited his looks, height and health, his dignity of feature: a high forehead, a long pointed nose, a full firm-lipped mouth. He had inherited, too, an ease of manner, a confidence that he would be obeyed, an air of authority that was increased by his exercise of that authority among a rustic and subservient peasantry. These he had inherited. By his training he had acquired an almost feminine curiosity about the world from which he had been excluded. It was easy to see how a girl like Julia would appeal to his imagination. He had led the life of a male Cinderella. Just as Cinderella, while she swept passages, washed pans, scrubbed floors, dreamed of the coloured-sounding world that lay beyond the narrow tether of her kitchen, so Martin, as he inspected leaking roofs, interrogated cottagers, supervised in their proper seasons the lambing, the picking of the hops, the ploughing of the wheatfields, had speculated on the nature of the world, glimpses of which periodically reached him through such books and magazines and newspapers as his grandmother and sisters tolerated in their drawing room.

Cinderellas focus their dreams of the world from which they are excluded upon one person who symbolizes that world for them: an athlete, a prince, a film-star. To Martin, the tenth Lord Bishopsbourne, London and all that London stood for in glamour, adventure, richness of experience, was symbolized by the garish personality of Julia Thirleigh.

I looked forward with the liveliest interest to their meeting. What happened in real life, I wondered, when Cinderellas met their dreams?

Very much what happened, I was to discover, in the simplest fairy tale. When Julia came into the room, a peroxidized mane of curls upon her neck, her face as smoothly white as a magnolia, decorated with a mouth that bore no relation to the actual contours of her lips, her finger-nails pinked to match the bright ribbon of her hat—'Really,' I thought, 'she's gone too far. This is not the way to dress for a small cocktail party in a one-room flat.' But on Martin's face, as he rose to greet her, there was the look of a man who has met his fate.

It was not, however, a moment of tongue-tied rapture.

'You are the one person in London that I've really meant to meet.' That was his first remark to her. The second: 'You are even more beautiful than I'd thought you'd be.' The third: 'Let's go over into that corner where we can really talk.'

He led her in his most authoritative manner to the far corner of a many-cushioned divan, and there proceeded to behave as though there were no party, as though there were no one else in the room beside themselves. He allowed me to fill his glass from time to time; but the attempts of one or two of Julia's friends to disturb his monopoly of her company were frustrated by a

144

frontier of passive resistance. They came up with their 'Hullo, Julia!'s. They stood expectantly, waiting to be included in the conversation. But he behaved as though they were not there. The river of his talk flowed on. Once, over his shoulder, Julia caught my eye. She made a half-comical gesture of resignation, a 'What-on-earth-am-I-to-do-about-this?' look. But rescue was not possible. When at last, ninety minutes later, the colloquy was broken, it was at his side that she rose to her feet, at his side that she left the room. 'We'll dine at the Jardin,' he was saying with that same odd mixture of masterfulness and boyish eagerness.

Early next morning she rang me up.

'That's an astonishing young man,' she said.

'You're telling me!'

'It's like nothing that's ever happened to me.'

'Hasn't anyone ever made love to you at first sight before?'

'Oh, yes, of course. But—well, not like that. He seems to think—oh, I don't know—that I've nothing else to do except spend my entire time with him. There's no refusing him. Today I'm supposed to be lunching with the Gregsons, but I find I'm not; I'm motoring with him to Bray. I'd meant to play golf this afternoon. I'm not; I'm going on the river. I had thought I was going down to Pratings for the week-end; but I find I'm going to the first night of *Canary Bird*. And as far as I can see, he's already made plans for tomorrow, and the next day and the day after that.'

She hesitated. She tried to explain. Yes, of course, she had been made love to before at a first meeting. But invariably by the kind of man who was too busy to delay attack. The kind of man who was continually consulting a little diary that was black

145

with entries—'Yes, let me see now—Monday—Tuesday—Wednesday—what about Friday, then?' The kind of man who had to make full use of his few unmortgaged moments. Julia had known that type. She had also known the type whose diary was a blank page for her to write on. 'Now, what are you doing tomorrow—the next day—well, what about the day after, then?' A technique which was, she had come to realize, less a proof of devotion than a need on their part to have their minds made up for them. Martin was not like that. He knew his mind, all right. His diary was a blank sheet. He placed it at her disposal. He assumed that she would reciprocate; that hers, too, was blank. That was what puzzled her; his naïve assumption that what he wanted, she must want as well.

'He's the oddest creature I've ever met. I don't know, precisely, what it is he's driving at, but this I do know: he's serious about it.'

She was not to be left in the dark long. On the sixth day of their acquaintance—and so concentrated had their acquaintance been that she felt she had known him all her life—he invited her to spend a week-end in Kent. 'It's all right,' he explained. 'My grandmother will be there.'

Then she knew.

It had been an odd courtship. It was an odd proposal. Strictly speaking, there was no proposal. Martin assumed that they were engaged. As the car turned from the main road through the lodge gates, he pointed to the wide, gabled house at the end of a long curving drive.

'You'll probably think it a little bare. But we could arrange some herbaceous borders.' He took her into a large bow-windowed room, its long table littered with papers, its corners stacked with guns and riding-boots. 'This is my study. It's very untidy. But it's light and airy. I expect you'd like to have this for your drawing room.' On the first floor he led her into a room of pleasant proportions that would have appeared large had not the greater part of the floor and wall space been occupied by a vast, four-poster bed. 'You'll like this,' he told her confidently; 'it faces south.' That was surprising to Julia; but he had an even greater surprise in store. There was a door across the end of the passage. It opened on to a separate wing. 'This is immediately above the kitchens,' he informed her. 'It will make a pleasant nursery.'

For the first time since she had been very young, Julia found herself in a situation that was beyond her scope. In a long trailing telephone talk, she poured out to me the recital of the day's adventures.

'I've never met anybody like him in all my life. He's the very last person that I could have imagined myself marrying. Still, if he can cajole that gorgon of a grandmother into accepting me as the daughter of the house, I suppose he does deserve me.'

Julia had no doubt of the reception that Martin's announcement of his intention to marry her would have at his grandmother's hands. Nor had I. But Martin, where his own wishes were concerned, never considered other people's plans. He produced his news with a bland and cheerful confidence.

'Well, Grannie, I've not taken long in following your advice.'

'What do you mean, Martin?'

'Julia, of course.'

'Julia who, and Julia what?'

'Julia Thirleigh. We're going to be married.'

'The young person who lunched here yesterday?'

'Yes.'

There was a long pause.

'I will discuss this matter with you one week from now,' said Lady Bishopsbourne.

Within three days her grandson had been summoned to her presence.

'I am afraid that I have painful news for you,' she said.

'Oh?'

'Exceedingly painful news. It will be impossible for you to marry Miss Thirleigh.' 'Why?'

'I have made inquiries about her. She is not the kind of girl you think she is.'

'What makes you say that?'

'She has been extremely wild.'

'I know.'

'You misunderstand me. I don't mean headstrong, wilful. I mean that there have been men, a great many men in her life.'

'What else do you expect? She's very pretty.'

'Don't be silly. I don't mean in that way. I mean that she has had what the young people of your generation, euphemistically call "affairs", but for which in my generation we had a very different word.'

'That's no news to me.'

'What?'

'Nobody worries about that now.'

'What!'

'It's not what a girl's done before she's married, but what she does when she becomes a wife, that matters.'

'Martin …'

There was a pause; then with the authority of one who has not known opposition of any sort for fifty years, Martin's grandmother spoke. It was a long harangue. She spoke of family and tradition, of the race and of the future, of woman as the guardian of the race, of woman as the sacred vessel of the race. It was a full quarter of an hour before she abandoned generalities and approached the personal implications of the problem.

'I cannot imagine how a man with any delicacy of feeling can contemplate such a marriage. Do you expect your grandmother and your sisters to live in the same house as such a woman?'

'Certainly not. I'm going to have the dower-house done up.'

That evening he wrote to Julia telling her that she would see the announcement of their engagement in the next morning's issue of *The Times*.

Julia shrugged her shoulders. 'Well, if he feels that way about me—but I can't think why he does. I suppose,' she added, 'that Freud would have an explanation.'

Which is the kind of explanation that would be sought in an age which believes that human nature has been recast in the mould of Austrian psychology.

The wedding-day was fixed.

London was frankly and unanimously sceptical. It regarded the whole business not only as the season's best, but the century's best joke. 'Julia in orange-blossom!' It refused to believe that it could last three years. 'What else can happen?' scoffing voices argued. 'A girl like Julia. Think of the life she's led! We're not saying that a girl of her age shouldn't have *some* experience. You'd expect her to on the whole. If a girl is not married by twenty-five, it's probably because she's been in love with someone that for some reason or other she couldn't marry. Nowadays that usually means one thing. But Julia—well, you've only got to see what's happened to other girls of that type who've married. Three years: that's the limit. Still, at the end of it, there'll be a nice comfortable wad of alimony. The girl's on velvet.'

That was what London thought. But I was not certain. For the most part I sat silent when odds of eight to one against were laid.

In the main I was not certain, because in the last analysis I did not really know what manner of girl Julia was. Though I had known her for so long, she had never been quite real to me. She had remained a type: she typified innumerable things, but what she was herself I did not know. I could not even guess how her marriage would turn out, because I could not guess at the kind of person that marriage would reveal to Martin as his wife.

Martin, who had puzzled me first when I met him at Lord's, had become a comparatively simple problem; but Julia, about whom I had then scarcely bothered, had become, now that I had really started to consider her, an inscrutable enigma.

Her behaviour during their engagement was altogether different from what I had expected. In view of her reputation, I had anticipated a flaunting and defiant manner, a head held high in self-vindication, lips curled with an unspoken, 'Didn't I tell you so? I've got the thing both ways: have had my cake and have it still to eat; have played the town and am marrying a peer.'

That's what you would have expected. But not at all. She grew quieter, dressed less stridently, arranged her make-up in approximate conformity with the contours of her face. At times she would sit quite silent at a party, an abstracted look upon her face. As the marriage day drew close, her moments of abstraction grew so frequent that her manner became almost trance-like. One would have said, had she been anyone but Julia Thirleigh, 'A young girl in love for the first time!'

So marked indeed was her manner that when I met her two days before her wedding at a cocktail party given in her honour, I could not help exclaiming: 'Julia, you look like a bride!'

150

Her answer came back pat. 'I feel like one.' It was the obvious answer, but the tone of voice and the look that went with it made me feel that there was a meaning behind her words. I looked at her quickly, interrogatively. 'I've every right to feel like one,' she added. Then I knew there was a second meaning. I took her by elbow. 'Now, what's all this about?'

It was the kind of cocktail party where there is so much noise, so much crowding of people into a confined space that no serious conversation is considered possible, or is, indeed, intended by its organizers, but which provides in actual fact the best of shelters for two people who really want to talk intimately to one another.

Julia chuckled as I led her toward a window-seat.

'Come along,' I said. 'What is it?'

Her chuckle became a laugh.

'I've always wanted you to know. I'd wanted to tell you when you wrote that novel. But I thought: No, I'd better wait. I've waited so long that I can afford to wait a little longer.'

'I don't know what you're talking about.'

'No, you wouldn't. It was what you said about my looking like a bride. I feel like one. I've every right to feel like one. I've as much right to wear orange-blossom as any Victorian damsel that walked up an aisle.'

'I still don't follow you.'

'Of course you don't. You got me wrong. Everybody got me wrong. I let them. I encouraged them. All those things you wrote about me—it's not true, any of it. I'm not like that at all.'

'But—'

'I've been wild. I know that. But not in *that* way.'

I stared at her uncomprehendingly.

'But those men, those love-affairs?'

She shook her head.

'No, not one.'

I stared blankly. Had I been offered proof of Queen Victoria's frailty, I should not have been more astonished.

'But how, when, why, where, what—' I stammered.

She laughed: the kind of laugh that comes from the depths of a great happiness.

'It was shyness to begin with,' she explained. 'All the girls I knew were talking about their affairs, I felt ashamed of not having any. So I pretended that I had, just so as not to seem out of things. I expect that a great many more girls than one would ever suspect are like that too. There's more talking about things than doing things. Perhaps if I'd ever been attracted by anyone, really attracted, I'd have had a real affair; but I wasn't, so I just pretended. And when one starts pretending, one can't stop—even when one realizes that it's gone too far; as I knew it had, of course. But I couldn't have told anyone then. I should have looked so silly. Besides, it was fun, too, in a way, deceiving every-one. I used to chuckle when people warned me, when they told me that I'd never find anyone who'd want to marry me. I knew that some day someone would come along who would be so much in love with me that he wouldn't mind what I'd been, who'd want me for what I was. I knew that would happen. But what I never had suspected, was how completely I was going to fall head-over-heels in love with him myself.'

The smile on her lips and in her eyes was touching.

I had listened to her in silence; stupefied at the start, but with a dawning sense of comprehension. It was rather like the sensation one gets from a good detective story, when the least suspected person is revealed to be the murderer. You say: 'Oh, but that's impossible.' You feel fooled and cheated; then gradually, as clue after clue is stated, you recognize that you have not been fooled, that the clues were there if you had had the sense to spot them; that subconsciously, indeed, you had spotted them; that no other conclusion would have fitted *all* the facts. Astonishing though Julia's confession was, it did explain all that had puzzled me before. I could understand now why she had never seemed quite real: why she was someone who had done things rather than somebody who was something. She had been acting a part. No wonder she had seemed a type.

Her confession explained a lot. It did not, however, appreciably determine the outcome of her marriage.

'Are you going to tell Martin this?'

'Naturally. I've been keeping it as a surprise for him for the wedding-night.'

'You think he'll be pleased?'

'What man wouldn't be?'

I answered her obliquely.

'Have you ever read a book called *Tess of the* D' *Urbervilles?*'

'No. What about it?'

'It was much discussed in my parents' day. It's about a dairy-maid who had an illegitimate child that died. Several years later, she married. On her wedding-night, her husband discovered the secret of her past. He was so shocked that he left her there and then.'

'That was very silly of him.'

'It was very natural. Angel Clare—that was the husband's name—had thought he was marrying an innocent girl, the daughter of peasant stock. He had to reconstruct his entire picture of her when he discovered that she was not that at all, that she was the descendant of degenerate aristocrats, that she

153

had already borne a child. He had fallen in love with her, not knowing her for what she was. He had to adjust himself to a strange woman. He could not do it.'

Julia looked puzzled.

'Well, what about it?'

'Don't you think it might be just as much of a surprise to Martin to discover that you were completely without experience?' She laughed out loud.

'I suppose it's by putting things like that in your books that you claim you're a psychologist.'

I tried to explain to her. I argued that if Martin had fallen in love with her, believing her to be a certain kind of woman, when he discovered her to be another kind of woman altogether, she would have become a stranger to him, a stranger with whom, very possibly, he would not be in love.

She listened mockingly. Then she asked in great amusement:

'What do you think'll happen? Will he get up and leave me then and there, like the hero in that novel?'

'It might spoil an idyll.'

She shook her head.

'Novelists are nearly always wrong when it comes down to a problem in real life. You got me wrong. You've probably got Martin wrong as well. What are you suggesting that I should do? Say nothing?'

'Yes.'

Into her face came a look of real indignation.

'I've been saving up this secret for five years. If you think I'm going to miss the best chance I'll ever have of spilling it, you're stupid.'

She left me in a fine fury.

It was, in its way, a quite grand wedding. Julia had produced from an estate in Norfolk an unsuspected and quite distinguished parent. Lady Bishopsbourne had seen to it that the family's first public appearance in twenty years should not lack splendour. Rarely had the altar of St. George's been more opulendy bowered with unseasonable blooms. The mansion in Chester Square which had been requisitioned from an exceedingly distant aunt, was feudal in its parade of footmen. Every acquaintance of any consequence had been invited. Curiosity had led to the acceptance of ninety-seven per cent, of the invitations. An attendance fully twice as long as the invitation list, sweeping like a tidal river in its armada of long, low, shining cars, forced the lorries and taxi-cabs of Belgravia into inextricable traffic blocks in the remoter reaches of Grosvenor Place. An entire floor was required to display appropriately the generosity of the guests.

Unquestionably it was a grand occasion. And there, at the end of the long L-shaped drawing-room was the young couple—so blissfully, so blindly absorbed in one another that only two glasses of champagne were needed to render me tearfully wistful over the fate that threatened them. Something must be done. They were such innocents! I had brought them together. I was in a way responsible for their future. I had pondered the problem during the long, inaudible address. I had believed myself to have discovered a solution—if, that is to say, I could find an opportunity to propound it; or rather, if I should have the courage to make the opportunity. A third glass of champagne gave me the courage.

I pushed my way through the crowd to Julia.

She welcomed me friendlily. Two days earlier she had been angry. But on a day like this she had forgotten that. Besides, it was I who was responsible for her happiness.

'Julia, I must have one word, just one word, alone with you.'

She pouted. 'Darling, not that again!'

'It won't take two minutes.'

'Very well, then.'

She let herself be led away. I kept my promise: it did not take a minute. I knew exactly what I had to say. I had phrased it very carefully during the address.

'You said that you'd been saving your secret for five years: that you wanted to make the most effective use of it. You're right. You should. But let me assure you of this. Now is not the time. Within the first year of marriage there comes the first big quarrel, when each turns on the other and flings every available recrimination at the other's head. On the outcome of that quarrel depends the course of marriage. You'll want every possible weapon then. Keep your secret till then. It'll torpedo any opposition.'

'Is that really true: about the quarrel, I mean to say?'

'Invariably.'

'In that case, then, perhaps—' She was half convinced; but there was still a pensive, puzzled look upon her face. She hesitated. Then suddenly she looked up, and with a brilliant flush, she asked me a question so naïve that I could have kissed her.

'But on a point like that, could one really make a man believe one wasn't what one was?'

I reassured her. 'Him, you could.'

'Oh, well, then in that case, perhaps—perhaps it would be best to wait … And, thank you, anyhow.'

She turned away, caught up by her obligations as a bride: the cake to be cut, the toast to be responded to, the innumerable good wishes. She was only half convinced, but I was pretty sure

156

that she would not say anything that night, nor the one after, nor ever, probably, till the time had come when their relations with one another were so firm-knit that no premarital confession could disturb it.

They were together now, he and she. As they stood answering the stream of congratulations, her fingers plucked at his trouser seam, signalling for the hand that crept down to hers ... They stood there, their fingers interlocked. It was very touching.

Perhaps no one nowadays would care to offer long odds on any marriage lasting, but these two had had as the prelude to this moment so much of self-doubt and of anticipation; there was so much for them to reveal to one another, so much of themselves to learn for the first time, so many things to share, that I would have been prepared to lay, well, seven to one on.

I turned away, to climb the flight of stairs to the higher floor on which was set out the imposing tribute to the young people's prominence and popularity. Usually at such a wedding it is with some diffidence that I walk past the long high-piled tables in the hope that my modest contribution of book or brooch has not had its modesty too markedly accentuated by the adjacency of ancestral candelabra. But on this occasion I did not care. I felt that the advice I had just forced upon the bride was a more valuable wedding-gift than the studded circlet of the Bishopsbourne tiara.

'Ambition' Bevan

I was responsible for his nickname.

I had found it for him before he had been at school a week.

He was my junior. But as the head scholar of his group, he had passed into a form that it had taken me a year to reach.

His existence had been announced to me by the headmaster's wife a week before the term began.

'I should be very grateful,' she wrote, 'if you would keep an eye on Bevan. As the only new boy to pass straight into the Upper School, he is bound to feel rather lost his first few days. He will be in the same dormitory as you, so it won't be difficult for you to give him hints.'

The letter did not predispose me in Bevan's favour. Nor did Bevan's personal appearance. He was lankily over-grown, with a sallow complexion and a pimply chin. His collars were too high, his trousers were too short, his shoulders were spotted with a snow of scurf. He had filled his pockets with so many objects that the coat sagged sideways in heavy grooves. His hair fell forward from his crown, to be swept off the forehead with one sweep of a damp brush. He moved with a loose loping stride as though his ankles were in splints, with all the spring coming from his knees and hips. He wore powerful spectacles.

He introduced himself to me on the first evening after hall.

'I'm Bevan: the chap you are looking after.'

I looked him over slowly.

'Are you?' I said. 'Am I?'

He took my remark literally. He peered at me with a bright, hawk-like eagerness.

'Yes, that's right, and the first thing I want you to explain is the system by which set subjects are organized in relation to form promotion. As far as I can see ...'

Convention decrees that a new boy does not ask questions. He may only answer them. But Bevan was beyond convention. There was no side of school life on which I was not cross-examined. At first I thought he was timidly anxious to avoid mistakes. Later I fancied that he was just inquisitive. It was a week before I understood. Then I gave him the nickname that lasted him right through his time at Fernhurst. It was simply that he was ambitious; fantastically, overweeningly ambitious; that he was resolved to be a success and appreciated the value of discovering in advance the precise nature of the race that he was running.

Fantastic and overweening are the only adjectives that can describe ambition such as his.

A single example will suffice.

I had explained to him that when a boy had once reached the Upper Sixth, the form order did not alter; that prefectship was decided by a process of automatic seniority. He pondered that thoughtfully.

'Then, in that case I must get ahead of anyone who's likely to be a rival before either of us reaches the Upper Sixth. I'm ahead of the boys of my own year. I ought to be able to stay ahead of them. But it might suit me to go up to Oxford at eighteen. I

159

mean to be Head of the School first. Now, I wonder if there's any one from the year before that's dangerous. There's Parkes in Claremont's. He's in the Upper Fifth. I ought to try and catch up with him during the next year, and pass him while we're in the Lower Sixth together. Then I shall be head of the school in the autumn of 1916.'

It was in September 1912 that he said that. I could not help laughing at such far-sightedness.

'My dear Bevan, if people are going to start looking that far ahead, I might as well be wondering whether I or someone else is going to be Captain of the XI in 1917.'

'And so you should. As far as I can see Evans is your chief rival.'

He was no less methodical in the planning of his private life. One Sunday afternoon I found him starting on a solitary walk.

'All by yourself?' I asked.

He nodded. 'As usual,' he replied.

It was a strange admission. Most boys are shy of being seen alone. It makes them look unpopular. I felt sorry for 'Ambition'.

'I should have thought you'd have got to know one or two of the new men by now.'

'I haven't troubled.'

'What!'

'One has to be very careful about making friends. Unless your friends belong to the world in which you propose to move, you have either to drop them when that world has become accessible, or remain in a world that you dislike.'

'I don't follow that.'

'No? I should have thought it obvious. There are larger and lesser ways of living. One should try and live in as large a world as possible.'

He spoke in a petulant, slightly patronizing, slightly irritated voice. But I did not understand: not then. I just thought, 'Poor old "Ambition". He's potty.'

Which was how most of us felt about him. We thought him mad and left him to go his own way unmolested. Strangly enough, he was not bullied. Bizarre though his appearance was, there was nothing of the buffoon about him. He was guarded by an unapproachable, dignified reserve. He went up the school at the rate that he had prophesied, a solitary figure, too absorbed by his ambition to share the communal interests and enthusiasms of house and school. Every term he was the winner of some prize. It was all turning out to plan. But he never seemed particularly happy. Occasionally the eager hawk-like look came into his eyes. But for the most part his face wore a driven, preoccupied expression. He was invariably alone. He availed himself of the Sixth Former's privilege of a study to himself—a privilege rarely taken. The only person in whose company he appeared with any regularity was a weedy, elegantly languid boy in another house, of no particular distinction in work or games, whose father was vaguely 'county', his grandmother having been the third daughter of a peer. Myself, I saw very little of him after those first weeks. We seldom met in the classroom or on the field. His eyesight made him a poor footballer, and a worse cricketer; while my scholastic career followed a desultory course to the safe harbourage of the history Sixth. We went up the school by parallel tracks, always just out of hailing distance of one another.

So little, indeed, did I see of him that I had to think twice before I could place the writer of a letter that I received a year after the war, on the notepaper of the Oxford Union. The handwriting was ornate; so was the style.

'I am now,' it informed me, 'for my faults, follies and lack of courage, directing the embryo literary enthusiasms of putative poets. As their controller, adviser, mentor, I from time to time cajole, flatter and otherwise intimidate those from the larger world "whose foreheads wear Apollo's wreathed crown", into succouring, guiding and generally supporting their uncertain ambits with counsel, exhortation, and such animadversions on the craft and aims of letters as may seem appropriate to their broader knowledge. May I therefore as a simple Osric, courtier in this cloistered city, humbly supplicate a Prince of Henrietta Street to pass rapiers of dialectic with an ill-harnessed Laertes of the Alpha and Omega Society on the 29th May?'

On a third reading I realized that this was an invitation to take part in the debate of a literary society of which Bevan was the secretary.

'Well!' I thought.

It was not so much the phraseology of the invitation as the fact that Bevan was responsible for it that surprised me. I had pictured his Oxford career in very different terms: long hours in the Bodleian and the lecture-room: a permanently sported oak. It astonished me that 'Ambition' Bevan should be wasting his time on literary societies.

If his letter has surprised me, his appearance did even more. He had been sixteen when I had seen him last. He had by then out grown his untidy coltishness, but I did not expect to be met at the station by a willowy, elegant, almost distinguished figure in a pale blue jumper and a green tweed jacket, who peered at me through horn-rimmed spectacles and spoke in a high, slow and very mannered voice.

Nor had I expected to find in Bevan's room a photograph of himself in uniform.

'I never thought they'd pass your eyesight,' was my comment.

'Nor did I.'

'Did they send you overseas?'

'I got gassed and wounded.'

'Didn't all that upset your plans a little?'

He shrugged his shoulders.

'I hardly think so. I am reading a short course, you see.'

I raised my eyebrows.

'I had always pictured you as a Fellow of All Souls.'

He laughed at that.

'Fellowships, that nursery nonsense!'

He spoke disparagingly of scholastic achievement. A man, he argued, must be educated, must be informed on men and manners. But the scholar lived in blinkers. What was the point of slaving to get a first in Greats only to become a glorified Treasury clerk? One might get a long row of letters after one's name. But what did that amount to? It wasn't what a man did but what he was, that mattered. He spoke airily, condescendingly. It all sounded very odd, coming from 'Ambition' Bevan.

I asked him if he saw any of the other men from Fernhurst who were up at Oxford then. He shook his head.

'We've nothing in common. I never bothered to make friends with any of them there, why should I here? Fernhurst: well, after all ...' he hesitated. He did not want to say anything against his old school. But that pause struck a very precise note of tolerant disparagement. It was as though he were saying, 'Fernhurst was a small school. Really prominent men could only regard it as a stepping-stone.' 'No, no,' he said, 'Barlow's the only one I see at all. I don't know if you remember him? In Claremont's.'

I nodded. I remembered him. The tall languid figure in whose society alone Bevan had appeared to take much pleasure.

'I see quite a bit of him. He's, of course ... well, how shall I put it? …' He pursed his lips in the attempt to find the correct phrase of qualified denigration, failed, shrugged his shoulders. 'He's a restful companion. It's pleasant week-ending with his people. But, come now, don't let us waste our time talking about Barlow. There's so much I want to ask about your life in London. Tell me, what sorts of people do you see?'

As he put the question that old hawk-like eagerness came into his face, as though once again he were asking me to map out for him the geography of the road he had to travel.

It was a question that I did not find it particularly simple to answer.

'As many different kinds of people as possible,' I said. 'A novelist ought to be like the centipede, with a foot in a hundred worlds.'

My answer was clearly not of the kind he wanted.

'Yes, yes; of course, that is the great advantage of being a writer. You can go anywhere, yet you are received. Tell me now, which of the younger writers would you say counted most?'

'Hugh Walpole sells a lot.'

'I don't mean that.'

'What do you mean?'

'I mean really *counts*. What writers, for instance, would be invited to a reception at Londonderry House?'

'I haven't the least idea.'

'What!' He stared at me as though I were an unclassified disease. 'You don't know?'

'Why should I?'

'Merely from the professional point of view. I should have thought that you would have been curious to know how your rivals and contemporaries were faring.'

'I don't see that invitations to Londonderry House have

anything to do with *that.*'

'No? I should have imagined that even in these commercial days a writer would have valued the privilege of mixing with the big world.'

He spoke in part pontifically, in his bored, superior Oxford manner; in part with the fretful impatience that had come into his voice at Fernhurst. Clearly, we were talking at cross-purposes.

I changed the subject.

'What are you going to do when you come down?' I asked. 'Take a flat in London and look round till I find something that really suits me.'

He spoke with an airy confidence.

That evening I made inquiries about him at the College of which I was the guest. There was a titter when I told them how we had nicknamed him at school.

'The only ambitions he's shown any signs of here are social. He's the most crashing snob that ever walked,' they told me. 'He'll only know peers and honourables.'

'Does he know many?'

'A good few. It's not difficult in a place like this. If that happens to be your racket.'

With this information I felt better equipped to deal with Bevan.

When we met next morning, I directed our conversation into a social channel. He expanded, readily. A society columnist could not have been more full of gossip.

I nodded and smiled and interjected an occasional remark. It was easy now to realize what had happened. Bevan was a provincial; with a provincial's anxiety to mix in the great world, to make a name for himself, to be a figure. He had naturally regarded a small school like Fernhurst as a stepping-stone. He had avoided friendships that might prove a hindrance to him later, concentrating upon the classics, recognizing that to have been head of his school and a scholar of Balliol would make an effective start to a career at Oxford. But that start once made, he had found it possible without further calls upon his scholarship to mix with members of the world that dazzled him. I watched his face as he spoke of his acquaintance with the aristocracy. He was sunning himself in the light of his achievements. Although he had been content to read a short course instead of becoming a Fellow of All Souls, he clearly regarded himself as unqualified a success at Oxford as he had been at Fernhurst.

He seemed, however, to be no happier here than he had been at school. His face still wore that driven look: the fear of being late for something.

I had proof of this before my visit ended.

We had gone into Blackwell's to buy a copy of the recent Newdigate. A tall, loose-limbed young man wearing an old Etonian tie came over to us. Bevan introduced me. As the introduction was one-sided, I did not learn his name. I did notice, however, how completely Bevan's manner changed. It was hard to say in what particular. But there was a general atmosphere of constraint, of self-consciousness. A tightening up, a talking for effect.

'Who's that?' I asked when we were in the Broad again.

'That? Oh, that's Harry Marshall, Lord George Marshall, you know. The Marquis of Patrixbourne's younger son. A delightful fellow.'

A rich note of satisfaction like the purring of a well-stroked cat had come into his voice. Yes, I thought, you get an enormous kick out of reminding yourself that you know these people, but you're not in the least happy when you're with them.

What, I wondered, would happen to him when he came down? He had a private income of some five hundred pounds a year. A sum on which it is possible to make an adequate display at Oxford, but which does not see a social climber very far in London. I also knew how well-stocked London was with young men from Oxford demanding employment worthy of themselves. It would be amusing to watch the outcome. Not that I supposed I should see much of him. I was not nearly grand enough.

Nor was I. Neither should I, had not a friend of mine chosen to fall in love with him. Her name was Lucy Martin. And I can best describe her by saying that she was a typical 1917 club product. She was, that is to say, in the early twenties. She had become politically conscious during the last months of the war when Liberal opinion was turning towards the Labour Party in protest against a capitalist continuation of the war. She was pretty, in the hour's fashion: dark, bobbed hair, be-jumpered; with the smoke of innumerable cigarettes drifting across her eyes. Her slogan was 'personal liberty'. Politically, she was extremely narrow, angrily intolerant of every shade of opinion except her own; but in herself she was genuine, warm-blooded, open-hearted. She was in addition admirable company. She had a zest for life. She always enjoyed what she was doing. I saw a good deal of her during the first half of the 1920s.

She regarded me as a kind of father-confessor. She had, however, the habit of describing her acquaintances by their Christian names, so that I had no means of identifying the 'Raymond' of a long, inconclusive, unsatisfactory saga. For weeks she had told me about him: how handsome he was, how

167

brilliant, how misunderstood. 'He could do anything, but anything; only in the way that society's constituted now there isn't anything for him to do.'

I asked her what he did do.

'Nothing, as yet. He's waiting till he finds work that's worthy of him. He's bound to, soon, of course. But in the meantime you can't be surprised at his being rather bitter, when he sees third-rate people succeeding everywhere.'

He lived in a maisonette flat in Bloomsbury, spent his mornings in the Museum Reading-Room, devoted his afternoons and evenings to a round of parties. 'He thinks that the best way of finding the kind of work he wants. It's degrading for a man of his talents to be forced to that kind of strategy. It'll be different when the Socialists are in power.'

None of which particularly predisposed me in 'Raymond's' favour.

'Is he very much in love with you?' I asked. She shook her head.

'No. That's what makes it all so wretched. There's someone else.'

'Who is she?'

'I've never met her. But he's got her photograph all over his rooms. She must be the explanation. There couldn't be any other. I think you ought to come and see him.'

It was not till I was actually inside his rooms that I identified 'Raymond' as my old friend, 'Ambition' Bevan.

It was three years since our Oxford meeting. But Lucy's account of him, a glance round the room so typical of Bloomsbury with its long rows of bookshelves, its Van Gogh reproductions, its Wyndham Lewis etchings, its bright striped curtains, gasfire, many-cushioned divan; a quick survey of the physical change in

Bevan, the loose collar, and tie, the long hair, the sneering expression of the mouth, the pitch of voice, mannered and supercilious, told me what had happened in those three years.

He had come down from Oxford with his inherited income of five hundred pounds. He had no job. He was going to look round for one. And that is a bad platform for a young man in London. A young man earning four hundred a year can have a better time in London, which is a man's city, than anywhere in the world. A man with four thousand a year and no profession can have an exceedingly amusing time in London, spending it. An independent income of four hundred pounds can be of incalculable value to a young man of industry and ambition, at the start of a career. But the one fatal combination is no job and a small unearned income. Particularly in the case of a young man from Oxford with ambitions, but undefined ambitions. Before Bevan had been long in London he had been forced to realize two things: that jobs are not easy to find, and that he himself with no job and very little money counted for nothing in the large vortex of London's interests. It was not surprising that he had grown bitter. He was, in fact, the most vindictively bitter person under thirty that I have ever known.

Lucy had said that it exasperated him to watch the success of third-rate people. It would be truer to say that he was obsessed with the desire to prove that all success was of a third-rate nature. Before I had been talking to him five minutes he had provided me with an example of his resolve to disparage and diminish the value of the most mild good fortune.

'By the way,' he said, 'I saw a story of yours in some magazine the other day. I should imagine that that kind of thing brings in a lot of money.'

'No. But it clothes and feeds me.'

'Really? That's most interesting. Just what I'd have thought. Now, a writer like Ronald Firbank would not have made enough out of all his books put together to buy a cabinet of cigars.'

'I should doubt it.'

'Strange, isn't it? And there's not the slightest doubt that in twenty years' time Firbank will be recognized as the one really important writer of this decade.'

The only writers for whom he had a good word to say were those with three-figure circulations, who could not win a footing in such periodicals as paid contributors.

His interest in the social racket was as keen as ever. When we discussed any former acquaintance, one of his first questions invariably would be, 'What kinds of people does he go about with?'

We happened to mention a certain Soho restaurant. I told him that I liked it, that I went there often.

'Would fashionable people go there?' he asked.

I told him that I did not imagine so.

'Who do go there then?'

'It's hard to say. Quite a number of my friends.'

'Writers and that kind?'

'More or less.'

'Quite, quite. You are very wise to move among the people with whom you feel at ease.'

It would be difficult to convey the exact note of patronizing contempt on which he made that comment. He placed side by side my capacity to sell stories to the illustrated magazines and my preference for the company of such people as frequented the Café X. By this standard I was judged and was dismissed.

It was extremely difficult to remain in his company for long and keep one's temper. It was absurd that a girl as nice as Lucy should have chosen to fall in love with anyone so sour.

'I can't imagine what you see in him,' I said.

She shrugged her shoulders.

'I don't know. He's so unhappy, he's such a mess. And it's such a pity. It's all so unnecessary. Such a very little thing is needed to put it straight.'

The remedy was not destined to come from her, however. Bevan let her come to his flat, curl up on a rug before his fire, smoke innumerable cigarettes, read his books, make Russian tea for him, argue about politics and the new world. But his attention was entirely focused on the girl whose photographs adorned his room. I knew her slightly. She was one of those bored, listless, amoral creatures of whom the novelists and the playwrights of the period made such fertile copy. Her hair was cut close about her scalp; she walked as though she had no backbone; her voice was so low-toned and drawled that you felt that she would never have the strength to carry a sentence to a full stop. She was well calculated to make supremely wretched any man who pursued her with 'honourable' intentions.

'Why not chuck it?' I advised him. 'You won't get anything that's worth having there. And there's a really nice girl who, for some incomprehensible reason, thinks a lot of you.'

He shrugged his shoulders.

'Yes. I know. Poor little Lucy. But … oh well, one can't get mixed up with somebody like that.'

'What do you mean, "somebody like that"? And what do you mean, "mixed up"? Lucy isn't the kind of girl to start running you into a registry office.'

'I know, I know, but … oh well, we really haven't anything in common. And in a thing like that, it has to be the real thing or no thing.'

The old Bevan: with his insistence on the two worlds; and his resolve to get the one ticket in a lottery.

But I did not see very much of him. He was too acid a companion. It was pointless to subject one's self-confidence to the incessant pinpricks of his irritation.

I preferred to keep track of his movements through Lucy Martin.

So that it was indirectly, from her, that I learnt of the disaster that in terms of poetic justice was an appropriate corollary to his career.

Weary of doing nothing, acutely conscious of the low level at which his social stock was standing, he had sold out his War Loan and invested the resulting capital in a motor business with young Barlow as his partner. He had hoped to kill two birds with one stone. With Barlow's connexions he would at the same time make money and move in the world from which his lack of prominence was rapidly excluding him.

To a certain extent and for a time his hopes looked likely to be fulfilled. Barlow did bring clients, the majority of whom were listed in *Debrett*. Unfortunately, they bought their cars on credit. When a slump came, they handed their cars back. Bevan was not the man to litigate against a peer. A day arrived when he was forced to recognize not only that his capital had vanished, but that on certain of his transactions a most unpleasant construction could be placed in a court of law. He was advised to leave the country.

In a fine fever of indignation Lucy brought the news to me.

'He's been swindled, that's quite obvious. Those fine friends of his are making him their scapegoat. I've told him so, but he won't believe it. Instead of showing them up, he's saying how grateful he is to them for having got him a job with the police.

With the police, indeed! That's what they've done for him, a job with the police: a man like that. In a place like Malaya too! That's where they're sending him; they would: they want him out of the way. It's disgraceful. What a waste of talent. But it's no good telling you. You never liked him. You were never fair to him. But … oh, it's tragic to think of a man like that being sent to a place like that. It proves that the world wants turning inside out. The way things are run now, a man of real talent doesn't stand a chance …'

Fumingly, the flood of words poured on. 'It's good luck for you,' I thought. 'You're well rid of him.'

That was in '26.

During the next four years I don't suppose I thought of him three times; and one of those times was when I read the announcement in *The Times* of Lucy Martin's engagement to an exceedingly eligible young stockbroker. I had actually been in Malaya a couple of months before it occurred to me to ask whether anyone had heard anything of a man called Bevan.

It was in the Penang Club that I set that question. I was conscious of a stir round me of inquisitive amusement.

'We' ve got a Bevan here all right,' they said.

'If it's the same one, I was at school with him.'

'Would it be R.F. Bevan?'

'R. F.? Yes, it might,' I hesitated. 'It sounds absurd, but I'm not certain of his intitials. We always called him by his nickname.'

'What was that?'

' "Ambition". We called him "Ambition" Bevan.'

There was a laugh at that.

'There's not much ambition about him now,' they said. 'He's the manager of a second-grade plantation, with a half-caste wife and a couple of coloured brats. There's not a white man between Siam and Singapore with less to boast about. "Ambition" Bevan, indeed!' I stared at them amazed. Bevan, the man who had thought himself too grand to have an affair with Lucy Martin, married to a Malayan half-caste.

'How did it happen? What on earth made him do a thing like that?' I asked.

The answer was given with a guffaw of laughter.

'His father-in-law's right arm.'

'Tell me the whole story, please.'

Up to a point it was a conventional enough story. Bevan had come out with a job in the police. It wasn't a particularly good job, and it wasn't likely to lead to much. But it was a *'pukka sahib's job'*. It was official. And in English communities men with a *pukka sahib's* job have got to obey the conventions of their caste. They must not, that is to say, get ostentatiously drunk. Nor must they flaunt a liaison with a coloured girl. Which was what Bevan did: in Kuala Sumut, a smallish river station half-way between Port Swettenham and Penang.

Even then it might have been all right if he hadn't boasted about it in the Club.

The girl's father was a man of over sixty. He was the old type of planter: the third son of a West Country baronet who had run up debts, caused scandal, been sent to the colonies with a draft on a Penang bank for a thousand pounds. He had come to Malaya in the rough days, before genteel society was established; when it was a man's world; when women were left behind in Europe and a man as a matter of course established a native girl in his compound. 'The good bad days,' old Penton called them. He had made money, he had lost money; he had stood no truck from anyone. Now, at the end of his life, loud-voiced, a heavy drinker, generous and quarrelsome, he was a man that Kuala Sumut regarded on the whole as a credit to itself. He was a figure, a character; with his broad shoulders, his blue-veined cheeks, his mane of white hair, his loud voice, his great hearty laugh, his capacity to drink men half his age beneath the table.

Old Penton was too big for prudery.

He wouldn't have minded what happened to the youngest of his Eurasian daughters, as long as the girl wasn't badly treated. But he was not prepared to hear late in the evening, when he was quarrelsome with a succession of late nights and livery mornings, a bored supercilious voice remarking, 'I suppose I mustn't keep poor little Sally waiting any longer. A little waiting's good for her. But not more than half an hour.'

That was more than old Penton was prepared to stand. He rose from his chair. He lurched slowly towards the bar. He was not taller than Bevan, but because of his breadth of shoulder he appeared to tower over him.

'You ought to think yourself lucky to have a girl like Sally waste her time on you.'

He glowered at Bevan. He had never much liked the man. There was something namby-pamby about him; something supercilious and superior. He was in a bad temper, in need of a focus for his spleen.

'I suppose you think you are so damned important that you can keep her waiting. I suppose you consider yourself her superior?'

His eye ran Bevan up and down. He was in a mood with which every member of the Kuala Sumut Club was well familiar, which most of them had cause to dread. Bevan was nervous, but he was not a coward, he knew how to put a face on things. He replied in his most Oxonian manner.

175

'Well, really, after all ...' He paused. It was said in the pitch of voice to which a monocle would have been appropriate. It increased Penton's irritation. That a weed like this should speak in that tone about *his* daughter.

'I suppose you think you're too grand to marry anyone like Sally.'

There was an angry glint in his eye. He was in a mood that could only have been treated in one way. A hearty laugh, a slap upon the shoulder, an affectionately jocular, 'Now, what is all this about, old boy? Let's have a drink and talk it over.' But affectionate jocularity was not Bevan's line. The Oxford drawl came back into his voice.

He never got further than that first 'Well'. Penton had banged his fist down on the table, his face an apoplectic scarlet.

'You middle-class rat. You think my daughter's not good enough for you. My daughter? Young man, I tell you this: either you'll have married my daughter within two days or as far as Malaya's concerned, you're broken. Get that straight.'

There was a silence in the room, as he lumbered back to his seat at the bridge-table. Everyone knew that he meant what he had said. They only wondered whether he would remember next morning that he had ever said it.

He did.

He was waiting on the porch of the Club when Bevan came in for tiffin. He lifted himself slowly from his chair.

'Have you made your mind up, young man?'

'What am I to take that to mean?'

'You know! Are you going to marry my daughter or are you not? I give you three minutes to decide. I count for something here, and this I promise you: while I'm alive and I don't mean to die just yet, you aren't going to feel safe walking into a single club in the F.M.S.; because if I were to see you there, I'd pitch you straight into the street. Your life, if you stayed on, wouldn't be worth living; that's if you don't marry Sally. If you do, officially you'll be ruined, but you can come on my plantation. I'll give you a house. You can live, like others of your breed, on the generosity of your father-in-law. What of it?'

There were quite a number gathered round the Club veranda. Half of them expected Bevan to cringe, to apologize; the rest thought he would try and bluff it through with an Oxonian superciliousness. None of them expected him to capitulate without a fight: to say, 'I'll marry Sally. I'll be glad to,' in a quiet voice, on a note almost of relief.

That they had not expected.

Yet that is what had happened. He'd married her, resigned his job, gone to work on his father-in-law's plantation. He had two children now. As far as anybody knew he'd not left K.S. from that day to this.

'In that case,' I decided, 'I'm going to Kuala Sumut.'

Kuala Sumut is a night's journey from Penang. You travel down in a pleasantly neat motor-ship. Provided you don't strike 'a Sumatra' it's a cosy journey. There will probably be another half-dozen saloon passengers, a couple of Chinese planters, a European salesman, an English official. Most of the ship is given up to cargo and steerage passengers. But the saloon is comfortable. You settle down to your *pahits* as the sun goes down. By the time the Chinese boy has begun to lay the dinner, life wears a friendly look. You wake at six to find the ship anchored in the bend of a river, against a wooden jetty. There is a scattered village, attap huts for the most part. On the hill there is the white, wide-verandaed bungalow of the District Officer. Half-way up the hill is the corrugated roof of the Rest House. The sun has just risen across the bay; the village wears a clean, clear look. Its single street is busy with chattering figures.

I had as a travelling companion a young Englishman called Blunden, who was doing the grand tour before settling down to his father's business. We had brought with us a letter of introduction to the District Officer. We strolled up to his bungalow after break fast to present it.

The D.O. was a man of about forty. He was short and bald and stocky. He had served in the war and risen to the rank of captain. He wore an old Marlburian tie. His white ducks were spotless and his trousers creased. His face was very red. He was a bachelor. I pictured him as the kind of man who would settle down every night to steady drinking, but who would never lose control of his tongue or faculties.

He shrugged his shoulders when I mentioned Bevan.

'Poor devil, he's done for himself out here. Done for himself in every way, in fact. After all, even if a man makes a mess of his own life, he does get a kind of second innings in his children's lives. He can say to himself, "Well, anyhow, I can protect my boys from making the mistakes I made." If they do come through all right, one can feel that one's own life's not wasted. But in Bevan's case—what is there for those kids of his? The best his boy can hope for is to become a minor clerk—and that girl of his, who'll want to marry her? She'll become a white man's mistress or a Eurasian's wife. No, poor old Bevan, I'm afraid he's finished.'

I wondered what manner of man I should encounter.

It was ten years since I had seen him. I remembered the savage, spiteful, snarling creature whose acquaintance I had willingly let drop. If he had been bitter then, heaven knew what these last ten years would have made of him.

I was to find that out soon enough; the very next morning, as I was sitting in the club over a gin *pahit*. I recognized him at once, though quite possibly I shouldn't have unless I had been told that he was there. He was very different. He was in typical planter clothes: khaki shorts, bare knees, brown and scratched; a cotton shirt, not too clean and open at the neck. He was still thin, though considerably stouter than when I had last seen him, with the straining of his linen coat suggesting that he was likely to grow a paunch. His face, that had been pimply and pallid, was sallow now and sunburnt, with blue veins breaking out under the eyes and round the nostrils. Physically he was very changed. But it was not his physical change that I noticed so particularly. It was mentally that he was changed. He was at ease, affable, open-handed. The moment he recognized me he came across with outstretched hand, and a broad grin of welcome.

'My dear fellow, what a nice surprise. Why didn't you let me know you were coming? Then you could have come and stayed with us. You'll be much more comfortable at the Rest House, but you'd get much more copy staying on a plantation.'

It was precisely the same speech that he might have made ten years back. But the tone, the spirit, were altogether different. Ten years ago he would have sneered at the writer's search for copy; he would have been on his guard against a comparison between his bungalow and the Rest House. He had still a distinct Oxford accent, but it was genial, not supercilious.

'Anyhow, you've got to come and have a meal with us tonight. Are you alone?'

I told him about Blunden.

'Fine! Bring him along, too,' he said.

Ten years ago Bevan would have been on his defensive against

179

a new acquaintance.

'He seems happy enough,' I told the District Officer.

The District Officer shrugged his shoulders.

'Heaven only knows what he's got to be happy over.'

I looked forward to the evening with excitement and curiosity. We had arranged to meet at the club for a *pahit,* as soon as was convenient after sundown. In Malaya there is no fixed hour for dinner. Dinner is something that happens when one is tired of drinking *pahits.* At eight o'clock there was still a crowd of us seated round the large centre table.

The District Officer touched my shoulder. 'There's something I want to show you.'

He led me to the veranda.

'Do you see that?'

He did not point, but faced in the direction of a dusky figure that was standing twenty yards away. She was alone. She was bare headed. She was dressed in European clothes: a cheap kind of printed cotton that made her slight figure seem shapeless and dumpy. In the dusk I could not tell if she was pretty.

'That's Bevan's wife,' the District Officer told me. 'She's always here if he's not home by eight. She's not allowed in, of course. She just stands there. Sooner or later one of us sees her and tips him the word. If she has to wait over half an hour he has hell to pay when they get back.'

'They quarrel?'

'Like hell. She despises him for having married her.'

I took another look at her. She was a forlorn, pathetic figure, standing there in the dusk, between the Club which was forbidden her and the native village from which her marriage and her white blood had excluded her.

180

'She looks pretty shabby,' I remarked.

'It's the best that Bevan can afford.'

By the bar Bevan, the better for six *pahits*, was recounting a metropolitan anecdote that concerned a peer and his own discomfiture.

'No,' I thought,'I don't begin to understand it,' as in spite of the warning shoulder-tap from the District Officer, he proceeded to order another round of drinks.

Nor was it in any mood of bravado that he guided us across the compound to the gravel square where he wife was waiting beside an exceedingly battered Morris-Oxford. He rested his hand affectionately on her shoulder.

'We've kept you waiting, Sally old girl, I know. I'm sorry. But this is an occasion. We don't have guests so often. Up you get, both of you. We'll be there in seven minutes.'

His wife got in the back, with Blunden. She made no comment. Bevan talked cheerfully the whole way home. Either he was deliberately ignoring his wife or was so used to her moods that he did not notice her.

'Here we are,' he said.

It was the kind of house in which you would expect to find a coloured overseer rather than the white manager of a plantation. It was one-storied, wooden, with a wide flower-hung veranda. At its back was a small grove of coconut palms. In front, running right up to the porch, was the broad park of rubber-trees, set out like soldiers, in even rows. Less than fifty yards away were the lines where the Tamils slept, the factory where the rubber was made into sheets and packed. From the outside an overseer's house. And inside, was the bareness, the lack of personal possessions that you would associate with an Eurasian employee. No curtains, no flowers, two garishly vivid oleographs, and a framed advertisement poster for cigarettes. A long refectory table, some straight-backed wicker chairs, a couple of long rattan chairs, two or three occasional tables littered with magazines. The floor was covered with grass mats. The long cushioned window was littered with children's toys, sewing, newspapers. There were not more than a dozen books in the corner of a set of shelves that served the treble purpose of dresser, sideboard and cocktail cabinet. The whole room had a slatternly appearance. I remembered the punctilious neatness of Bevan's flat in Bloomsbury, the long stretch of bookshelves, the black-framed etchings, the John Armstrong lampshades. Yet here Bevan had none of the self-conscious defensiveness with which ten years earlier he had in the same breath apologized for his flat, and informed you with the greatest truculence that if you didn't like his scheme of decoration you were an ignorant and tasteless moron. He had never had then, as he had now, the easy relaxed manner of the host.

'There's whisky on that shelf there, if you want it. I'm going to splash some cold water over myself and change.'

It was then that his wife spoke, for the first time.

'If you do that, the dinner'll be even more spoilt than it is already.'

She spoke in a resentful tone, with a whine that was in part the expression of her mood, in part the natural sing-song note of an Eursasian. It was the first time I had seen her in the light. I was surprised to see how plain she was. One usually imagines that when a white man goes native he receives physical attractions of the highest order in compensation for the loss of caste, of social standing. But Bevan's wife was infinitely less attractive than the average sales-girl that you would see in a London or New York store. She was not particularly young. She had a shapeless kind of face. Her hair, which was straight, parted in the middle and

182

drawn tightly behind her ears, gave her a severe appearance. Her eyes were fine: large, dark, long-lashed. Her teeth were white and even. But her general effect was definitely unprepossessing.

'I'd prepared dinner for eight o'clock. It's quarter to nine. You can guess what it'll be like by now.'

'In that case it won't be any the worse for waiting another fifteen minutes.'

As he pushed back the mosquito-netted division between the main living-room and the bedroom, her voice whiningly implored him not to make a noise and wake the children. And this, I reminded myself, was the man who had thought himself too good for Lucy. I walked over to the dozen or so books that now constituted, apparently, his entire library. They were dog-eared and well-thumbed, all of them. But they were not the kind of books I should have expected. There were no signs of the Bloomsbury influence: no Eliot, Firbank, Virginia Woolf. Instead, there was a Horace, the *Iliad,* Palgrave's *Golden Treasury,* the *Oxford Book of Victorian Verse,* the Everyman Shakespeare in three volumes. There were only two novels: *Spring Floods,* and *War and Peace:* the kind of library one would have expected to find on the shelves of a school prefect during his last term.

I was still looking at them when Bevan came through from the bathroom. He wore a grey cotton, short-sleeved open-collared shirt, a Javanese sarong of imitation Batik. His hair was wet and brushed in the careless way that I had known it first, the sweep of a damp brush across the forehead.

'Not much of a library, is it?' he remarked. 'But I must say it's all I want. Everything I need is there.'

It was the kind of remark that I could have pictured him as making ten years ago. But then it would have been made with a superior exclusiveness. He was now stating a fact, uncontentiously.

'Let's eat. Come on, you two.'

The other two had been seated in the window. They were laughing as they came towards us. Blunden was one of those rare people who bring out the gayest side of whomsoever they happen to be with. Now that Sally was laughing, I could see her charm. She had become another person. She was carefree, irresponsible, the kind of person who could sing and dance out of a mere zest for living. Blunden had that effect on people. He was like the sun; people were warm, happy, at ease, when he was with them. He made friends quickly. I never knew anyone who could count speedier conquests in the lists of gallantry.

Sally remained standing as we took our places at the table.

'We've no servants. It's a Tamil feast day: Deepavali: I gave them the day off. If I hadn't they'd have all got drunk. I've had to serve the meal as well as cook it,' she explained; the surly whining note had come back into her voice.

Blunden jumped to his feet, instantly.

'I can't let you do that. I must help.'

'Oh, no, no!'

'But yes, I insist. I'm a good cook, too, if anything gets spoilt. Come along.'

She was laughing again now.

'That's absurd, really,' she protested.

But he had taken her by the hand, and led her towards the kitchen. There came the sound of clattered plates, of laughter, of several, 'No, I'll take this.' 'No, that's yours.' 'Now, be careful there.' When they came back into his living-room, Blunden gave an imitation of a butler. Sally, who had rarely seen a white man relaxed unless he was half-drunk, was bent double with that kind of cackling laugh that only coloured people can produce. All through the meal Blunden continued his clowning. They had a grand time together. Which was as well. It kept down the friction between Bevan and Sally, and it also prevented us from realizing quite how bad the dinner was. For it was without exception the least satisfactory meal I can remember. Such merit as the soup had ever had, had been long since boiled out of it. There was some fish that might have been hot at eight, but for at least an hour had been left to congeal in another part of the oven into a cool flabby paste. The joint on the other hand, had sustained the full force of an hour's extra heat. Its blackened crust was half an inch thick, there was merely a core of unburnt meat about the bone. The dessert, apples from a tin, alone was unexceptional. Moreover, there was no cream, nor had Sally remembered to put the beer and soda-water bottles in the ice-chest. We drank lukewarm whisky with disrelish. A shocking meal. Bevan, however, who had once deliberated so pensively on the rival merits of pre-phylloxera clarets, did not seem to notice that the meal left anything to be desired. He talked affably, easily; asking questions about London, about mutual friends. Usually, his questions had a social bias: which writer moved in the big world, who was 'received', which were the fashionable restaurants, what was the fashionable dining hour? But the questions were set on a note of detached curiosity. There was never the note of personal acrimony that previously had made his questions ring like the stages of a cross-examination.

When the meal was ended, the villainous coffee drunk, he rose to his feet with the grateful sigh of one who is at ease after good fare.

'Let's stroll down to the beach,' he said.

Blunden turned to Sally.

'Have you got to wash up?'

'Naturally.'

'I'll stay and help you.'

She burst out laughing. The idea of a white man washing plates was ludicrously amusing.

'You'll smash them all.'

'Bet you a dollar that I smash less than you.'

'I never smash them.'

'We'll see.'

It was the kind of badinage that you used to hear on Bank Holidays on Hampstead Heath in the days when the costermongers used to drive up in their donkey-carts and pearly coats. Bevan and I left them giggling among the dirty crockery.

'It isn't far,' he said. 'A couple of hundred yards, at the outside.'

We walked in silence. It was warm, so warm that one could leave one's coat unbuttoned. But a breeze was blowing, cooling one's cheeks. There was a moon, silvering the palm fronds, drawing a broad line of silver across the bay, veiling with a poetic dusk the humped shoulder of the far peninsula. The air was scented with frangipani and the small white blossom of the tropics that is half tuberose, half gardenia. On all sides was the murmur of a tropic night: birds, crickets, the rustle of branch on branch. It was the tropics such as one dreams of finding them.

The coconut grove ran right down to the grey-black powdered sand. The tide was full. We sat beneath a casuarina-tree, watching the successive waves quiver in long phosphorus-shot ripples among the rocks. It was one of those tropic nights for which the traveller, returned to northern latitudes, is for ever a little homesick. The kind of night on which it would be easy to believe that Bevan had found ample compensation here in the exchange that he had made.

I had been long enough in the tropics, however, to know the actuality of that exchange. At that very moment mosquitoes were biting at my ankles, and the mosquito is the symbol of all the malice and poison that lies hidden in the seeming softness of a tropic scene. The climate that seems so much kinder to man than that of our northern latitudes is actually robbing him of his health and strength far faster, far more surely and cruelly than frost and cold and rain. In Europe there is glamour in the idea of a man's 'going native'. But actually, a man's life with a native girl is the equivalent of a man's marrying a woman whom his friends' wives refuse to meet. Neither more nor less than that. I had no illusions about the exchange of Bevan's life.

In silence we sat on there. The mosquitoes had begun to worry at my ankles. Unless I did something about it soon, there would be a swollen rash of irritation by the morning. I stood up.

'I'm going back to the bungalow for a sarong. I shan't be more than a few minutes.'

I walked back along the path. Between the bending palms the lights of the bungalow shone friendlily. I hurried across the porch; then paused astonished.

In the window Blunden and Sally were seated side by side. The washing-up was finished. They were close together, in the dusk. As I stepped into the room, they moved quickly away from one another. Blunden turned, saw who it was, put his hand to his left ear and tugged it. It was a secret sign between us. It meant, 'Keep away from here. And see that other people keep away for at least an hour.' It was not by any means the first time that Blunden had made that sign. I had little doubt as to the outcome.

Without a sarong I walked back to the beach.

Bevan was seated as I had left him, seated on the root, looking

187

across the bay. There was about his pose an irritating quality of complacence.

'I don't know what you've got to be so pleased about,' I said. He looked up, surprised.

'What do you mean?'

'You know what I mean. You were the most ambitious person that I've ever known. You were so ambitious that you never allowed yourself to have any fun, so ambitious that none of the things that were good enough for the rest of us, the friends, the lovers, the books, the careers, the way of life, were good enough for you. You were wretchedly unhappy because you weren't getting the things you wanted, you made everyone you met uncomfortable. Yet, now, you seem completely happy. I can't think why.'

The moment I had said it I was sorry. It was hitting a man when he was down. But I'd never liked him much. He had never placed any latchet on his own tongue. Besides, I was inquisitive.

I had thought that my outburst would bring another outburst. It didn't. It brought a question. 'What do *you* mean by happiness?' It was a rhetorical question. As I hesitated, he went straight on. 'I've never had any doubt about that you see. Happiness lies in the right work, in the right friends, the right way of life, the right position. You look at my life now, you say it's nothing. Of course it's nothing. Do you think I don't know that: work that is un congenial, no position, acquaintances who speak another language, a foreign climate, a marriage that is not even friendship. I know how I've finished up. And there's no hope: not the slightest. I don't need telling that. But, even so … no, even now … I don't think that I was wrong.' He paused. He was looking at the panorama of his past: with a detached, impersonal interest: so that he could speak of it with his voice level, with no note of

188

acrimony.

'It's like this, as I see it,' he went on. 'The fact that one person fails does not mean that there is no such thing as success. Because one is driven to do work one hates, that does not prove that there does not exist the work in which a man can express his nature. Some men have found it. In the same way there's such a thing as friendship even though your friend betrays you; such a thing as love though your wife deceives you; such a thing as talented intellectual society though your lot has cast you among boors. Those things do exist. And I wanted them so desperately. While there still seemed a chance that I might get them, that I might pick up what I see now is the thousandth ticket in a lottery, well, naturally, I was difficult. I saw things slipping from me that I couldn't bear to lose. It's hard to be philosophical when your life's in the making. But when it's once made, when it's spoilt, irremediably, why, that's another thing.'

He paused; then said about the truest thing that I have ever heard about the lot of human beings on this planet :

'It's quite easy to be happy, when once you know you never will be happy.'

The Second World War

M *y life, like so many others', was completely disrupted by the war. As an officer on the Reserve, I was recalled to my regiment immediately, and after a few months of regimental duties was posted as an Intelligence Officer to the B.E.F. in time for the early stages of the Battle of France. In June 1940, my wife, an Australian, took our three children with her to Melbourne. I, after a year's Staff Captaincy in London in the Ministry of Mines, was posted to the Middle East; at first to Beyrouth as a liaison officer in Spears Mission with the Free French Forces, later to an Intelligence organization in Baghdad. I remained there till I was demobilized shortly after VE day.*

When I arrived in New York in September 1945, a friend of mine asked me if I had had a 'chic war'. No, I told her, mine was obscure and undistinguished, but it was interesting. I saw a part of the world with which I was unfamiliar; I made friends among the Arabs; during my three years in Baghdad, I was in close touch with the Police authorities and the experience I acquired was to prove very useful when I returned to novel writing.

I wrote practically nothing during the war. When it began I was halfway through a West Indian novel. I finished it during the phoney war when I was stationed at Dorchester. But when I was transferred to Staff work, I found that after eight hours at a desk I needed relaxation. In Baghdad, however, Robin Maugham bought me, as a Christmas present, an elegantly bound manuscript book. It was so pretty that I felt I had to fill its pages; so every morning I jotted down in it, in the form of a continuous narrative, a series of wartime sketches that were eventually published under the title of His Second War. *It contained a vignette called* 'Bien Sûr'.

Bien Sûr

Lazy, lackadaisical, and Lebanese, an uncatalogued, unclassified orderly at the military hospital, she shuffled around the dormitories in heel-less slippers, carrying trays, making beds, filling water bottles—neither sister, nor nurse, nor kitchenmaid—a general factotum, always occupied but never busy; always on the move but never hurrying; friendly, good-natured, willing; almost but not quite competent.

She was short and plump. Her hair was black, worn low upon the shoulders as the fashion was. A grey-green apron was knotted about her waist, her sleeves were rolled up to her elbows. She had a pale, almond-coloured skin. Her chin was a little heavy. When she was not smiling, she gave the impression that she was scowling. But even when she was not smiling you were conscious of her eyes. They were dark and long-lashed and lustrous. They made all those similes of pools seem reasonable. She was eighteen years old.

I met her for the first time in the hall when I visited a brother officer. 'I've come to see Captain Boot,' I said. She nodded.

'He is here?' I asked. Again she nodded.

'Perhaps you could direct me to him?'

'*Bien sûr,*' she said.

She was a person of few words, or at least she was a person with a limited French vocabulary, and I knew little Arabic. But even among her friends she was for the most part silent.

It was fun, though, talking to her. It was fun trying to see how often one could take that scowl away and make her smile. It was a kind of game, an amusing game—a game that grew on me, a game that I found myself playing with increasing frequency; twice a week to begin with, then every other day, finally every day. A visit to the hospital, with its twenty minutes' walk, filled in conveniently the slack ninety minutes between the end of lunch and the opening of my office. And she could usually be persuaded to dawdle over the tray of tea with which hospital visitors were entertained.

One afternoon I arrived late. I had lunched at the French Club in congenial company. They served no half-bottles at the Club. A bottle was put before you. When you had reached what you judged to be half you would, if you were strong-minded, call the waiter and ask him to remove it. There was invariably a point when you wondered whether you had reached the half or not. There was a point half a minute later when you wondered whether you could honourably call what was left in the bottle half a litre: a thought to which every so often came the inevitable corollary: 'Would it not be better to retain one's honour and finish the bottle where it stood?' At this particular lunch, however, I had not reached the punt of the bottle by any such process of deliberation. I had ordered a whole bottle right away. It was in an anapaestic mood that I made the mile between the Club and the hospital in fifteen minutes.

She was crossing the hall as I arrived. She was carrying a tray of tea, for which someone presumably was waiting. She was never too busy, however, to stop and talk. She paused, resting the tray upon her hip. It looked a very heavy tray. Too heavy a tray, I thought, for a young girl, when the carrying of that tray was not just one excursion, when that tray was one of many. It couldn't be much of a life for her, I thought. I wondered what her home was like. I wondered how much fun she had. 'What about our going to a cinema?' I asked.

'*Bien sûr,*' she said.

We dined at Saad's—a restaurant that had a feel of London: that was a single narrow room with a balcony at the far end of it; a restaurant where there was no table-d'hôte, where you could order Arab dishes—*kibbe* and curries and curdled milk; a restaurant that was out of bounds to other ranks, that was expensive and quiet that the majority of British officers considered dull, that was patronized by the Lebanese rather than by the military.

She was there within five minutes of my arrival. Her hair and eyebrows glistened with oil. She was wearing white network gloves and a white muslin blouse. She had a black, long-sleeved woollen cardigan that she pulled off the moment she was seated. She looked round her, caught the waiter's eye, and smiled. From the manner of their greeting, they seemed old friends.

What would she like to eat, I asked.

'*Quelque chose de bon.*'

She did not listen, though, to what I ordered. She had begun to introduce herself. She was, she said, the eldest of a family of six. She and her elder sister had been born in Brazil, where her parents, like so many other Lebanese, had hoped to make a speedy fortune. But her father could never have made a fortune anywhere. He drank. Brandy had absorbed the *dot* he had taken out with him. Back in Beyrouth, Arak had consumed the capital

195

that his parents left him. Nothing was left now except the house; which was her mother's and which he could not touch. It was lucky, she explained, that he had six children. If he had not so many to look after him now that he was getting old, heaven knew how he would have managed.

She shook her head when she spoke about him. He was very difficult, very ill-tempered, always about the house, ill half the time. So difficult, so ill-tempered, that she had never dared to tell him about her marriage. Oh yes, she had been married. The day after her sixteenth birthday. It hadn't worked—gambling was all *he* cared about. She had stood it for five months, then she had got divorced. It was quite easy in the Greek Church to get divorced. You just went and asked. Her parents had never guessed. She had gone on living at home all through it. There had been the afternoons. And now she was half-engaged, she told me, to a young French sailor, who had been wounded in the July campaign, whom she had nursed in hospital. His right shoulder and arm were shattered. No, she did not think she was in love with him, but she just did not see how he was going to manage without someone to look after him.

She told her story with her habitual phlegmatic calm; cheerfully, but casually, as though there was nothing remarkable about this record. She finished her story and was silent. It was my turn to talk. I was uncertain of what to say. It was the first time I had been alone with her. I had no idea what her tastes or interests were. I began to talk about Beyrouth, about its cinemas and cabarets, about the brother officer who was sick in hospital, about … but she was not listening. I soon realized that she had something on her mind. Was it the food? Wasn't this fish mayonnaise her idea of *quelque chose de bon,* or the wine? Would she rather have had beer or Arak? Were they really all right? I asked her.

'*Bien sûr,*' she said, and indeed she was making steady progress with the course.

'I wonder which film you'd like to see?' I asked. 'There's the French film at the Rialto.'

She seemed, however, to take little interest in her choice.

'*N'importe,*' she said and relapsed into cogitation. Really, but this was being rather a bore, I thought, as I returned to a dissertation on the resemblance between Beyrouth and a similar town on the Riviera. 'The chief difference that I can see,' I started, but she interrupted me.

Where did I live? she asked.

'On the edge of Regent's Park.'

'Regent's Park.'

I began to explain about London's parks. She shook her head. No, she hadn't meant that: she hadn't wanted to know where I lived in England, she wanted to know where I lived here …

'I've got a flat,' I said. 'Just …' But she was not interested in knowing where it was. Her face brightened. Her preoccupation left her. The thing, whatever it was that had been worrying her, had ceased to be a problem. She could now enjoy her evening. She was prepared to discuss the film that we were going to. An American film, she said, with a lot of action.

We took an arabana, and she slipped her hand into mine. 'I'm glad you've got a flat,' she said. 'A hotel or a *pension*—if my mother were to hear of my going into a hotel or a *pension*, she would never have forgiven me.'

Her eyes were bright, her expression animated, as we took our seats. This was a great treat for her, she said. She was hardly ever taken to the pictures. Before the film had been running for five minutes, however, she was fast asleep. She slept right through the show, soundly and soundlessly. The moment the film stopped she was awake, her eyes were bright, the animated expression was on her face. 'What about coming back for a moment, for a drink?' I asked her.

'*Bien sûr,*' she said. But she was not thirsty.

A dying moon was rising out of the sea as we walked back to her home. The streets were quiet and ghostly in the partial black out. The snow on the mountains glistened. It was hard to believe that Beyrouth was in a forward area, that all down the coast guns were manned against invasion, that all that day I had been busy with the provisioning of those defences with ammunition.

'You will come back again?' I asked.

'*Bien sûr.*'

The next night she dined with me. And twice in the next week. Then she broke a date. Her small brother, a boy of seven, was waiting outside Saad's with a message that she could not come that night, but she would next day. Next day at the last moment I found myself on duty. I went round to her house to tell her so. She lived, she and her family, on the ground floor of a house that could with little renovation have been converted into what is called a mansion in the Lebanon. It was a typical small house. A large, central living-room with doors opening off it. Her mother was sitting over an open charcoal fire, puffing at a *narghile*. She received me graciously. Her daughter would be back in a few minutes, she explained. She wiped the mouthpiece of the *narghile* and offered it to me to smoke. A girl of about twelve brought out two cups of coffee. A small boy of six came in, was introduced, stared at me, then ran out of the hall, and stood half-concealed behind a door peering at me. Behind another door there was another urchin watching.

We dined together on the following night. But when I went round to Saad's two evenings later her brother was waiting with a note. She was busy and suggested Thursday. On Thursday, however, she was not there. She frowned when I called round on the following morning. Her mother, she explained, was not happy about my seeing her so often, afraid of her getting talked about.

But how otherwise, I asked, could we arrange it? My friend was no longer in the hospital. I had no longer an excuse for calling there, and if I could not call for her at home … I paused, waiting for her solution. She pondered, the surly phlegmatic expression was on her face. Then her face brightened. It was difficult for her, she said, to fix things in advance. Sometimes she was kept at the hospital. Sometimes she was tired. Sometimes she was not in the mood. But if I would dine alone at Saad's every Wednesday and every Friday she would join me whenever she was able.

Sometimes she came, sometimes she did not come. And when ever she did come I had the consoling knowledge that she had come because she wanted to. How often, in London and New York, had I not found myself taking out young women whose distant manner had suggested that they were only there because they had made a date six days earlier, and that when the day had come they would have given anything to have stayed at home and written letters and washed their stockings—or gone out with someone else.

It was a very satisfactory arrangement. Whenever she came it was to the certainty of a happy evening. And when she did not come … well, I am someone who has spent a good deal of his life alone; I like dining by myself.

All through the winter and that spring every Wednesday and every Friday I dined at Saad's at the same table underneath the gallery.

1942

A Luckless Lebanese

When I met her first, within a few weeks of my arrival in Beyrouth, Annette Drollet was twenty-one years old. She was little and slim and dark, pale-skinned, with her hair worn loose upon her shoulders. In appearance she was typically Lebanese, and her problems were of a kind that only a Lebanese would have. The Drollets were a patrician family; a network of cousinship, every strand a gilded one, linked them to the Surcock aristocracy. Annette was the youngest of three sisters, both of whom had married Frenchmen. She should have gone to Paris for her finishing year in the first autumn of the war, and had been highly indignant when her father refused to let her go. Even now, with Paris in German hands, she felt ill-used. Her sisters, judging from their letters, were having all the fun that they could use—theatres, dances, the shop windows full. It was just British and Free French propaganda that painted Paris as a city of the dead. Besides, the war could not go on for ever.

She had a grievance, not against Hitler or Mussolini, not even against Roosevelt or Churchill, but against life in general. She had been cheated. She had been promised that finishing year in Paris, and the chance that it would have given her to marry the best kind of Frenchman. She was not, however, a sulky girl. She was making the best of a bad job; had taken a post-graduate course at the American University and, since her chances of marrying a Frenchman had considerably diminished, was looking round to see what England had to offer. On one point she was resolved—not to marry a fellow countryman. In all of which she was typically Lebanese.

I met her through Blanche Ammoun. And it would be impossible for me to write of Lebanon without making a reference to the most charming and the most talented friend I made there. Married now to a French officer, the mother of three children, Blanche when I met her first was in the middle twenties. Her father had been a minister in the Turkish days; her mother, a Baghdadi—whose nieces, the Ghannams, were later in Iraq to become my friends; her brother Charles, a barrister with an interest in politics that has since brought him prominence. Blanche was, however, very much more than a member of an important family. An excellent painter, she has written and illustrated a history of the Lebanon, which is no less a serious work of scholarship because it is told lightly, almost frivolously: she was the first Lebanese woman to be called to the Bar. In addition to all of which she was extremely pretty, in the Lebanese fashion of pale skin and glistening black hair worn loose upon the shoulders. She was very small, and by her right nostril was a small black mole, the dimensions of which in self-portraiture she was at pains to magnify. She was so elegant and neat and small that it was possible at a first meeting to classify her as just another very pretty girl: it was only later that I came to realize how much character she possessed, to guess at the amount of ruthlessness and resolve that must have been required for her to develop her talents in two such different directions. By her compatriots she was held in respect and she was held in awe. She was able to make her own rules for her own conduct. Herself of exemplary behaviour, she was able to ignore convention. The chaperone is one of the major nuisances of Lebanese society. Not only is it impossible for a man and a woman to go out alone together, but when two men take out two girls they are invariably disconcerted by the sudden and uninvited appearance of a brother or a cousin. Blanche refused to tolerate such constraints, and so great was her personal prestige that even the mothers of marriageable daughters were forced to accept her point of view and concede that it 'really was all right provided Blanche was there'.

It was as a friend of Blanche's that I met Annette, but it was because another member of the Mission, Michael Sinclair, fell in love with her that I saw so much of her.

Sinclair was thirty-five years old, a captain in the Economic Section, in private life a barrister not only of promise but achievement; he was tall, round-shouldered, with a long neck and beak-like nose and spectacles. He looked all wrong in uniform. He had been commissioned in the Munich period, through local influence, in a Territorial anti-aircraft battery. On the outbreak of war, his commanding officer had been retired to a sedentary occupation, and a new brisk Regular Army colonel had quickly decided that Sinclair was the last type of officer he wanted, had sent him on a gas course and arranged for his transfer in his absence. For eighteen months Sinclair was in a constant process of being moved from one command to another. He had made the mistake that many civilians do, of imagining that the Army is an affair exclusively of service; you offer yourself to discipline, and the army, knowing its own needs, decides in what direction it can make best use of you. Actually the army is a career like any other. You have to plot the graph of your own future, identifying your personal interests with the army's needs. A general once said to me, 'In every officer's career there comes the offer of an appointment that in his own ultimate interests he must refuse.' It is of course only the minority of civilians who take the army seriously, in terms of self-advancement. Indeed, the more ambitious a man is as a civilian, the more likely is he to regard his four or five years in khaki as a sideshow, to accept what is offered him, to say, 'These fellows are professionals, they know where I fit in. I'll do as well as I can whatever they may put me on to.'

It was an attitude that Sinclair had found the easier to adopt since he had, as a barrister, been precluded from soliciting work and had acquired a belief in his capacity to familiarize himself quickly with the essentials of almost any subject. A new appointment was only a new brief to be mugged up. During the first eighteen months of the war he filled seven separate posts. His knowledge of Greek had got him posted to Middle East, but Crete had been evacuated before he arrived in Cairo. Since his French was good, a place was found for him in the Mission, but the only available appointment was in the Economic Section, the very one for which by taste, temperament, and training he was the most unsuited. He had a suspicion that he would not remain there long. 'As soon as I've learnt one job,' he complained, 'I'm posted to another.' And he was, of course, a hard man to place, with his unsoldierlike appearance and his air of scholarship. After thirty months of this kind of thing, his face had assumed a bewildered look. He was not at all the kind of man to appeal to a girl like Annette, who pictured romance in terms of cocktail parties, dances, and a smart escort to show her off. Moreover, he was married.

It was not a happy marriage; divorce proceedings had, indeed, begun when war broke out. The delay was only temporary. But

Blanche laughed when I explained this to her.

'That's what every married man says, particularly in war-time. Let him get divorced, then let him start talking.'

But I already foresaw that long before that could happen his opportunities of speaking would have passed. Annette quite liked Sinclair; his attentions flattered her; he was a good conversationalist to the extent that he had a barrister's capacity to tell an effective story, but he could not hope to compete against a rival such as Major Franklin.

Hugh Franklin was everything Sinclair was not. He was twenty-eight, tall, dark, with a small moustache: athletic with a breezy manner; good company, easy to get on with, always laughing, always the first to stand a round of drinks. He had served as a gunner in the Western Desert; not for very long, but long enough for him to be able every now and then to remind his audiences that though he might now be holding down a staff appointment, he was not, as were the majority of officers in Beyrouth, a chair-borne warrior. No one knew exactly what he had been doing before the war, he talked familiarly of London restaurants and the Riviera; but he never talked about his home or school. He was the kind of man, we thought, who gets his chance in war-time. He was efficient, without being officious; popular both with the men and with his seniors. He would almost certainly finish up with red flannel on his lapels. An American might say of him: 'What a relief to find a typical Englishman who's not standoffish'; while the Colonel Blimps might say: 'A Spanish grandmother, I suppose.' It was inevitable that Annette should think him wonderful. Their engagement was announced shortly before I left Beyrouth. A year later in Baghdad I saw in an old copy of the *Tatler* a picture of their wedding Franklin, I noticed, was a half-colonel.

By the time I went back to Beyrouth on leave, eighteen months later, they were in Cairo. Blanche had had a postcard from Annette describing ecstatically their flat with its view over Gezira. I asked Blanche whether she thought the Drollets had provided a handsome *dot*. She smiled. A Frenchman, she suggested, would have driven a better bargain, but I did not fancy that Franklin was grumbling, even so. Sinclair by this time had left the Mission: no one quite knew where he was. He was in the Advocate-General's department, someone said. Somewhere in India they believed. His divorce, by the way, was through. I smiled a little wryly when they told me that. If only it had come through a few months earlier! But even if it had, I did not imagine that Sinclair would have stood much chance; not against Hugh Franklin—he and Annette were so very thoroughly each other's tea.

That was in the autumn of 1943, and that was the last I heard of any of them until one evening in the summer of ' 46 I ran into Michael Sinclair on the steps of the London Library. It was close upon six o'clock. He was living in Albany, he said; wouldn't I go back and have a drink.

We soon got on to the subject of Annette. Yes, he'd seen her; only a few months before. They'd come, the pair of them, to a small cocktail party. Was marriage suiting her? I asked. He nodded. She was more static, more fulfilled, he said. She had a daughter;she was beautiful now; as a girl she'd been merely pretty.

'And she still likes Franklin?'

'She dotes on him.'

'And what about England itself. How's she liking that? Austerity and all those restrictions?'

He laughed.'I don't think they're worrying her much; but I'm afraid that novels had given her a rather rose-coloured impression of English life—she'd pictured it in terms of royalty and country houses. She can't think why she's not on the Buckingham Palace invitation list.'

I wondered how Sinclair himself had struck her, in these changed surroundings. He was no longer the bewildered and ineffective economist of the Mission. He looked much better out of uniform, in a dark pin-stripe suit, a loose-collared shirt and a Sulka tie. Annette must have been impressed by the atmosphere of Albany: the uniformed and cockaded porter, the cloistered privacy of the Rope Walk, the dark panelling of the chambers; the Queen Anne bookcase; and Sinclair would surely have been at pains to select fellow-guests who would enhance his own position. Moreover, he was now divorced. I wondered whether Annette had felt any qualms, whether she had doubted, if only for a second, whether she had chosen wisely. I did not think she had. But possibly this thought may have struck her: 'If I'd known what he amounted to and if there'd been no Hugh Franklin, yes, I might have waited.'

'How's Franklin getting along?' I asked.

Sinclair shrugged. 'That's what I asked myself. It's just one of those things that puzzle me about post-war England. I don't know how that class of person manages. I know what happens to professional people like myself with very little capital, who earn quite large salaries, but aren't on anyone's expense account. We have to be very careful, with income tax at the height it is. What's left of my income won't run to double Martinis at the Ritz. I know what's happening to the class with large estates: half of them are committing *hara-kiri*; maintaining their old standards by cutting into capital. Probably they are wise. They may not be left with their capital for long. But there's another whole world of spivs and semi-spivs, people with expense accounts, who lunch at expensive restaurants, have all the petrol that they need, take trips abroad. Heaven knows how they work things out. They're the new privileged class. And Franklin's one of them.'

I was surprised. He was exploiting post-war in the same way that he had war-time conditions. The war had given him his chance and he had taken it. I remembered Turgenev's simile: 'When a gale is blowing the lower branches of a tree can touch the top ones.'

That was in '46.

It was a very different story that I was to hear on my return to Lebanon in the summer of 1950. So different that one of my first acts was to get in touch with Annette. I found her living in a first-floor three-roomed apartment, opposite the University, facing the tramlines: it was hot and it was noisy. I remembered her father's house—cool and dignified and quiet, with study and dining-room and bedrooms opening off the large high hall.

'Oh yes, it's true enough,' she said.

I asked her how it had all come about. She shrugged. 'That's something I've never understood. Perhaps you can help me.'

It had begun three and a half years ago. Up till then every-thing had been going smoothly. She was happy with Franklin, she was still in love with him. Business was good. No, she had never known exactly what his business was, something to do with the export drive, she fancied. They were partners to the extent that she had invested the greater part of her capital in it. It paid good dividends. They never seemed short of money. Then her father had got ill. She had decided to come out and see him, to take his granddaughter.

To her surprise Hugh had raised objections. It flattered her, but at the same time puzzled her; puzzled her because he would give no cogent reason; he strode backwards and forwards up and down the flat, as near hysteria as she had ever seen him. 'It'll be fatal if you go, fatal, fatal,' he had repeated. She begged him for a reason; any reason. He shook his head. He was obstinate, mulish: she almost lost her temper. For three days it had gone on like that. Then suddenly he had capitulated. 'O.K.,' he said. 'You go. You probably know best.' And he had become once again what he had always been with her, tender and considerate.

Their last week together had been a second honeymoon.

She was glad, more than glad on her arrival that they had parted on such terms. Her father was worse than she had feared, a final illness, through a long six months, a sad, sad time. 'Thank heaven,' she had written home after the funeral, 'I've you to come home to.' Just as she was packing, however, she had received a cable. 'Do not return yet letter explanation follows.'

The letter of explanation had told her little. Business had become suddenly very bad. He might have to close down his London offices and establish branches overseas, in Canada and South Africa. He would let her know. She did not understand what it was all about, nor did his subsequent letters make it any clearer. Owing to currency regulations, he could not, he explained, send her any money. But he assumed that since her father's death she would be in a position to support herself. Then he went abroad. Each letter bore a different address. He had advised her not to join him. It would not be fair on their daughter. There was also the financial problem. Things were very bad. She must have gathered from the papers how bad they were.

Every month there had been a new excuse. Then there had been the devaluation of the pound. It was the final blow, their business had been forced into liquidation. She had made out for him a power of attorney before she left, so that the transfer had been effected in her absence. There was some capital left, of which a part was hers, he said; but owing to currency controls, he could not send it out. But she could rest assured that it was safe. In the meantime, he presumed that she was not in any difficulties.

She was in despair. She did not know what was happening. The temptation to fly back was great; but the habit of obedience to the man of the family was hereditary and ingrained. She did not know where to turn. Then suddenly a few weeks ago the blow had fallen. He had written to tell her that he had fallen in love again, that he wanted to marry a South African, that he was planning to divorce her for desertion under the three years' law. He could trust her not to defend the case. He was certain that he was acting for the best in all their interests.

There was the story as Annette told it me. She spread out her hands helplessly. 'I had to do what he asked. What else was there for me to do?' she said.

It was a typical Lebanese reply. The feminine submission to male authority. 'What do you make of it?' she asked.

How was I to answer her? In a sense, the whole thing was as typically English as it was Lebanese. I knew no more than Sinclair did how this new spiv world marshalled its forces, organized its attacks and its retreats. I do not think that Franklin was crooked. He had taken her money, invested it, and lost it. But it was true that the currency regulations made it difficult, if not impossible, for him to send her money. I do not think he had behaved badly with intention—he was an opportunist; he had to trim his sails to the prevailing wind; he had tried to stop her returning to Beyrouth because he had known his business to be in a tricky state. He did not trust himself. He could not tell how in her absence he might behave if things grew desperate. Had she stayed in England, he would have done his best to make a joint show of it; with her away the temptation had been too strong. I did my best to put his case to her, not exactly in that way, but so that she might feel the happier about it all, so that she should not feel she had been tricked, that he had made use of her.

She shrugged. 'I hope it's true,' she said. 'And I was very happy for a time; happier than most people ever are. I should be grateful for that, I suppose, and even as things are I might be a great deal worse off. I've enough money to look after myself. I'm only thirty. I can marry again. I dare say I made a mistake, marrying someone about whom I knew so little, but how was I to know? People are so different when they're back in their own country. Look at Michael Sinclair, compare him in that nice apartment with all his books about him with the way that he looked here.' She paused. Then she said something that put in a nutshell not only her problem but her country's problems. 'It's so hard for us to tell what the people who come here are really like.'

That has been her country's problem all along. Lebanon has never quite known what her invaders were really like.

1950

Travel Years 1946–1952

*I*n the autumn of 1943, after the Germans and Italians had been driven out of Africa, a sense of frustration settled upon those troops who were still stationed in the Middle East. They developed a sense both of guilt and grievance. Their families and friends at home were living very different lives, subjected to different privations and to a different strain. Their own garrison life at the base was in many ways more comfortable. They thought that no one in Britain took any interest in them now they were not in action. They felt abandoned. They were afraid that when eventually they were repatriated, they would be treated as a kind of deserter, instead of being welcomed home as heroes. The letters M.E.F. were sneeringly held to stand for 'Men England Forgot'.

Most soldiers returned with misgivings after long service in the Middle East. Myself I found on my return to London, that I had lost contact with my old friends. We had no longer the same community of interests. For four years they had travelled in one direction, I in another. There was a difference of eight years between us. In time, no doubt, those differences would have disappeared and a new base of shared experience would have been constructed. But within two months of my return, I went to New York. The life of New York had not changed during the war in the way that the life of London had, and I picked up easily the threads of my old friendships and soon made new ones. Later when I began to travel I found that my four years in the Middle

East had given me a new sense of kinship with the administrators and busi-nessmen whose careers had been based on foreign service. I felt that I was more qualified to describe their lives and problems than those of the contem-porary Londoner. I arranged my life and writing in terms of travel.

My travels took me to the Caribbean, to the Seychelles and the Far East. At the start, I concentrated on travelogues and short stories, but recently I have needed a broader canvas and have written two long novels.

'Circle of Deception' is my last full-length short story. It was a lucky one for me. Written in March 1952, it was published in Esquire *a year later. During that year my fortunes had reached their lowest ebb. I had worked steadily upon short stories. They weren't any good. I did not sell one across the water. A novel by which I had set high store, though it did moderately well in England, flopped in the U.S.A. I wondered where I went from there. Then, to everyone's surprise, Hollywood became excited about 'Circle of Deception'. Twentieth Century Fox and M.G.M. bid against each other. Their bargain-ing left me with two years in the clear. I took a long slow breath, then started upon a long, fast novel.*

Circle of Deception *has taken a little while to reach the screen. The original script was unsatisfactory and it was made into a TV play in the U.S.A. starring Gene Tierney, Trevor Howard and John Williams. This version was shown as a fifty minutes' supporting film at a few English cinemas during 1956. Sir Carol Reed then became interested in the story, and Nigel Balchin was asked to write a script. But Sir Carol, when he learnt of the TV version, threw in his hand. At the moment of writing (August 1960) it is being shot at Walton-on-Thames, starring the exquisite Susy Parker.*

This film, which will presumably have been released before this book appears, is based upon Nigel Balchin's script. Authors usually complain that film directors alter their plots and spoil their stories. I think Balchin has improved mine. He contrived a twist which I wish I had thought of myself. I was tempted to rewrite the story in terms of it, but in the end I came to feel that I had been able to put over the character of my heroine more intimately by telling her story in the first person; so I have let the original Esquire version stand.

The story went the round of English magazines for forty months before it found a purchaser. Editors said 'Our women readers will be horrified at the idea that anything like this could happen to a man of theirs.' I have been asked if it was based on actual experience. It very definitely was not. During the Second War I worked for three years in Military Intelligence in the Middle East, but I was not Baker Street or Broadway, and the cloak-and-dagger boys will know what I mean by that. I was employed in Defensive Security; but in a remote outpost like Baghdad where we all knew each other, I got a glimpse into what was being done in other branches. I think something like this could have happened. I do not say it did. I hope it didn't. But it might have done. War is not a tea-party on a rectory lawn.

The Woman Who knew Frank Harris

The Seychelles Islands contain as many eccentrics as I have encountered anywhere. They are by no means only men. The colonel's widow was far from being the least remarkable.

I met her on my third morning in Mahe. I was writing in my room when my hostess put her head round the curtain, and with her finger pressed against her lips to ensure silence beckoned me into the sitting-room. 'I was sorry to disturb you,' she said later. 'But I couldn't have you miss one of the island's characters.'

The character to whom I had been introduced was a tall, plumpish woman, grey-haired, in a locally made straw hat, with a sallow skin and no noticeable features. She was, I imagined, one of those women who at twenty have the attraction of youth and health, a clear skin and supple movements, whom middle age and maternity rob of their figure and complexion, so that as early as their thirties people begin to say of them: 'I can't think what he ever saw in her.' Her eyes were bright and she had a deep, rich voice. She might have been any age over sixty.

She had called at the early hour of half past nine to enlist my hostess's support in an anti-Communist campaign. She had a full morning ahead of her. 'People are so unpublic-spirited,' she complained. 'There's the Attorney-General, now. He's a Roman Catholic. He ought to be one of the first to help. He says he's too busy. He says it's not his business. Too busy! Not his business! I ask you.' She struck a fine note of indignation and contempt. She paused. She looked at me interrogatively.

'I know you are only going to be here for a short while, but you could help, you know.'

I excused myself on the grounds that I was unpolitical.

She sniffed. 'Unpolitical. It's not a question of politics but of principles. That's the trouble with writers nowadays. They won't interest themselves in the things that matter.'

In the late 1930s I should have replied that the converse was the case. But maybe she was right today. I retreated to a different base. Did she think there was any real Communist danger here? I asked. I recalled my days in Military Intelligence when we had looked for a channel of communication. I could not see how Moscow was going to build a cell in Mahe. She had her answer ready. 'If the soil is ready, then a seed may fall. We must keep the soil unfertile.' She spoke with such conviction that I almost agreed to give a lecture on my visit to the U.S.S.R. in 1935. Almost but not quite.

'Tell me all about her,' I asked when she had gone.

She had arrived, I learnt, in 1937, with her husband, a retired Indian Army colonel. Their daughters were married and they were looking for a place to settle. They were debating between Tanganyika and a cottage in Devonshire. On their way to Africa they had decided to spend a month in Seychelles. They had liked it there so much that they had lingered on. Then the war had come. Though he was much over age, the colonel had insisted on going back to India; there must be something there that he could do. His ship was torpedoed: nobody was saved.

'And she stayed on?'

'She had no alternative at first. Later, well, I suppose she's got used to being here. There was rationing in England and a housing shortage. She was afraid of being a nuisance. She talks, now that things are getting easier, of going back to see her grand-children. But I doubt if she will. It's difficult to uproot yourself at her age.'

'And is this typical? This anti-Communist campaign?'

My hostess nodded. 'Typical but not general. Most of the time she lives quietly in her bungalow in the country. She hasn't got much money; she does a certain amount of what one used to call "good works": sits on church committees and helps us at Home Industries. Then every so often she goes off the rails.'

'In what kind of way?'

'In the kind of way that you'd expect of an Indian Army wife. That's what we call her, you know— 'the Colonel's Widow'. There was a disease among the dogs, hardpad, some time ago. She got very worked up over that. Then she wanted to start an orphanage, but the mission authorities said it would only make the Seychel-loise more casual. She wanted to hold a public meeting. Luckily her crazes don't last long. She's a very good-natured creature. You'll be seeing quite a lot of her, as a matter of fact. She lives near Northolme, and takes her lunches there.'

Northolme was a guest-house on the other side of the island where I was planning to spend the greater part of my seven weeks' visit to the Colony.

I was indeed to see quite a lot of her. Every day at lunch for seven weeks; under the worst conditions that is to say, with an attempt being made at general conversation by seven people sitting at solitary tables, talking across a room, each about five feet from the other; those lunches were relieved, however, by occasional visits to her bungalow.

It was a minute contraption: almost a 'prefab', except that it had a veranda and no labour-saving gadgets. Built of wood, roofed with corrugated iron, two-roomed, with a shower and a kitchenette, it was all she needed: it was all anyone required in the tropics. You do not need heavy upholstered furniture that damp and heat and cockroaches will eat away. You do not need pictures. You want your wall space to be windows so that every way you turn you can look out at the continually changing panorama of cloud and sea scape against a foreground of palm and sand, of rock and mountain. All you need of a bungalow in the tropics is that it should be cool and clean and neat and rain-proof. Hers was all of that.

She had light linen curtains and fibre mats. A few photographs; a collection of shells; a three-shelf bookcase. I glanced at it. A row of Book Society selections. I ran my eye along them. It is the fashion to sneer at Book Clubs: but glancing over the choices of a dozen years, I could see few among those I had not already read that I would not be glad to read. She was apologetic on their account. 'It's the best one can do out here, I had quite a library once, before I married; I left all my best books in England. I didn't want them ruined by the climate. The depository where they were stored was bombed.'

At the end of the top row was an uneven collection of volumes with stained and battered bindings—Palgrave's *Golden Treasury*, the Everyman Shakespeare, the *Oxford Book of English Verse*, *A Shropshire Lad*, Dowson's *Poems*.

'I wonder how many copies of that there are in this colony,' I said.

She smiled. 'I used to think him the greatest poet of all time. I used to write sonnets in his style.'

'Most of us have.'

'I got mine published.'

'Really. Where?'

'*Vanity Fair.*'

Vanity Fair. That was an echo from quite a long way back. In its own way it had had a rather special cachet. But my memory could not precisely place it. The title had been used upon both sides of the Atlantic. It suggested Conde Nast. But that was in the 1920s, and in America. I could not remember when the English edition left the newstands.

'Who was the editor then?' I asked.

'Frank Harris.'

I made a rapid calculation. Frank Harris held so many posts. The *Evening News*, the *Fortnightly*, the *Saturday*. Then just before World War I, that most improbable of ventures *Hearth and Home* with Hugh Kingsmill as his assistant. *Vanity Fair* must have been about 1906. That would place the Colonel's Widow in the middle sixties. Well, that tallied.

'Did you ever meet him?' she asked.

I shook my head. 'But I heard a good deal about him.'

When I arrived in April 1918, as a prisoner-of-war at the Kriegagefanginenlager, Karlsruhe, it was to find Hugh Kingsmill, who had been captured fifteen months earlier, a third of the way through a novel of which Frank Harris was, if not the hero, the central character. It was published later by Chapman & Hall under the title *The Will to Love*. It was a witty and satiric novel, and, had it been published a few years later when the public mind had been acclimatized by Aldous Huxley and Michael Arlen to flippant satire, it might have had a considerable success. It described the seduction by Harris of a schoolmaster's daughter, and ended with Harris blackmailing the father to the extent of £2,000. The picture of Harris is so vivid that when I hear people talk of Harris, I am confused between the Harris of fact and fiction. Maybe Kingsmill's Harris was the more real picture.

'I met him several times,' she said. 'I was just back from my finishing school in Paris. I sent him some poems. He asked me to call on him. Then he asked me out to lunch.'

'Where did you lunch?'

'The Café Royal.'

Yes, of course it would be the Café Royal, in the Domino Room, with its red plush banquettes, its mirrors, its gilt columns, its faded panels, and its frescoed ceiling; the Café Royal with all its memories of Wilde and Ruskin; and Harris, dapper and dark, declaiming in his great booming voice of the great men he had entertained there, dazzling her with his sense of power and importance, yet every now and again playing his other role of the unappreciated genius, ranting against the tycoons of Fleet Street, 'the Penguin Professors' who had no fire in their veins, who could never understand 'out of what dark forests of the tortured soul the sacred fires of art are lit'; then turning to the girl beside him, identifying her with his tirades. 'I can speak of all this to you, you will understand. I can tell it from your poems.'

'And I suppose he pointed out to you all the well-known people that were lunching there.'

She nodded eagerly.

'That was the fascinating thing about him, he knew everyone. Shaw, Wells, Middleton, George Moore; not only poets and painters, but politicians; men of affairs. He was wonderful company; I've never known anyone who could talk as he did.'

I nodded. They had all said that.

'And underneath it all, yes, whatever anyone may say, underneath it all he was so fine,' she hurried on. 'He had such high

220

ideals. I asked him once why he had written so little. He said that he did not care to publish anything that was not good enough to be set beside Maupassant and Turgenev.' She paused. She looked at me rather shyly. 'What do people think of him nowadays?' she asked.

I hesitated. I was not certain if I was the right person to be asked that question. I had just passed my fifty-second birthday, and one of the more disconcerting of my recent experiences has been the discovery that topics and personalities that once formed part of the rough material of conversation now mean nothing at all to a younger generation. I suppose this happens to everyone at fifty; but possibly it has happened to me in a more marked degree. By publishing a novel in my teens, I got off to a flying start; I found myself at the age of twenty associating with and meeting on equal terms men ten to fifteen years older than myself. Of the men I met most frequently in the early 1920s, not many are still alive. Harold Momo, Ralph Straus, C. K. Scott-Moncrieff, Luke Hansard, Norman Davey, W. J. Turner, Hugh Kingsmill, W. L. George, Stacy Aumonier, A. G. Macdonell, David Woodhouse, Edgar Walmisley—one by one they have gone.

In addition, the course of events was telescoped even more by the Second War than it had been by the first. During my last weeks in Mahe I had several lively and stimulating conversations with the wife of the new Administrator, Susan Bates. She is young, the mother of three children, vivid, pretty, with a lean, taut figure and a lean, taut mind. I was surprised at first by the contempt with which she dismissed the lighter novelists and playwrights of the 1930s. 'They've nothing to say to me,' she said. By our third meeting I had found a partial explanation for her disdain. Born in 1923, and sixteen years old when the war

221

began, she had never known as an adult person any other world than that of rations, uniform, queues, barracks, shortages, with happiness snatched at during the thirty-six hours of a week-end leave; brought up in the cold climate of necessity she had needed mentally something to try her teeth on, a hardier fare, a tougher nourishment than that which had sustained her seniors.

I have lived so much out of London since the autumn of 1941 that this was the first time I had met, long enough to cross swords with, an Englishwoman both of her age and mental calibre. It was an exciting experience. I had not realized how different is the young Englishwoman who grew up during the war both from her immediate predecessors and from her contemporary opposite number in America. I asked Susan how she would grade Frank Harris. 'Never heard of him,'she answered.

Probably it would have been surprising if she had. Most books went out of print during the war; only a fortunate few have been re-issued or found their way into Pan, Penguin, and the Pocket Libraries. The only book by Frank Harris that is still obtainable—and that only overseas—is *My Life and Loves*, and maybe as soon as a sufficient quantity of titles *plus cochon* have been discovered, it will slide out of print. In a few years Harris may be a mere legend, to become possibly, in view of his frequent appearances in the memories of his contemporaries, the subject of a valedictory *New Yorker* profile, like the Wilson Mizner one. To have achieved as much is to have achieved something. But it is a great deal less than Harris expected for himself; or rather than what he appeared to be expecting for himself. One never knew with Harris. That was the whole problem about him. He was such a liar.

Hugh Kingsmill published later a biography of Harris, but I fancy that he got nearer to the real man in *The Will to Love*; he explained there not only Harris's deficiences but also his qualities. He had Harris's pugnacity, his brashness, his vulgarity, his pushingness, his dishonesty, his boasting, his untruthfulness. Yet he had his other side, his moments of talent as a writer—'Elder Conklin' is a real short story—his flashes of intuition as a critic—he was one of the first to see the man Shakespeare behind the dramatist; his sincere respect for literature. Harris's snobbery was fantastic, but he placed the artist high in his hierarchy; it was better to be a poet than a duke. There was again his disinterested desire to be of help to writers, his fits of loyalty—he was a good friend to Wilde—and above all there was his immense vitality.

Arriving in London at the age of twenty-six, unknown, half educated, penniless, he was within two years editor of the *Evening News*. Very little later as editor of the *Saturday Review*, then a very powerful Tory paper, he was entertaining in his house in Park Lane many of the most prominent social and political personalities of the day. He went everywhere and saw everyone, and yet found time and energy both for his own writing and the conduct of innumerable intrigues. It had been suggested that his rapid progress was based like Maupassant's *Bel-Ami* on his success with women, and his first wife was a wealthy woman. But he was more than just another adventurer. He was a man of immense potentialities: yet it was all ruined—or mainly ruined—by the lie within himself.

Wilde said of him, 'Frank has dined in every house in London—once.' He could capture ground with a sudden assault, but he could not hold it. He lost his friends, betrayed their trust—no one could rely on him; and that same noisiness, that ill-bred forcefulness that made him socially intolerable, spoilt him as a writer. His actual writing is poor. I did not realize quite how poor it was till I compared the French with the English version of *My Life and Loves*. His books are only readable because their subject matter is sensational. He had in *The Man Shakespeare* something new and definite to say. In several of his short stories he struck an exciting plot. In his *Portraits* he wrote intimately and indiscreetly of persons about whom one is inquisitive. Unfortunately you cannot believe a word he says.

His anecdotes about Maupassant's priapism and Carlyle's impotence are typical. He takes two rumours which probably have a basis in fact and makes them the subject of a confession. The men who are reported to have made these confessions are no longer in the world to contradict him or defend themselves. And who could believe the scene where he pretends to have been completely ignorant of Wilde's inclinations until the scandal broke? His memoirs are valueless as history. If he survives as a legend, as part of a pattern, as a motif in the mosaic of literary history during the close of the nineteenth and the opening of the twentieth centuries—that is the most that can be hoped for. But his effect in 1906 on a twenty-year-old poetess must have been apocalyptic. He was then in the middle fifties. Though his political career was ruined, his literary reputation was still untarnished. He had not yet alienated many of his more worth-while friends. He was, however, conscious of the tide's turn against him. He needed the adulation of the young to restore his self-esteem. He took trouble over the very young.

'Did you always lunch at the Café Royal?' I asked her.

'Except the last time. We lunched at Kettner's then.' She paused, hesitated. 'Is Kettner's going still?' she asked. It was very flourishing, I told her.

'Is it still the same kind of place?'

'I suppose it is.'

'He took me to a private room.'

'I'm not sure if you'd find those still.'

Dinners in private rooms in restaurants went out with the modern flat. I saw the tail-end of their vogue. They would seem very unhygienic to a generation that is used to the centrally heated amenities of the modern apartment building, but there was a rakish rococo air about the whole procedure—the curtained stairway, the discreet waiters, the eighteenth-century engravings, the chaise-longue—that provided its own special stimulus; married couples got a kick out of going there and being mistaken for what they weren't.

'If that was your last lunch, I gather it wasn't a success,' I said.

She smiled, then flushed. 'I'm afraid he must have thought me very childish; girls weren't so sophisticated then. *Ann Veronica* seemed a very daring book. And besides, that room; it was tiny; I felt so big and clumsy. He was a little man, you know.'

She paused, smiled wryly. 'I must have been a disappointment to him. He never asked me out again. But he printed my poems: the poems I sent him afterwards. I was very happy about that. I should have been miserable if I'd thought he only accepted them because he had thought I was the kind of girl who might—' She checked; there was an abstracted look upon her face. 'Did you read *My Life and Loves?*' she asked.

I nodded.

'They say, don't they, that the things which you regret in middle age are not the things you've done but the things you haven't done. That's not always true, you know. I was so glad I hadn't, when I read that book. I used to wonder sometimes when I read his other books and when I read about him, whether if I had behaved differently he might not have been a different person. There was so much that was fine in him. It all seemed to be going to waste. I might have saved him. But when I read that

225

book, oh, it was all so materialistic, all that love-making and no conception of what love might be. I realized that I couldn't ever have made the slightest difference. It was too late, or I was the wrong person. I don't know which. Anyhow, I was very glad I hadn't.'

'You never saw him again, not after that last lunch?'

She shook her head. 'Very soon after that I went out to India: my sister was married to a civil servant.'

'You did not say good-bye?'

'I didn't tell him I was going. I dramatized myself. I pictured myself writing a tremendous poem on the way out. He'd be astonished to get an envelope in my handwriting with an Indian postmark. Then he'd read the poem. He'd be even more astonished. "I never realized she was capable of *that*," he'd think. My next poems would be better still. He'd be impatient to get me back. He'd write me beseeching letters. I'd go on postponing my return. That's how I'd punish him, for his own good. You know how a young girl daydreams.'

'And it didn't turn out that way at all?'

She laughed. 'The third day out I met the man I married.'

'And you wrote no more poems?'

'I wrote no more poems.'

Her bungalow was only five minutes' walk from Northolme. Most weeks I would drop in there for a gossip. Sometimes after lunch she would take her coffee on my veranda. Our conversation always came round to the same topics, the poets and personalities of the Edwardian decade. She could not ask me too many questions, about Wells and Bennett and Ford Madox Heuffer, and those 'left-overs' from the '90s—Symons, Le Gallienne, Davidson. What had happened to them all? 'I've not talked in this way for forty years,' she said.

226

It was probably in the main for that reason that now she talked of them so voraciously. But also it was in part, I think, because the early part of her life was now at the end becoming more real to her than the long middle section. In *The Linden Tree* J. B. Priestley had a moving conversation between an old man and a young girl, in which something was said about truth being found among the very young and the very old; they were nearer to 'the way in and the way out'. Perhaps 'the Colonel's Widow' was becoming again the young girl who had written Dowsonian sonnets. I began to wonder which was mattering more to her in retrospect—the long stretch of worthily spent years when she had been an irreproachable *mem-sahib*, or the months when she had lunched with a rake in the Domino Room at the Café Royal.

How long had it all gone on? I asked her. About a year. And how often had they met? Nine times. She was living in the country, it had not been easy for her to get up; she was closely chaperoned. Her parents would have been shocked to know that she was lunching with a married man. There was no telephone in her parents' house. Very few private houses did have telephones. 'But of course we wrote each other letters.' Or rather, I fancy, she wrote him letters and he acknowledged them.

It was not difficult to picture the situation. The poems that even though imitative had a quality of freshness; that would make an editor say: 'Well, there's a hundred to one chance she may amount to something'; poems that were promising enough, since they were signed with a girl's name, to make a man like Harris feel curious about their author. As she came into the office, a large wholesome-looking girl with fine eyes, fresh colouring and an engaging mixture of shyness and self-confidence, it was easy to guess how Harris thought, 'Yes, this is worth my time.'

He had many irons in the fire, so many plans and projects, literary, financial, amatory. But he was always ready to slip in one more iron, waiting for the appropriate moment. He was in no hurry. And then one day a mood of irritation, of loneliness, the need to rehabilitate himself in his own esteem would make him decide. 'It's high time I brought *that* thing to a head.' So he had booked the private room at Kettner's.

She had never been more than a sideshow; one scene in an unimportant sideshow, and when she had been 'childish' he had shrugged his shoulders. There were so many who were not child-ish. He probably barely noticed the cessation of her manuscripts and letters. Within two years if he had remembered her name, he would have found it hard with the mind's eye to recall her features. He would have been surprised could he have foreseen that half a century hence, in 1950, the year for which he had prophesied his own apotheosis, almost the only person south of the Red Sea to whom he was still a living influence was the girl he had lunched once at Kettner's.

She kept referring to him in her conversation. 'As Frank used to say …', 'Frank told me once …' All her original observations were put in that way into quotation marks.

'The artist suffers for the eventual benefit of mankind. The crucifixion is a symbol of the artist's treatment by the masses.'

'That sounds like Frank Harris,' I remarked. She flushed. 'Well, it's true, isn't it? And after they've persecuted him all his life, they bury him in the Abbey.'

A direct echo out of Harris. He had set the imprint of his mind on her. I thought of the heroine of Hugh Kingsmill's novel. Though he had altered all the circumstances, he told me whom he had had in mind. He showed me the letter of congratulation that she wrote him when the book was published. I have followed her career. It has brought her renown and riches, a successful marriage and proud progeny. How much of it does she owe to Harris; how often does she think of Harris, and in what way? So I brooded as I listened to her predecessor repeating sentiments whose truth had become discredited because they had been mouthed so often by one whose whole philosophy was warped with self-deception.

It was on that note of query that I had planned to end this sketch. I had half written it in my mind, during my walks along the shore, when something altogether unexpected happened; one of those storms in a teacup that make life in a small community at the same time stimulating and exasperating.

A guest at her house had noticed in the kitchen a collection of spills made out of the pages of a book. Opening out the spill he had noticed that the book in question was *The Struggle for World Power*—a sociological study written by John Strachey, in his pro-Moscow period. 'That's an expensive way of making spills,' he said.

'It's all that book's worth,' she retorted. 'To be burnt page by page.'

Her guest repeated the incident at the club. It quickly went the rounds. Finally it reached the ears of the Librarian. 'But that's a book she took out of the club library. She said she'd lost it. She was very apologetic. She paid the purchase price of it. Pretty decent of her, I thought, as we'd had it for years, and it was half in pieces. She lost two other books at the same time. She paid for both of them as well.'

'What were the books?'

'I can't remember now. I'll have to check.'

They were both Left Book Club publications. The inference was obvious. She had been weeding out the Library.

'I wonder if she's been doing the same thing at the Carnegie?' someone asked.

Enquiries were made; and it was found she had. *Das Kapital* had gone, and John Reid's *Ten Days that Shook the World*.

A member of the Club Committee called on her. She made no attempt to conceal her action. She admitted it and proudly. 'When you see a poisonous snake you kill it. Books like that should be kept under lock and key.' The club was on the whole indignant. Who was this silly old fool to decide what they could read and what they couldn't? That was the worst of these Indian Army people. Thought they owned the universe; all that *mem-sahib* nonsense.

So they argued. But something assured me that it was not the *mem-sahib* side of her that had turned a Left Book Club treatise into spills.

Next time I saw her I asked her what had started her on this anti-Communist campaign. 'Their censorship,' she said, 'their muzzling of the artist. There's no health in a country where an artist isn't free to speak out of his own heart.'

Muzzling of the artist. That was not 'the Colonel's Widow' speaking: any more than it had been 'the Colonel's Widow' who had wanted to found an orphanage. Her resentment sprang from a far earlier training: a loud brash voice booming across a restaurant.

'But aren't you yourself imposing your own censorship?' I said. 'Hasn't the other side a right to express its own opinions?'

She shook her head. 'Not when it's the voice of evil speaking.'

There was a fierce, resolute expression in her eye. At that moment she was a Colonel's Widow. 'They'll expect me to resign from the club, I suppose. But I don't care,' she said. 'It'll be a nuisance and I shall miss it; but I mustn't let myself worry about that.' She paused, and her expression changed, became soft and tender, so that for a moment I could see a flash of the girl that she had been—the girl who had written poetry, who had listened adoringly to that booming voice.'I don't care whatever any of them say. I'm right; I know I am, Frank would have said I was.'

1950

A Bunch of Beachcombers

Many years before the Vicomte Moreau des Seychelles assumed control of Louis XV's finances, there had been periodically washed up on the shores of western India and the Maldive Islands large heart-shaped nuts weighing as much as forty pounds. When the husk was removed there was revealed a double coconut, formed like the unlegged extremities of a woman—*mulieris corporis bifurcationem cum natura et pilis representat.*

So detailed and exact was this reproduction that the nut was held to have magic properties. As no one knew its origin, it was called *coco-de-mer*. Not until the end of the eighteenth century was it discovered that the parent tree grew wild in a horseshoe-shaped valley in the island of Praslin, twenty miles from Mahé. The tree from which it falls is a very straight, thin, tall palm; its growth is very slow, and as some of the trees rise to a height of a hundred feet, it is impossible to compute their age. The male palm reproduces with accuracy, but with considerably increased proportions, the masculine apparatus. Nowhere else in the world is this tree found.

General Gordon, a literal-minded man, was convinced in view of these facts that the *coco-de-mer* was the original tree of good and evil, and produced an ingenious genealogical argument that the Colony of Seychelles was part of a submerged continent, and that the Valle de Mai must be the Garden of Eden. He even found there an unusual serpent.

A few years later an equally literal-minded gentleman, a Monsieur M. Murat of Mauritius, opposed this theory on the grounds that Eve could not have climbed so high, that the husk was too tough for her to have broken, and that Adam would have found the taste of the nut insipid. This final argument is not in my view convincing; the nut when green contains a white jelly that is palatable in itself and excellent when mixed with brandy. Whether of divine origin or not, the nuts remain a source of profit to the island. Though the Indians, now its origin is known, can no longer regard it as holy, some three or four hundred nuts are annually exported. The kernel is ground up to form the basis of *nux medica*, while the shell serves a variety of purposes. The Moslems on their pilgrimages to Mecca are not allowed to take manufactured articles, and the double nut is a useful and unique receptacle. It is also used for baling out canoes.

Close though Praslin is to Mahe, the days are not so many on which from the hills behind Victoria its outline stands out clearly. Cloud and rain intervene. And the journey there is not one to tempt the unadventurous. You make it in a fifteen-ton motor-launch that presents every appearance of discomfort. A gale was blowing when I set out at seven in the morning in company with the new C.I.R.O., the officer in charge of income tax. As I watched the launch rock against its moorings, I recalled the villainous *Moneka* in which, two years earlier in the Caribbean, I had suffered so grievously between Montserrat and Antigua; luckily this time I was supplied with dramamine. It was the first time I had had occasion to take this much-vaunted drug, and when I arrived at Grande Anse three hours later, rested and refreshed, I felt that a whole new world was opening for me. Never again need I feel nervous of small boats. Cruising in the Caribbean, an activity I had previously avoided, would now hold no qualms for me. I am grateful for the trip to Praslin for that lesson. The launch rocked and rolled: everything and everyone was soaked: the groans of the suffering were louder than the creaking of the woodwork: children lay supine in their vomit. But I was ready on landing for a three-mile walk along the coast. It was well worth the journey to learn that.

But I should have been glad, anyhow, that I went to Praslin. Though it rained consistently during my four days' visit, I would not have missed the Valle de Mai, where the great *coco-de-mer* trees tower in lofty ranks: I would not have missed the three or four new acquaintances I made there. I would not have missed the chance of drawing comparisons between Mahe and its sister isle.

In rain and under cloud Praslin is a melancholy island, and even in the sunlight I suspect that it must seem forlorn. Though much less mountainous than Mahe, it has the same appearance—coconuts and granite and a succession of white-sanded beaches. There the resemblance ends. The bathing is not good. There is no club; there is no social life; there are no motor-cars. There is an administrative centre and a hospital, but the plantation houses are sufficiently far apart to render calling difficult. There is something, if not eccentric, at least out of the ordinary, about everyone who lives in Mahe: the types in Praslin are even more distinctively individualized.

There was the Brigadier for instance. A gunner who had spent most of his service in India, he resigned his commission in 1937 anxious to have two years' travelling before the war whose imminence was clear to him. Seychelles struck him as the likeliest place to settle in. As soon as the second war was over he came back.

He was a large man, stoutish but not fat, in the later fifties. His white stockings fitted over his calves without a wrinkle; his shorts were starched and stiff; the last quarter-inch of his short sleeve was punctiliously ironed back. He was the only Englishman in the colony who wore a solar topee. It was spotlessly white.

There is no hotel in the accepted sense of the word at Praslin. But there are a number of furnished bungalows along the coast that you can rent by the day or week. Maid service is supplied but you take your own cook with you. The best of these bungalows was rented by the brigadier. It consisted of two rooms divided by a passage, with a veranda at either end. He had given it an air of being lived in, but it was definitely not a home. He was, as far as I know, the only man in the colony who did absolutely nothing. He had no civic duties, he had no property, he collected nothing, he had no hobby, he had no vices. The C.I.R.O.'s boy made the most careful investigations and discovered nothing untoward. He was temperate; every evening of our stay he was either our guest or we were his. He drank two whiskies before dinner, and that was all.

On the one occasion when we dined together, he drank a single glass of wine and took a brandy with his coffee. He did not sail or fish or shoot. His exercise was walking. There is, as I said, no club in Praslin, but once or twice a week a French colonist bicycled over to play chess with him. He played with caution, devoting five to ten minutes to every move, whereas his opponent was a slapdash player, a persistent attacker, an improviser unwilling to plan farther than two moves ahead. Their friendship survived the strain of their respective styles.

A great deal of the day the Brigadier devoted to reading: his favourite literature being *Time*, the *Economist*, and *Illustrated*. During his military career, he explained he did not have enough time to think and read. He was making up for it now. For days on end he would have only his man to talk to and he enjoyed the opportunity of a talk. He had a firm military voice. He had an affliction of the left eye, the lids being joined in their centre by two threads of mattery yellowy skin. And when he fixed you with his right eye, the effect was minatory. But he was not by any means a violent man. On the contrary, he qualified his most dogmatic assertions with a conciliatory 'in my humble opinion', or a disarming 'of course I know I'm not intelligent'. He was a good listener. He would ask you your opinion, and when you had given it he would sit with his eyes half closed, his head lifted, ruminating over what you had said. 'That is most interesting,' he would say. 'I have so few opportunities here of exchanging ideas with anyone.'

His opinions were, however, definite. We were discussing a young Seychellois of good family who was an unregenerate ne'er-do-well. 'Only one thing to do for that kind of fellow,' the Brigadier asserted. 'Hitler was right: exterminate them. No good wasting good money on trash; too many people in the world already. Psychiatrists and all that rubbish. Some colonels used to say, "If you've got a troublesome fellow in your company, make him a lance-corporal." Nonsense. I never did. I waited for the fellow, caught him at it, then I jumped: break 'em. That's the only course. Bad blood always outs. You train racehorses, don't you? It's the same with men, in my humble opinion; rotten parent, rotten son. It always follows.'

It was difficult to argue with him because he jumped so quickly

236

from one topic to another. I suggested that some of the greatest men had been unfortunate in their fathers. He nodded. 'Were they? Now that's most interesting. I'm not an intelligent man. I want to learn, want to exchange ideas; what great man would you say had bad blood in his veins?'

To my chagrin I found that I could think of no one. I suggested Dickens, not feeling that I had chosen a fortunate example, but already he was off on another tack. 'If you ever find a shifty streak in a public figure, you can be certain that it's bad blood coming out. Look at that Labour fellow—a Spanish Jew, you know?'

The man in question could scarcely be called that since the alien streak had entered his blood three hundred years ago. But the Brigadier was not to be denied.

'That doesn't matter; it was there, waiting; biding its time. At last it's made its pounce. Look at all those company directors who evade income tax by taking salaries for posts they never fill.'

I do not know whether this was an extension of his anti-Semitism or whether I was receiving the benefits of his study of economics, but before I could decide he had switched again:

'I don't know why people should worry about laying up fortunes for themselves. Why can't they trust in God.'

That switch certainly surprised me, though I had noticed during the Second War that a high proportion of high-ranking officers were fanatically devout. I asked if he was a Roman Catholic. But he shook his head. No, no particular denomination. He never went to church. You didn't need to if you were on good terms with God. 'Just ask Him for what you want. You'll always get it. Provided you ask for the right things.'

I asked him what he meant by the right things. 'The things that are right for you to have.' To that there was no answer.

237

The most unexpected character in Praslin was not, however, the Brigadier. The C.I.R.O. was making an official visit to hear any complaints his recent assessments had occasioned. 'We might go and see Campbell,' he said. 'He's quite a person. He should interest you.'

I had heard of him and I was glad to go.

A married man in the early fifties, an ex-official in the South Kensington Museum, he had been seconded during the war to Delhi, to the India section of the Ministry of Information. He had now retired on a pension. In one sense he was a beachcomber. But he was by no means 'typical'; he was working a plantation; had rebuilt the plantation bungalow, and furnished it with pictures and books from England. Though he enjoyed a glass of wine, he was not a heavy drinker. Though he came over to Victoria every two months and spent the greater part of his time in the club, he had no special friends. He was not stand-offish, but he was impersonal. He had the reputation of being highbrow. He was respected rather than liked. I was curious to meet him.

His house was on the other side of the island, not far from the hospital above Bay St. Anne. Having chosen a remote island, he had certainly chosen the most remote section of it. There was no means of reaching it except on foot. He was wise in that, I supposed. If you are going to retire it is as well not to be reminded of the world from which you are an exile. We had sent over a letter the day before, warning him of our visit. He had been out when our messenger arrived; but he had sent a message the moment he returned inviting us to tea.

We found him awaiting us on his veranda beside a silver tea-tray. He was wearing cream-coloured linen shorts, sandals, and a white silk shirt. He was sunburnt, dark-haired, and had a very thin moustache. As he rose out of his chair I noticed that he was even shorter than I had expected. He was plump, and his walk was a mixture between a glide and waddle. He looked at me somewhat curiously when we were introduced. 'Was it you or your brother who wrote *The Loom of Youth?* he asked.

'I did.'

'And which of you wrote the book on Campion?'

'My brother.'

'That was a first-rate book.' Then he turned to my companion.

'I've desolating news for you. This is your last chance to prey on me.'

He spoke in a precise, modulated voice.

'What am I to take that to mean?' asked the C.I.R.O.

'I'm leaving, going back to England.'

'On leave?'

'For ever. I am disposing of my property. I'm delighted that you should have come out here. You can assist me on several points. But let's leave that till after tea.'

He had a silver kettle which he boiled himself. 'You can't trust even a Sinhalese to make you proper tea,' he said.

When I visited Lipton's tea gardens, I heard experts discuss the way in which tea should be made. I noticed that Campbell satisfied their demands—cold water in the kettle, the teapot and the teacups heated; one spoonful for each person and the one extra for the brew; the water poured the instant it was brought to boil; the stirring and the five minutes' wait. It was certainly an excellent cup of tea. It was accompanied by hot cakes and savoury sandwiches. It reminded me of Sunday afternoons in Cadogan Square a quarter of a century ago, and a grey-haired lady in a high-held whalebone collar; there was the same air of ritual. It was a full half-hour before he was ready to get down to business.

'Perhaps Waugh would care to look round my books while we talk our shop,' he said.

I could understand why his fellow-members in the club were a little restrained in their affection for him. He was not patronizing, but he had a *grand seigneur* air.

I walked over to his shelves. A small library is more revealing than a large one when, as in a case like this, it is the result not of haphazard purchase but selection. One has often played the game, 'If you were shipwrecked on a desert island, what twelve books would you prefer to have washed up beside you?' but the choice of the five hundred books that a man takes out with him to a lifetime's exile is much more revealing.

Not that this particular selection was original. There were the standard classics—Shakespeare in the Temple edition; the Oxford edition of the chief nineteenth-century poets; the *Oxford Book of Verse*; a few Russian novels; *Georgian Poetry; Poems of Today*. The novels included *Antic Hay, The Green Hat, The Prancing Nigger*. The kinds of novel that a young man would have bought in the early '20s. There were no erotica, not even among the paperbacked French novels, though I did notice a copy of *Si le grain ne meurt* ...

I walked out on to the veranda; coconut palms and granite boulders and the sea. There was nothing distinctive about the view. There was no reason why Campbell should have picked this site. My own view from Northolme with the perpetual back-cloth of Silhouette was worth a hundred of it. From the other side of the veranda a voice called out, 'We're through now. What about a drink?'

I crossed to where the income-tax expert was gathering his papers. A trim narrow-shouldered girl in an ankle-length white skirt had brought out a tray of drinks: the figure turned and I saw it was a boy; a Sinhalese, wearing a long-sleeved embroidered tunic with a high collar buttoning tightly at the throat. He wore his hair long with a tortoiseshell comb projecting like twin horns above his forehead. 'What'll you have? Something with gin, or whisky?' Campbell asked.

'Whisky, if you've any soda.'

'Of course I've soda.'

I looked at him with curiosity. Why on earth, once he had made the break with England, was he going back? 'Is it an impertinence to ask you why?' I said.

'By no means, it'll soon be common knowledge. My wife was killed in a motor smash. I'm going back to look after our two daughters.'

It was such an unexpected admission that there was no comment to be made. I waited for his amplification. 'We'd drifted apart before the war,' he said. 'Then when the war came, well, I was away five years, and once the strings are cut …'

'But why come out here? Why not live on in England?'

He shrugged. 'You know how income tax works out, how a husband and wife's income are joined and taxed as one. You can't lead two separate lives upon one income. You could before the war. You can't now. My daughters and my wife had become a team; I'd always been more of an uncle to them than a father. A complete break seemed wisest. I saw no reason why I should go through the squalid business of a divorce.'

'And having decided on a break, I suppose you thought that the further you could get away the better.'

He shook his head.

'Not altogether. The less I spent of the money that'll one day be theirs, the better.'

'But now your wife is dead …'

241

'Now of course I have to go back and take up my responsibilities.'

He said it in such a way that 'take up my responsibilities' was put into inverted commas.

'When are you leaving?'

'On the next eastbound boat.'

'That's the one I'm taking.'

'Good; then we'll see something of each other.'

He looked at me again with the appraising look that he had assumed at our first meeting. 'I'll enjoy that,' he said, 'though it's the last thing I could have foreseen myself as saying thirty years ago.'

Authors get used to having odd things said to them, but this was more than usually unexpected.

'May I ask why?' I said.

'That first book of yours. I disapproved of it. Subjects like that are better not discussed.' My first book as I have already explained in my Foreword, written at the age of seventeen, was a Public School story. It dealt in one chapter more realistically than was then considered prudent with the consequences of herding together in monastic seclusion boys who are almost men and boys who are almost children. It caused a *succès de scandale* at the time. Its scarlet passages seem very tame today.

'If you believe that, you've got one or two rather unexpected books on your own shelves,' I said.

'For instance?'

'*Si le grain ne meurt.*'

'Oh, so you noticed that.' He flushed. He paused. 'One's opinions alter. I said thirty years ago, remember.'

I looked at him thoughtfully. There was something odd about him, something that did not ring quite true, something that did

242

not quite add up. That story about his coming to live in Seychelles because of income tax. It seemed contrived.

Three weeks later I stood beside Campbell on the upper deck of the *Kampala*. We had embarked the night before. We were due to sail in half an hour. It was a grey, sunless morning, the peaks of Trois Frères were shrouded. Rain drifted intermittently like a series of gauze curtains across Victoria. Sailings at daybreak after a late night's pouring on the boat are an anti-climax. The familiar life of the town had started. We could see through glasses the bustle of early traffic along the esplanade.

No one was noticing the *Kampala*. As far as the island was concerned she had sailed when the last launch went. We were no longer a part of the life that we were watching.

The police launch left. The steps were lifted and the anchor weighed. The engines began to throb. I turned to Campbell.

'Two months ago this must have been the last thing that you foresaw?'

He shrugged. 'One's a fool to look ahead too far.'

I asked what he was planning for his daughters. My own daughter was just sixteen. She was going to Switzerland the following year. I explained about applying for currency in advance. He scarcely listened. He was following his own thoughts.

'I couldn't not go back,' he said. 'But the infuriating thing is that if that last time I bathed I had swum out by mistake too far and the sharks had got me, my daughters would have been no worse off; probably better off. Their uncle could have looked after them. They've always spent half of their summer holidays with him. He lost his son in the war. His daughter's married. He'd be delighted to have my kids. They know him better than they know me. They'd be better off with him. But because I'm alive, they'd not be happy there. They'd think they ought to be with me. It would look queer my being stuck out here, and that's the one thing that children can't stand, something that looks queer, that they can't explain to their friends.' He laughed, a short, wry little laugh. 'It's odd how often the best service one can do one's friends and family is to disappear, to die under conditions that would confer no disgrace. There's always something discreditable about a suicide.'

'The Romans didn't think so; they held that a man had the right to leave a party that had begun to bore him.'

'I dare say, but we're not Romans.'

He spoke impatiently.

We had begun to move; in half an hour we should be passing Praslin. Rain was falling steadily. 'Have there ever been times,' he said, 'when you have thought, "If I were to die now, everyone would be left with a good impression of me. Everyone would speak well of me. My family would be proud of me. But in the next fifteen years things may have happened to make them feel ashamed of me; I may have forfeited their pride and trust. If only I could make my exit now?" Have there been times when you've thought that?'

'Is there anyone in the world who hasn't?'

An idea for a story crossed my mind, of a man who has gone to seed in the tropics, who is afraid of going back to face the son who has made a hero of him; and who in order to preserve the son's memory intact swims out to sea to meet the sharks. I saw it as a possible short story.

I looked at Campbell thoughtfully. Confidences are usually made late at night, after many drinks. But they are also made on grey chill mornings upon station platforms. Had Campbell realized quite how much he had admitted, how much he had betrayed? Did he guess that he had taken me behind the scenes?

'What about that Sinhalese boy?' I asked. 'Are you taking him back with you?'

He shook his head. 'It wouldn't be fair to him, the climate— who'd there be for him to talk to? He's going to Colombo.'

I hesitated. There was something that had been puzzling me about Campbell all along. That story about joint income tax in England; there should have been a way round that. I had discussed it with the C.I.R.O. He thought there was.

'The C.I.R.O. seemed to think that you could have filed separate declarations.'

'My income-tax agent didn't think so.'

'Couldn't you have signed a deed of separation. I know one man who ...'

'Do you think I'd have come all this way out here, if I'd known of a single way in which it could have been avoided?'

He snapped it out and he was frowning. I had gone too far.

'What other reason could I have for coming here?' he said.

What other reason? I could think of one. I thought of his fear of going back; of that something happening that might destroy his reputation. I enumerated certain points—his precise modulated accent; the way he walked; the Sinhalese servant; *Si le grain ne meurt*; his attitude to my first book; the defensive mechanism of a man who instinctively, without knowing why, distrusts discussion of a dangerous subject. He might not have discovered until middle life that danger lay here for him. He might have discovered it in India. What if his wife had offered him an ultimatum—to leave the country for his children's good. It all fell into place.

I may have been completely wrong, but I noticed that Campbell avoided me for the remainder of the trip.

1950

The Wicked Baronet

I hesitate when friends ask me to recommend hotels in the West Indies. A change of management can transform a hotel within a year, making or ruining it. I have not been to St. Thomas since 1953 and I have no idea what kind of hotel the Harbour View is now. I can only testify that in 1950 it was a very congenial place for any one who enjoys elasticity in his time-table.

It had, from its long, wide veranda, one of the best views in the island, and was run on the European plan. Lunch was not served, and although those who have to catch an early plane could rely upon being fed before they left, there was no fixed hour for breakfast. There were a few small tables and a long central one. At the large table breakfasts were still being served when it was time for the first rum swizzle. In the evening, when there were sufficient guests to justify the serving of a dinner, there was an air of parade, with well-appointed tables and long dresses. But for the most part the atmosphere was that of a casually and friendly run country house, with someone always on the veranda, reading, or playing Canasta, darning a stocking or sipping a highball. It was the right kind of place for people who prefer to leave their plans vague till they can see what the day is like and

246

how competent they feel to face it.

At the back of the veranda was a large courtyard kind of hall, built on the Arab plan with bedrooms opening off it and a staircase leading to the upper storey. On my last afternoon, as I was crossing this hall on my way upstairs, I was checked by the sound of a long, loud, masculine guffaw. I paused. I had heard only one man laugh in quite that way. I was in a hurry. I had my packing to get done, but I had to make certain first. On rubber-soled shoes I moved across the hall. I stood in the shadow of the entrance; and there, at the far end of the veranda, seated on the balustrade with one knee drawn up, with his hands clapsed round it, was a large, heavily built man, florid with blue-veined cheeks and a handlebar moustache. He was wearing white shorts and a white short-sleeved shirt. A yachting cap was tilted over his left eye. He was in the middle fifties. It was over ten years since I had seen him, but no, there was no doubt about it—he was Reggie Thayne.

Some years ago the *New Yorker* magazine, in the course of a 'Where are they now?' article, printed a list of thirty names, each of which had made the headlines, in a sensational manner, in the last thirty years. How many of these names, it asked, would have any concrete significance to the contemporary reader? Personally, I remembered four; and I would doubt if there is a single American, and not more than two or three Englishmen, who would today connect anything definite with the name of Thayne. Yet for a few weeks in the summer of 1938 Colonel Sir Reginald Thayne, Bart, was as much discussed as anyone in England.

'Grave charge against a Wessex Squire', that was how the headlines ran, with the letterpress below double-column photographs explaining that a seventeen-year-old village schoolmistress had pulled the alarm-bell of a railway carriage to defend her honour against an alleged assault by the owner of Winchborough Hall, a man of forty, an M.F.H., the husband of Lord Wilmot's daughter, and the father of two daughters and a son. It was as big a scandal as the neighbourhood had ever known.

Personally, I was especially interested in the case because I had been in the habit for several years of going down into that part of the country and working in a small hotel. I knew the Thaynes quite well, and I was as much surprised as anyone. The whole thing seemed to me, and to everybody else there, inconceivable.

It was not so much that Reggie himself was the last person whom you could imagine in that kind of mess. On the contrary, he was a healthy, full-blooded creature, a sportsman, a man's man, a moderate drinker but a heavy eater, loud-voiced and always laughing, whether anything particularly amusing had been said or not. And even though he had been for twelve stolid years the champion of law and order, Winchborough's hereditary figurehead, captaining its cricket side, opening its bazaars, reading the lessons in church, presiding over its committees, serving as Lord-Lieutenant of the county, forty is a dangerous age. No one can count himself immune. It was something altogether else that made Reggie's predicament so astonishing—the fact that he was Sybil's husband.

As that he was something special, very special; or rather it was Sybil herself that made him special. It was not just that she was singularly lovely, slim and small with corn-coloured hair and cornflower-blue eyes, a peachbloom complexion and a voice that lilted—there are, after all, a number of lovely women in the world—it was an interior intrinsic quality, a quality that I can only define obliquely.

It was easy to explain why we dislike a person. It is easy to make a catalogue of unpleasant traits. But how are you to indicate what it is about a woman that gives you when you are in her company the sense of having been transported into another country, another climate, where the sun is warmer, the breeze softer, the colours brighter? That is the effect that Sybil had on you. The moment she came into the room the world seemed a more pleasant place.

You could imagine Reggie Thayne, but you could not imagine Sybil's husband making a pounce at a village schoolmistress. Poor Sybil, we thought, I wonder how she'll take it.

We had not to wait that answer long. Every summer on the last Saturday in June the Duke of Wessex entertained the county. It was the biggest social function of the year. His impressive terraces welcomed some five hundred guests. Most of us imagined that Sybil would stay away.

She did not. Nor could she have been less abashed.

It was a hot, almost too hot, a day, but she looked very cool in flowered muslin under a floppy hat, so cool that you felt a breeze was blowing.

'What a heavenly day,' she said. 'Isn't Francis lucky! He always has this weather for his parties. We were so sure that it would be fine this week-end that we'd arranged to go over to Le Touquet, and now of course we can't owing to this absurd mess of Reggie's. I suppose you saw about it in the papers? Yes, of course you did. One always does see that kind of paragraph. So instead of sunbathing on some lovely beach, we've got to spend the week-end with the lawyers. Aren't you a nuisance, darling!'

He laughed one of his loud, hearty laughs. She raised her hand and patted him playfully upon the cheek.

'We've briefed Patrick Forrester,' she said. 'I do hope that you are all coming over to hear the case. It ought to be quite amusing. Sir Patrick is *such* a pet.'

I was in court on Wednesday. The old oak hall where, on so many occasions in the past, Reggie had officiated as Lord Lieutenant gave a curious dramatic irony to the whole affair. This friendly and familiar room, with its time-stained panelling, its tattered banners, its gilt-framed portraits, had been the scene of many of his proudest moments. Was it now to prove the setting of his disgrace?

It was, indeed, in its own way one of the most dramatic mornings I can remember. I had watched so many court scenes on the screen that it was an odd experience to meet one in real life. It was all so leisurely, so casual, it was hard to believe that there was so much at stake.

Nor could anyone have looked less like a screen character than Patrick Forrester. Tall, thin, tired, he was more like a family doctor than a barrister. His appearance was, in fact, his greatest asset; his chief skill as a cross-examiner lying in his capacity to lull a witness into a state of false security. He never bullied a witness. He never rounded on a witness. It was not until his final speech that a witness realized the extent and nature of the admissions that had been drawn from him.

I shall always consider Forrester's handling of that case a master piece.

The schoolmistress looked, I must say, the last kind of girl whom you would expect to inspire that kind of enterprise. She had come with her parents, and she had put on, presumably under their instructions, a tailored dark-blue coat and skirt that would have been more suitable to a November than an August morning. It made her look uncomfortable. She was of medium height, with a featureless, pudgy face. No doubt when she was in a cheerful mood she had the natural prettiness of youth. But she had no distinction of line and feature. She looked glum and sulky. She gave her evidence in a toneless voice.

She had gone into the town on market day, she said. She had meant to get home for lunch. She had reached the station early and all the carriages in the back coach were empty. Her carriage had remained empty until, just before the train started, Sir Reginald got in. She of course knew Sir Reginald well by sight, she had often talked to him at village fêtes. They said good morning to one another. As is not uncommon in local railway lines in England, there was no corridor to the train. He had sat across the narrow compartment, in the opposite corner, facing her. They exchanged a conventional comment about the weather. Then he opened out his *Times*. She had a book and she resumed her reading of it. After a little while, Sir Reginald put down his paper. 'It's rather warm,' he said. 'Do you mind if I let down the window?'

'Of course not.'

He rose to his feet. He crossed the carriage. He stood by the window. He paused. He turned round towards her. He stared at her. His eyes became very bright. His face got hot. Suddenly he pounced at her with his hands spread out. She was terrified. She wriggled free. She ran to the other side of the compartment. She pulled on the alarm cord. She put her head out of the window. She shrieked for help. She didn't know what she said.

That was her story as she told it; quietly, sulkily, undramatically. She was a girl whom everyone in court had known since childhood, whose parents everyone respected. Not a word had been breathed against her ever, or against her family.

I looked at Sybil. She was in profile and I could not read the expression on her face. It had been one thing to brave it out last

251

Saturday. It was altogether different now. I wondered how Reggie would behave when his turn came to take the witness-box. His face was flushed. He was no fool. He knew that everyone in court was sorry for the girl.

Sir Patrick sensed this atmosphere. His voice was urbane, encouraging; there was to be no bullying, no intimidation; he led the girl slowly through her evidence, step by step. He asked her about her meetings with Sir Reginald. When had she met him last? How often had she seen him in the last six months? He was one of the governors of the school. Did he visit the school often? Six or seven times a year; indeed; and when he did, he usually exchanged some gossip with her? Had he ever said anything to suggest that his feelings for her were not strictly such as were correct between a man in his position and a girl in hers?

It was obvious that he was going to point out later that, if Reggie had ever had any intentions towards the girl, the ordinary routine of his life would have given him ample opportunities of indulging them.

Sir Patrick then began to question her about Reggie's behaviour in the train.

'You have told us that when Sir Reginald entered the compartment he said, "Good morning."' Is that correct?'

'Yes, sir.'

'Can you remember his exact words?'

'He just said, "Good morning."'

'Is that all he said?'

'Yes, sir.'

'Was there anything unusual in his manner?'

'No, sir.'

'What were you doing when Sir Reginald came into the carriage?'

'Reading a book.'

'Did you go on reading?'

'Yes, sir.'

'What did Sir Reginald do?'

'He opened out his paper.'

'How soon after Sir Reginald had arrived did the train leave the station?'

'In a minute or two.'

'And you went on reading?'

'Yes, sir.'

'Did the jolting of the train disturb your reading?'

'Not very much, sir.'

'But it did a little?'

'Only a very little.'

'Your attention was, in fact, concentrated on your book?'

'Yes, sir.'

'You took no notice of Sir Reginald?'

'No, sir.'

'You were not embarrassed at being alone with him in a compartment?'

'No, sir.'

'Did Sir Reginald make any attempt to enter into conversation with you?'

'No, sir.'

'Did he do anything to make you feel embarrassed? Did he stare at you, for instance?'

'No, sir.'

'He read his paper quietly all the time?'

'Yes, sir.'

'There was complete silence in the carriage, that is to say, for some fifteen minutes?'

'Yes, sir.'

'While you read your book and he read his paper?'

'Yes, sir.'

'And the first time that silence was broken was when Sir Reginald asked if he might open the window?'

'Yes, sir.'

'Now I want you, if you will, to explain to the court exactly what did happen. You say he stared at you. Did he do this before or after he had opened the window?'

'Before.'

'He walked, that is to say, over to the window, then paused?'

'Yes, sir.'

'Did he make any attempt to open the window?'

'I don't think so, sir.'

'You mean he had not even put his hand on the leather strap?'

'I don't think he had, sir.'

'Are you quite sure of that?'

She hesitated, but he did not press her. 'We'll let that wait for a moment. Can you remember how his feet were placed?' He asked a number of questions on this point. Was Sir Reginald facing the window; was he, that is to say, looking at her over his right shoulder or was he at right angles to the door; in that case he would be staring straight at her.

'I am anxious to recreate the exact sequence of events,' he said. 'Let us assume that this desk is the window and that these two chairs represent the corners of the carriage. Am I to understand that this is how Sir Reginald behaved?' Sir Patrick walked from the chair over to the desk. This part of the questioning took a little while. The girl hesitated, contradicted herself; finally agreed that Sir Reginald never touched the window strap at all, but as soon as he reached the window turned at right angles, facing her.

'At right angles to the window, facing you. I see.' There was a smile on Sir Patrick's face. It was easy to see the line of defence he had in mind. A large part of his defence would consist in his demonstration of the unlikelihood of Reggie having made such an attempt, at such a place, at such a time. But his chief line clearly was going to be that Reggie, a heavy man, facing the engine and consequently unbalanced, had been thrown forward by the jolting of the train, and that an inexperienced girl had been frightened by what had been a mere mischance. It was a possible if not probable explanation. Whether or not the court believed it, depended, I presumed, entirely on Reggie's behaviour in the box.

Sir Patrick's next series of questions left no doubt as to his ultimate intentions.

'I am most anxious,' he said, 'to learn the exact form taken by this alleged assault. I should like the plaintiff to show us exactly what she claims the defendant did. I think it would be easiest if she were to give a demonstration. Suppose, for instance, her mother were to sit in this seat here, then the plaintiff could give a demonstration. She must be able, I am sure, to recall in vivid and separate detail exactly what took place ...'

He took the girl by the hand. He led her in front of the chair where he had placed her mother. 'Imagine,' he said, 'that you are Sir Reginald and your mother is yourself. Will you show us exactly what happened next?'

The girl hesitated and there was a silence. Sir Patrick looked at her thoughtfully, kindlily, then turned towards the magistrate.

'Perhaps, your worship, in view of the nature of this case, the plaintiff would prefer not to have this demonstration made in public. Perhaps we might clear the court. Perhaps ...'

But before the magistrate could answer, the need for him to answer had been removed. Suddenly the girl collapsed, falling forward into her mother's arms, bursting into tears, crying out between her sobs, 'He didn't do it … It's all a mistake … He didn't. He never did.'

Yes, I shall always say that Sir Patrick's handling of that case was a masterly performance.

When I met the Thaynes three days later, Sybil was at her liveliest.

'I feel so sorry for the poor girl,' she said. 'She's a case for the doctor. It was pathological. She's full of inhibitions and timidities, and then finding herself alone with Reggie—all the novels that she reads feature a wicked baronet. She lost her head and then she was frightened of admitting it. Perhaps she didn't even know she was lying. The imagination of an adolescent can be so vivid. I'm terribly sorry for her parents. I'm trying to persuade them not to leave the village. They've lived here all their lives. I suppose Susan will have to go, but I've written to a school where Reggie's got a pull. I'm sure they'll be able to find a place for her. Of course we're paying all the expenses of the case. But it *is* tragic for them.'

There was no note of triumph in her voice, not a suggestion of vindictiveness, of resentment that her own name had been dragged into a scandal; for she was sufficiently a woman of the world to realize that some measure of scandal would attach to her for ever.

'I'm so glad you were all in court,' she went on. 'You know how it's going to be. People always say that there can't be smoke unless there's fire; I suppose that the younger generation, who'll never have a chance to get the facts right, who'll just have heard backstairs whispers, will soon be referring to Reggie as 'the wicked baronet'; of course, one only had to look at the girl to realize that there couldn't be anything in it, or for that matter,' she paused and laughed, 'for that matter one only had to look at my dear sweet Reggie.' She raised her hand and gave his cheek a pat. It would have been impossible for her, we all agreed, to have carried the thing off better. And when we learnt later that not only had Susan Carter found a post in a school in Wales but had become the wife of the headmaster, it was generally conceded that what had promised to be a tragedy and a disgrace could not have turned out more satisfactorily for everyone.

But that was in the summer of 1939; within a few weeks not only had every trace of such a scandal been washed from memory, but the whole way of life typified by Winchborough had been relegated to the past. 'The power of "the big house" '—all such feudal survivals as 'the Lord of the Manor' and 'the squire' had become anachronisms. I have not been to Winchborough since. I heard sometime in late 1940 that the house had been requisitioned by an evacuated ministry. But the following September I was posted overseas to Syria, and in the vast concentration camp of the Middle East I heard no Winchborough gossip. By the time I eventually returned to England it was as a kind of Rip van Winkle to find that I had lost touch with more than half of my friends.

That, indeed, is one of the minor tragedies of the war. For six years we were isolated by the particular kind of war work we were doing. It was almost impossible to pick up the threads.

But melancholy though it has been to lose touch with so many friends, there has been, in compensation, the surprise every now and then of meeting an old friend in a totally unexpected place, and it very certainly was all of that to meet Reggie Thayne in St. Thomas on the veranda of the Harbour View Hotel.

I hurried over. 'My dear Reggie, what a surprise,' I said.

He took my outstretched hand, but his stare was blank. He had not the least idea who I was. Which is another of the melancholy things about that eight-year gap: you do not realize how much you have changed yourself until an old friend fails to recognize you.

I introduced myself. 'Of course, the writing fellow. Sybil kept telling me I should read your books. Never quite got round to it. You had McCartney's, hadn't you?'

I hadn't. But I let it pass. I asked him about Winchborough.

He shrugged. 'I couldn't afford to keep it on. A place like that has to be run properly or not at all. And if I wasn't running Winchborough, what was there for me to do in England? I couldn't just sit around in White's all day. Besides, England's no place for a wife, washing up dishes all day long.'

'Where are you living now?' I asked.

'In St. Kitts of course.'

The 'of course' amused me. There is a certain type of person who expects his friends to be informed about the details of his own career at every stage of it, though he himself is completely indifferent to their doings; St. Kitts happened to be an island in which, at that time, I had never spent more than half a day. I recalled it as a plain of cane-fields, backed by hills. I asked him how he liked it.

'Grand. Just the life for me.' He had a schooner-type yacht, he told me. One of his guests was an American. That's how he happened to have dollars to spend in a hard-currency port. He raised sugar and was trying experiments with secondary crops. He sat on the Legislative Council. He was clearly leading in the Caribbean a life of public responsibility very similar to his former one in Wessex.

'Does Sybil like it as much as you?' I asked.

'Sybil? How does she come in?'

'Didn't you say something about not wanting to have your wife wash up dishes all the time?'

258

He roared with laughter.

'I don't, but my wife's not Sybil.'

'You're divorced, you mean?'

He nodded. It was the first that I had heard of it. But then that was not surprising. With newspapers reduced to four-sheet dimensions during the war, only the most sensational cases had been reported.

'Who's Sybil married to?' I asked.

'No one, as far as I know.'

'How did it all come to happen then?'

He shrugged. 'The war gave me a good excuse: having to give up Winchborough, I mean to say. It made a break and the break once made … I knew I never could go back.'

I looked at him interrogatively. When I had come across to him, he had been in a group, but the others, seeing that we were talking 'about old times', had moved away. We were alone and out of earshot.

'You mean that you broke it up?' I asked.

He nodded. I was astounded.

'I always thought you were so happy.'

'So we were till that damned case came on.'

'But I thought she was so marvellous about it all.'

'That was the trouble. She was too marvellous.'

Then I understood, or thought I did. I had read once a restoration comedy called *A Woman Killed by Kindness*. This was that drama in reverse; the case of a man, or rather of a marriage, that kindness killed. Sybil had been too marvellous, too gracious, too forgiving. It was more than a man's dignity could stand … Yet if Sybil had been too forgiving, there must have been something to forgive; or at least Sybil had thought there was.

'Then she didn't believe your story, after all? She pretended to in public, but when you were alone …' I checked. No, no. That couldn't be the explanation. Under these conditions the question of magnanimity could scarcely have come in. Wasn't there another explanation? Had Reggie really made this insane assault, had he confessed to Sybil; and had she accepted his guilt with a graciousness that he had found humiliating? Was that the explanation? I waited, curious, expectant.

He shook his head.

'She never doubted my word for a single instant. That was what I couldn't stand, living with a woman who just couldn't believe that it would be possible for me to behave like that.'

'Then you really did …?'

Again he shook his head. 'Was it likely—with a station only five minutes off! But when I got up to let than window down … it was a warm June day, there was a scent of summer in the carriage, she was wearing a loose cotton blouse. It was low cut. I was standing over her. She looked so cool and white and soft. It took me off my guard. At college I'd knocked about a bit. But since I married … well, that kind of thing dies down in marriage. I'd been completely faithful … that's why it knocked me off my guard. I stared. She look up and our eyes met. I could see at once that she knew exactly what was in my mind. Sybil was right, no doubt, about her being pathological. She was hysterical and inhibited. She stared at me, dazed, hypnotized like a rabbit with a snake. I had the feeling I could have done anything, any damned thing I wanted with her. I can't begin to tell you what I felt. It was the most violent sensation that I had known for years. Then suddenly she screamed, dived across the carriage, and before I could stop her she'd pulled the cord and was screaming her head off through the window.

'Yes, that's what happened. But could I explain to Sybil? Could I hell! You saw how she behaved in public. She was just like that with me. "How tiresome for you. That poor silly girl. I wonder who'd be the best counsel to defend the case." She scarcely listened to what I had to say. "But of course you didn't; no one who knows you could possibly doubt that, for a single instant." That was what the trouble was. I had learnt more about myself in those two minutes than in all the twenty years that I'd been adult. I felt I'd been a stranger to myself all my life. I felt I'd been living with a stranger all those years. But to Sybil I was the same person that I'd always seemed. I stood it as long as I could for appearances' sake. But I couldn't keep it up. My whole life was a sham. I was pretending to be something I was not. I couldn't be myself with Sybil. I couldn't help remembering that that girl in that one moment had read right into my very soul. She learnt more about me in that one minute than Sybil had in a dozen years …'

He paused. He looked away. He drew a long, slow breath.

'I hadn't anybody else in mind when I insisted on that divorce. I didn't expect to marry again. But I knew that if I did, I'd want a wife who'd know without my telling her the kind of person that I really was or could be. I never knew I'd have the luck … but look, here is Diana.'

He had risen to his feet and his eyes were shining in a way that I had never seen them shine before. A tall and youngish woman had just come on to the veranda. She was dark-haired, dark-eyed, with a dead pale skin. She must have been nearly six feet tall. She moved in a kind of glide—there was something of a panther's quality about her.

'Isn't it nearly time that you were thinking of buying me a drink?' she said. Her voice was a deep contralto. It would have been hard to find anybody more unlike Sybil.

1950

Circle of Deception

For one who has led as I have done, a scattered, travelling life, middle age has its own special compensations. I have, for example, acquired by now so wide an acquaintance that I never board a boat, check in at a hotel, disembark at a foreign port, without the thought, "Whom out of the past shall I run into here!' It is fascinating to see how people change over the years.

One of the most exciting encounters of this kind came my way in the spring of 1950. I had been commissioned to write a series of articles on the smaller British West Indian islands. I was already familiar with them, but there were several that I had not visited since the war. I went to St. Kitts, Montserrat, Antigua, then I booked a passage for St. Vincent. I boarded the boat in the late afternoon; by the time I had unpacked it was close on six and I went into the bar. In the doorway I checked, delighted. There are few people I could have been more glad to meet unexpectedly than Lily Martyn.

I had seen her last in Baghdad, in the last year of the war, when we were both employed in Military Intelligence. She still looked twenty-four, but that did not surprise me. She was the type—tall, slim, dark-haired, clear-skinned—that does not alter between eighteen and forty; I was, however, surprised to see her drinking Coca-Cola. In Baghdad, though she took wine with meals, she refused cocktails. She did not trust hard liquor, she explained; she might give away State secrets. It was a wise precaution. Whisky was in short supply and Cyprus gin and Persian vodka were a lethal mixture. But that was wartime and in Baghdad. This was peacetime in the Caribbean.

She was alone and I sat beside her. 'Still on the wagon, then?' She smiled.

'It's as hard to break yourself of a good habit as a bad.'

'What are you doing here?'

'My mother died. I came into some money. I'd an idea of coming out to settle. I thought I'd have a look and see. I'm trying Dominica first.'

That meant she would be getting off next morning. We would only be fellow passengers for half a day.

'We must make the most of it,' I said. 'Let's dine at the same table. Tell me about yourself.'

'There's not much to tell. I stayed on in Baghdad another year after you'd left. Then Daddy died. I came home to look after my mother.'

'You've not remarried?'

'No.'

It was strange she hadn't. She was the type that attracted men and her husband had been killed on the Dunkirk beaches. She ought to have got over it by now. But then from the start she puzzled me.

From the very start.

As the liaison link between my branch and hers, I had met her at the Baghdad Airport.

'Tell me about this place,' she said.

It was then late April and I described the long, hot, arid summer that lay ahead, with the temperature hovering between 100° and 120°, one day like the last and no hill station, the desert on every side.

'How about the flies?' she asked.

'There are none after June. The heat kills them off.'

'What about the people?'

'Baghdad's a large Arab city with a small British community living on its fringe. There's the Embassy and the men in oil and the men in trade. At the moment it's a G.H.Q. with all that goes with that.'

There was plenty of social activity, I told her. There was the Alwiyah Country Club with its tennis courts and swimming pool and Saturday-night dances. The British residents were hospitable and most weeks one of the messes threw a party. 'The males outnumber the females by thirty-five to one,' I added.

She let that one pass.

'What do you make of it yourself?' she asked.

'I've been here twenty months. I loathed the first three weeks, but the place grows on you. You are so far from everything. It gives you a sense of comradeship, like shipwrecked sailors.'

'An island in the desert. That might suit me very well.'

It was a strange thing to say; it was said too in a strange tone of voice. I started to feel curious.

I felt more curious as the weeks went by. I saw quite a lot of her. My office hours were long, eight to one and half past four to eight, and I was always glad of an excuse to leave my desk. She worked on the east bank of the Tigris in a dignified old Turkish house. It was pleasant to row across the river in the late afternoon when the heat of the day had lessened and a sun-shot, dust-laden haze lay over the mosques and minarets, over the low

264

ochre-brown mud-houses and the blue-tiled domes; and it was more than pleasant when our 'shop' was finished, to sit gossiping on her veranda in the cool of a shaded courtyard in which a fountain played. She was agreeable company, even-tempered with an occasional unexpected flash of wit. We soon became good friends. I went there oftener than our work required. One way and another I met her on an average three times a week. Yet when a year later I left Baghdad, I knew her no better than I had when she arrived.

I was not the only one she puzzled. To the many young and eligible officers who had been deprived for upwards of two years of feminine society, she was a cause of considerable concern. She was not shy. She seemed to have no inhibitions. There was nothing spinsterish about her. She was after all a widow. Yet her many suitors were given very clearly to understand that 'that' was 'not her game'. I rather fancied indeed that she showed such a flattering preference for my company largely because I was neither young nor eligible.

Several of my friends brought their perplexities to me. 'I can't make head or tail of her,' they'd say. 'She was only married a few weeks. Her husband has been dead four years. She ought to have got over it by now. One ought to be resilient at twenty-four, particularly in wartime.'

They all made the same complaint. She didn't look cold; they didn't believe she was cold. She was just not interested. What did I make of it?

I was as much in the dark as they were. On the surface she was a straightforward person. The facts of her life were in *Who's Who*: her father an admiral who had been knighted, her mother the daughter of an Indian civil servant; two brothers and a sister; a place in Devonshire; no scandal, no divorce. But I could not forget that first remark about 'the island in the desert'. Surely it could only have been made by someone with something on her mind.

She was also, I suspected, on her guard. Did she really refuse cocktails on grounds of military security or was she afraid of giving herself away.

I only caught one clue as to what might be worrying her. At the time that England was being attacked by buzz-bombs, someone made a remark at a mess party about wishing the Germans would fight clean. She flared up instantly.

'Fight clean! We aren't living in the days of the Crusades and the Knights of the Round Table. War's filthy. Let's accept the fact. Let's win by any weapons we can find: bomb hospitals, poison drinking wells. Use everything that'll end it quickly. Thank heaven the Germans are realistic. Let's hope we follow their example.'

It was said indignantly, and there was an awkward pause. She recovered quickly.

'I'm sorry. It's the heat,' she said, 'and that's a hobby-horse of mine. I'm off it now.'

It was an unexpected outburst. But the mess discounted it. 'No wonder she feels bitterly,' they said. 'She's lost her husband. She loathes the whole idea of war, thinks of it as a crime. That's why she's the way she is. She lives on the surface, friendly but not more than friendly. Now and again the surface cracks.'

I nodded in agreement. It sounded plausible. Yet somehow I did not feel the explanation was so simple. The outburst had been so very vehement and I could not forget that phrase, 'an island in the desert'. I could not rid myself of the feeling that she was trying not only to get over something but to escape from something. It would be interesting, I felt, to see what she did after the war. It was surprising to discover now that she had spent four years buried in the country with an ageing mother.

'Wasn't it very dull?' I asked.

'There was no one else to do it.'

Or rather there was nothing else she thought more worth doing. People don't sacrifice themselves unless they want to. I watched her as we talked. There were lines now between mouth and nostril. In a way it was a more interesting face, but there was an air of strain. She refused a cigarette. 'I only smoke after meals,' she said. Was that in self-defence to stop being a chain-smoker? Because her hands were idle she had developed a trick of twiddling a curl of hair behind her ear. A sudden gust of wind blew a plastic ashtray on to the floor; she started. Her nerves were definitely on edge.

We had champagne for dinner. 'This is like old times,' she said. We chattered about mutual friends, reminding ourselves of this and the other joke. She was gay and friendly. By and large she was the friendliest person I have ever known. It is easy to explain why you dislike a person, it is not difficult to explain why you're in love with someone, but it is very hard to explain what it is that makes you really like a person. I think that in her case it was that warm, fresh friendliness. I wished that I were disembarking in Dominica.

'Why don't you? It's not too late to change your mind,' she said.

I shook my head.

'I'm on a job. I've got all the dope I need on Dominica.'

'You know it well then.'

'As well as you can know any place where you haven't lived.'

'Tell me about it.'

I shrugged.

'It's a funny place. It's an island of contradictions and of contrasts. Its mountains are its pride and beauty. When the sun shines you wonder how green can have so many shades, but half the time you can't see the mountains because of cloud; the mountains attract the rain, and the rain makes the valleys fertile; the best fruit in the world is grown here, but the rain washes away the roads and the peasants can only market their produce by carrying it to the coast upon their heads. One thing cancels out another. The island's always in the red. It's a curious place. It attracts misfits and eccentrics.'

'Misfits and eccentrics.' She repeated the phrase in the same way that six years back she had repeated the phrase 'an island in the desert' as though it were the clue to something.

'When were you there last?' she asked.

'Two years ago.'

'Did you meet a man called Douglas Eliot?'

'Indeed I did.'

In a way he was a typical Dominican, an ex-Army officer on the edge of thirty who had come out with a pension and a small private income and large plans to make coffee pay. The plans came to nothing, but he stayed on. He was tall, blond, with a florid complexion and large features. He walked with a roll. He looked and probably was an athlete who was letting himself grow flabby. I had enjoyed his company. He had been a prisoner in the Second War; I had been one in the First. We compared experiences, we discussed books about prison life. I asked him if he'd read E.E. Cummings's *The Enormous Room*. 'No,' he said, but he knew Cummings's poetry. He had read a surprising amount of modern poetry. We were talking about Dylan Thomas when someone interrupted us.

'What's he doing there?' she asked.

'Not very much.'

'Is he married?'

'He wasn't then.'

'Any entanglement?'

'Nothing of any consequence.'

'What does he do all day?'

'His place has an acre or two of ground. That means some daily chores. He plays a little tennis. He's in the club every night.'

'Is he drinking?'

'Everyone drinks in Dominica. He does his share. Why are you so interested?'

'I briefed him for the Commando mission that he got captured on.'

'I didn't know he was a Commando.'

'No? Well, he might not mention it.'

She said it on an off-hand note, but it had an undercurrent of something I could not place. I had never seen her so absorbed by anything.

'It shouldn't be difficult to find him, should it?' she continued.

'The easiest thing possible. He's at the Paz every morning by eleven.'

'What's the Paz?'

'A bar attached to a hotel. You might call it "The Beachcombers Arms".'

'Will you take me there tomorrow?'

'Of course. It's where I'd have gone anyhow.'

My ship sailed for St. Vincent in the afternoon. The Paz was the likeliest place for me to pick up the threads of gossip.

We dropped anchor next morning soon after eight.

It was not actually raining when we went ashore, but the sky had a sodden look and mists lay low along the valley.

'Is it often like this?' she asked.

269

'Too often. It's what gets people down. They feel imprisoned, shut in by all these mountains that they never see.'

She booked into her hotel, then we toured the town. Roseau with its low dun-coloured houses and its puddled streets looked dingy. Even the market-place was drab. Within an hour we had seen it all.

'Let's go to the Paz,' she said.

Though it was only a little after ten, already there were seven men at the bar. They were variously dresssed in khaki trousers, bush shirts and shorts. They were white or white enough to pass as white. In the centre of the line was a man in a gabardine suit that though unpressed was relatively clean.

'That's him,' I said.

'I know.'

'Shall I bring him over?'

'Please.'

I walked across. I let my hand fall on his shoulder. He lifted his head, blinked, tried to focus me. I introduced myself. 'Of course, it is. Why, what the hell,' he said.

'Will you have a drink?' I asked.

'Why not.'

Because he was fair-haired, it was not immediately apparent that he had not shaved that morning. His polka-dot red tie was knotted so high that its first inch was crumpled. He was not so much grubby as ill-kempt. He smelt, but not offensively, of rum. Two years ago he had looked flabby. He was bloated now.

'What'll you have?' I asked.

'The wine of the country. Rum and water.'

I gave the order to the barmaid.

'There's someone here who knows you. Would you like to join us?'

He swung round on his stool, glanced, then stared, then started.

'Why, so there is,' he said. He walked across to her. 'Why, look who's here,' he said.

They did not shake hands. They looked at each other very straight.

'The small back room near Baker Street,' he said.

'The small back room near Baker Street,' she echoed.

There was a sudden dramatic tension in the air. I remembered that the London Headquarters of her outfit had been near Baker Street.

'You haven't changed,' he said.

'Nor've you, at least not much.'

'We can cut that out, can't we?'

'I spotted you at once.'

'That's a relief, anyhow.'

His voice had a half-sneer to it. The barmaid brought the drinks and he sat down. He put both hands to his glass. They were long, narrow-fingered, wide, short-nailed, well-cared-for hands.

'Only my second today. I'm never quite normal till I've had my third,' he said.

'I've always wondered what had happened to you,' she said.

'The Germans got me.'

'I knew that; but afterwards.'

'They put me in a prison camp.'

'And then?'

'That was all there was to it.'

'I see.'

'What else could there have been to it.'

'I don't know. I wondered.'

271

'What could you have heard to make you wonder.'

'Nothing. I just did wonder.'

'You've not been sent here by those boys in Baker Street,'

'How could I?'

'Aren't you with them still?'

'I don't even know if they exist.'

'What happened to you, then.'

'I was posted to Baghdad. I was there two years. Then Daddy died. I came home to look after my mother.'

'What are you doing here?'

She told him what she had told me. There was a pause. He seemed to want to say something, but thought better of it. She took up the lead.

'That small back room near Baker Street. February 1944. Six years and it seems yesterday. I'll never forget the way you looked when you came in; so buoyant, on top of everything.'

'And so I was. Is that so surprising? After all those months of training to have the chance I'd prayed for, a genuine commando mission: to be dropped behind the lines in France. And it all turned upon this interview. Did you guess how desperately keen I was to make a good impression?'

'That's why they chose me for that job, because I could spot those whose hearts were in it.'

And as part of that job, she had taken, as I had for mine, an interrogation course. We had both learnt how to extract the truth from prisoners and from suspects. I knew what she was doing, creating a mood in which he would find himself making admissions without knowing it.

'You were the exact type that we were looking for,' she said.'I knew that from the start. There wasn't any real need for an interview, but I was having such a good time gossiping.'

'Don't you think I was too.'

'Do you remember saying …?' She had started him on a trail of reminiscence, leading him to recall this, to recall that. I might not have been there at all. I signalled to the barmaid for another round. He barely acknowledged its arrival.

'How long did we go on gossiping?' she said.

'Over forty minutes.'

'And with all those other candidates outside.'

They laughed together. He was utterly relaxed, and off his guard. The tension gone. She had done a lovely job, got him where she wanted him.

'Do you remember your promise that if I came back safe, my first night home you'd dine with me?' he said.

'Of course.'

Their voices had grown soft. His face wore a brooding look. He had become in memory the volunteer of twenty-five on the threshold of high adventure. What had happened in six years to turn that brisk young officer into this rum-sodden beachcomber? Why had the bright steel rusted?

'As I walked away up Baker Street,' he said, 'the sun was shining. It was one of those miraculous February days when summer seems round the corner. The world lay at my feet. In a week I should be across the Channel. It was a short mission, a few messages to be delivered, a few reports to be received; by the end of the month I should be back, dining at some corner table. Life was a shop window waiting to be rifled.'

He paused and shrugged. 'I haven't felt that way since,' he said.

'Was it all that bad in prison?'

'Oh, no, it wasn't that.' He checked. He looked at her enquiringly.

'You really haven't heard?' he asked.

'Heard what?'

'What happened afterwards.'

'What could I hear?'

He shrugged, laughed ruefully.

'And I'd supposed you had. I'd assumed you had. That you must have, being in that racket. I'd wondered how you'd felt. I dreaded to know. Yet I ached to know. It was the one thing that mattered, how you felt about it, how you judged me. And now to realize that you'd never heard.'

'You'd better tell me, hadn't you?'

'I suppose I had.'

He leant forward across the table, on his elbows, his glass between his hands. Yes, she had got him where she wanted him. He was hypnotized. I felt I had no business there, but was afraid that if I moved I should break the spell.

'Have you read *Odette?* he said.

'No, but I know about it.'

'You know what the Germans did if you had any information they could use. Well, I broke down under it.'

It was the most sensational admission I had ever heard, and it could not have been made less dramatically; there was no self-pity in his voice.

'I'd always thought that when the pain became too great you just passed out,' he said. 'I didn't, and my nerve broke.'

'What happened then?'

'Nothing. I'd served their purpose. I'd told them all I knew. I was a prisoner like any other.'

'No special treatment?'

'I could have had, I suppose. But they didn't press me. I was a coward, not a traitor. I wouldn't broadcast for them. I was sent to an ordinary camp. You can imagine how I felt after the D-day landings, wondering how many Englishmen I'd killed. I wanted to get away by myself, and of course I couldn't. I wanted to get drunk, but I was only allowed to cash small cheques. I could only afford to get drunk once a week.'

'And after the war?'

'Something I've never understood. When the Germans collapsed, I started to worry on my own account. I'd got over my sense of guilt, or at least the acuteness of it. What was done was done and we were winning. In a few weeks I should be back in England. I began to wonder how much was known about me. Surely something must be. I'd given away valuable information. References must have appeared in Intelligence reports. Some of them would fall into Allied hands. I was really frightened.

'Can you imagine how I felt back in England, being fêted as a returned hero, having to lie and lie? Each week I read about some new traitor who'd been arrested; someone who'd talked over the wireless or given away information. Sooner or later they'd get round to me. I pictured the disgrace, the court martial, the prison sentence. I toyed with the idea of suicide. I avoided my old friends; I sat in a dark corner of my club drinking the afternoon away. I'd talk to strangers in a bar. I made no effort to find myself a job. I laid in a store of sleeping pills instead. And then the surprise came—a letter from the War Office, awarding me the honorary rank of captain in recognition of my exceptional services, and an annuity of £500.

'It was a mistake, of course. But I'd have been a fool not to turn it to account. I'd no need now to hunt myself a job. That pension with the small private income that I had would let me escape from England, away from my fellow countrymen and all their talk about the war and what they'd done in it. I got my atlas out. The West Indies were a long way off. The war had scarcely touched them. There'd be very few ex-soldiers there. If there had been no currency regulations, I'd have gone to a French island, Martinique or Guadeloupe. But Dominica's not too bad a substitute. And that's what put the water into this coconut,' he concluded.

He had told his story quietly, calmly, his eyes fixed all the time on her, completely indifferent to my presence.

'What about your music? You told me that you wanted to become a pianist,' she said.

He laughed. 'That's another reason why I decided to come out here. I wanted to forget that ambition by making it impossible.

A piano won't stand this climate. Insects eat the felt.'

'So you don't do anything?'

'Nothing that I'd have called anything ten years ago. I'm thirsty.

Won't you change your mind and have a real drink now?'

She shook her head. 'Too early, I'm afraid.'

'Too early. I'd have thought too late. I can't drink alone. I'll rejoin my friends.'

He rose and held out his hand, his long, well-tended hand that alone had survived the change.

'I've always hoped we'd meet again,' he said. 'I've often thought about that small back room near Baker Street, and the man I was that day. You are the last person who ever saw that man; I'm glad to have got this off my chest. You're the only person in the world I could have told it to. I'm glad you haven't changed, that nothing's happened to make *you* different. I wished I could have made that date. Good luck.'

He moved over to the bar, perched himself upon the stool and

276

caught the bar-girl's eye. He didn't give an order. She took his glass and filled it.

'Let's go,' Lily said.

We had been barely an hour in the Paz, but Dominica, in that short time had staged one of its transformations. The sky had cleared. The clouds had lifted from the lower mountains. The puddled streets were glistening in the sunlight, the dun-coloured buildings wore a gleam of gold.

'Let's take a drive,' I said.

We drove out to the Morne, a high hill behind the town. There was a seat there, and we left the car. Below us stretched the broad green valley with its neat rows of lime trees divided every twenty yards by the tall thin galba trees that stood as windbreakers. It looked very fresh and clean after the rain, and Roseau had lost its lack of colour with the general effect of amber relieved here and there by the bright scarlet of the tulip tree and the vivid canary yellow of the Poui.

'Do you see how this place could grow on you?' I asked.

She nodded. During the drive out she had scarcely spoken.

'What did you make of all that?' she asked.

'Did he really look the way he said in '44?'

'Yes, just like that.'

'That talk about a date, was it all on his side, or did you feel something too?' She pursed her lips.

'I lied when I told you that I came out here with the idea of settling. I didn't. I heard he was here. I came out to see him.'

I had the sensation of something under my heart going round and over, an acute sense of sympathy and fellow feeling. Basically her life must be all wrong. Otherwise she wouldn't have let herself vegetate in a Wessex village, otherwise I should not have noticed those signs of strain. It was pathetic to think of her, wondering during those long slow passing years whether that bright young officer met for forty minutes in a small back room near Baker Street might not be the solution to her problems; to think of her corning all that way, and to find this; now she had nothing left.

I sought for the right words of sympathy; sought and could not find them.

She spoke first.

'Did anything in that story strike you as odd?' she asked.

'That pension did.'

'I thought it would. Exceptional services indeed. I'll say they were. They were worth five divisions to us, at the least. You saw something, didn't you, of "deception" when we were in Baghdad?'

I nodded. 'Deception'—the giving of false information to the enemy, was a highly organized industry in World War II. Myself, I only touched its fringe. But I saw enough to recognize how intricate a game it was. We once found an enemy agent with a wireless transmitter. We put him behind bars and continued to operate his set, sending misleading information to the Germans. The Germans discovered we were doing this; so we had to start sending a different kind of information. We had, in fact, to start telling them the truth, because they would not believe it. Had they discovered later that we knew they knew, we would have returned to telling lies. It became most involved. But, as I said, I only touched the fringe. She was right inside it. I waited for her explanation.

'In February 1944,' she said, 'during D-day planning, it became highly important to confuse and mislead the Germans. Some very ingenious devices were employed. You've read of the actor who was dressed up like Montgomery and sent to Gibraltar. His presence was reported to Berlin. The Germans couldn't believe an invasion was imminent when the British Commander-in-Chief was in Gibraltar. There were quite a few plans like that. My chief thought out a very pretty one. We'd drop behind the lines a Commando volunteer whose nerves we had reason to believe would give way under torture. We would prime him with false information that he would believe was true; then we would warn the Germans through one of our double agents. He would be captured at once.

To begin with, he'd be brave enough. When he broke down, his subsequent sense of guilt and of remorse would be so acute that the Germans would be convinced that he had told the truth. The success of the scheme depended on the prisoner's own belief that he had betrayed his countrymen.'

'You couldn't be sure he would break down.'

'I know, but even so his capture would be useful. That double agent was worth two divisions. The Germans were getting restive. It was high time he reinstated himself with a piece of genuine information.'

Inside myself I shivered. I had known that such things were threatened, I had been told such things were done, but this was the first actual example I had had.

'I thought I was unshockable,' I said. 'I'm not.'

'How do you think I felt? At first I wouldn't touch it, but they talked me into it. War was war, they said. You couldn't make an omelette without breaking eggs. Generals made feint attacks, sent whole battalions to their death. "Suppose," they said, "you, as a general, had ordered a feint attack upon a certain hill. The attack could only be effective if the regiment making it was convinced that the whole issue of the battle depended on its success. You'd lie to the colonel, wouldn't you?" That was the argument they used and they were right. War's basically a crime.

Use the sharpest weapon.'

She spoke bitterly in the same tone that I had heard her use at Baghdad all those years ago when she had defended the use of buzz-bombs.

'What made you suspect he would break down?' I asked.

'Did you notice his hands? He told me that he wanted to become a pianist. The artist, in the last analysis, will sacrifice anything, even his country, for his art.'

'Was that all you went on?'

'No, of course not. I had to make more certain first. You only heard half the story. It was true about that date when he came back, but there was a whole lot more to it than that. We had a date that very evening. I forced his hand on that one. He asked me where I'd like to dine. I suggested Boulestin. It was underground and there was spasmodic bombing. It was a very cosy dinner. I felt that I had known him all my life. "Now what about a night-club?" he suggested. I shook my head. "My flat's quite close. I've a piano. Let's go there." I had it all planned out, you see. I wanted to hear him play.

'He played … well, he was out of practice and I'm no judge but I watched his hands, the way his finger-tips now struck, now caressed the keys … I had no doubt at all he had the artistic temperament. He played to me for half an hour. "Now you deserve a drink," I said. I had an open fire and we sat before it. "I promised not to talk shop," he said. "But won't you put me out of my misery. Do I get that job?" "Of course you do," I told him. Perhaps I made a mistake in telling him. It was just too much for him: pride in his own achievement, the imminence of danger and of parting, the growing intimacy between us, it was too heady a wine. He started to make love to me.'

She paused, she shrugged. 'He was going to danger and I was

sending him—to worse than danger. I owed it to him to make his last hours happy. Women have a sense of sacrifice to men going overseas; they want to give something too. Besides, in my case, how shall I put it, but that side of things … I loved my husband. I was in love with him, but when you're young and inexperienced and unformed … it's more general I think than women will admit … the actual act of love meant nothing to me, except for the happiness it gave him. I wondered why there was so much talk about it … You can be very nonchalant, you know, with regard to something that means very little to you when you know that it means a lot to someone else; so that when Douglas started to make love to me, I thought, "I must give him all the happiness I can." But then …'

She paused again.

'I don't know what it was,' she said. 'The moment, the mood, the music, something special about him, his hands perhaps, that sense of touch, but suddenly, deliriously, I knew what all that talk was about in books. It shattered me.

'He had to leave early in the morning to get back to camp. Can you imagine how I felt as I watched him go down the street; to have found him at last and then to have to lose him and under such conditions? Can you imagine the torture that I went through all that day? I tried to console myself with the thought that I wasn't sending him to death. I repeated the arguments my seniors had given me, that we weren't living in the days of the Crusades, of Arthurian tournaments. What was one Commando officer against five divisions? I reminded myself that I had taken on this job, that I was a sailor's daughter, that I had been trained to believe in duty, that my father had risked his life, my husband given his life for his country. Who was I now to shirk my duty?

'I believe actually, in the last analysis, that if I hadn't been involved myself, I'd have called the whole thing off, told my superiors that it was a dirty business and walked out on it, but my own personal happiness was at stake. I couldn't put that before my duty. I sent his name in. A week later he was in German hands.'

She paused. She smiled wryly.

'Maybe it was telepathy,' she said. 'Maybe we should find if we could get the exact day and hour, that it was at the precise moment his nerve broke that mine did too. It was a complete collapse.' She shrugged.

I had the explanation now of all in her that had puzzled me, that had puzzled all of us.

'You know what happened after that, or you can guess,' she said'I couldn't take it any more. I had to get away from all that office stood for, as far away as possible. That's why they sent me to Baghdad. I might be able to forget in a whole new world. I couldn't, though. I never have. All the time it's haunted me, the memory of that small back room and what I did there. I wondered what I'd done to him, but I didn't dare find out. I made my mother's old age an excuse for staying where I was, but I had to face up to it in the end. Do you understand now why I came out here? I had to know the answer.'

And now that she knew it, what came next, I wondered. I offered such consolation as I could.

'You shouldn't feel too badly,' I began. 'There's every kind of casualty in war. Think of the men who are maimed and blinded, who'll never know a painless hour till they die. There are many worse lives than a beachcomber's.'

She made no reply. She leant back against the seat, her hands clasped behind her head. I had no idea what she was thinking.

'Listen,' I said. 'Why not move back on to that boat, come on to St. Vincent with me and let's beat it up. There's a lot of fun

282

going there.'

She shook her head. 'He's here because of me; he's my responsibility.'

'Surely it's rather late ...'

She interrupted me.

'He's barely thirty-two, he's basically strong. He's not an alcoholic, simply a man who drinks too much. He could snap out of that. If he had a reason; most illnesses are mental. You know that.'

My spirits sank. There it went. That psychopathic jargon. The belief that a man was cured the moment he knew what was wrong with him.

'Do you really think it's going to make all that difference to be told that he saved five divisions, that he did perform exceptional services.'

'Are you mad? How could I tell him that?' She swung round and her eyes were angry. 'What effect do you think that would have, to be told he'd been hand-picked for cowardice? If anything would drive a man to drink that would.'

'What are you going to tell him then?'

'That I've never loved anyone but him, that I've tried to forget him but I couldn't; that I've come out only to see him, that I don't care what he did: that he showed more courage in attempting that kind of mission than ninety-nine men in a hundred. I shall remind him that we're both young, that we've the whole of our lives ahead of us.'

I was appalled; that persistent belief of women that they could reform a man; all those films and novels about the bad man being redeemed by the good woman's love, and the way it was all confused with the maternal instinct and woman's capacity for sacrifice. I could see now where it had been so important that the admission should come from him.

'Do you think you'll be able to make that sound convincing?' I asked her.

'Of course I shall. It's true.'

There was a look in her eyes that I had never seen before. 'Do you think I've come out only on his account? You're crazy. I can't do without him. They talk about the one man for the one woman. I don't say that's true. I think for some women, certainly for myself, there are a dozen men who might be right. But when they have found a man who is right for them, they're spoilt for the eleven others. When they've found that man, they've got to stick to him. That's what I've got to do.'

She rose to her feet. She stood straight like a spear. Her eyes were shining. She was transformed, passionate, vibrant, vivid. For the first time I was seeing the real woman.

'Do you think I'd have come here, if I wasn't desperate; if I hadn't experimented, tried every device, yes, every one. I'm as much a war casualty as he. But we can save each other. We've got to save each other. I can save us both.'

Her voice rang like a challenge, like the proud acceptance of a challenge. Behind her the mountains towered in the sunlight, their jagged peaks were sharp against the sky, deep green against deep blue. It was hard to believe that only an hour ago the landscape had been grey with cloud, a symbol of despair and gloom, a fitting backcloth for a beachcomber. There was a sense now of a whole world reborn.

'I've got to make a go of it,' she said. In her voice there was the glow of victory.

'You will,' I said. 'You will.'

1952

Sources

'A Stranger.' First published in *Pleasure* (Grant Richards, 1921). Copyright Alec Waugh 1921.

'An Unfinished Story.' First published in *Myself When Young* (Grant Richards, 1923). Copyright Alec Waugh 1923.

'The Making of a Matron' and 'The Last Chukka.' First published in *The Last Chukka* (Chapman & Hall, 1928). Copyright Alec Waugh 1928.

'Tahiti Waits.' First published in *Hot Countries* (Chapman & Hall, 1930). Copyright Alec Waugh 1930.

'A Pretty Case for Freud' and '"Ambition" Bevan.' First published in *Eight Short Stories* (Cassell, 1937). Copyright Alec Waugh 1937.

'Bien Sûr.' First published in *His Second War* (Cassell, 1944). Copyright Alec Waugh 1944.

'A Luckless Lebanese,' 'The Woman Who Knew Frank Harris,' 'A Bunch of Beachcombers,' and 'The Wicked Baronet.' First published in *Where the Clocks Chime Twice* (Cassell, 1952). Copyright Alec Waugh 1952.

'Circle of Deception.' First published in *Esquire* magazine, March 1953. Copyright Alec Waugh 1953.

A NOTE ON THE AUTHOR

Alec Waugh was born in London in 1898 and educated at Sherborne Public School, Dorset. Waugh's first novel, *The Loom of Youth* (1917), is a semi-autobiographical account of public school life that caused some controversy at the time and led to his expulsion; Waugh was the only boy ever to be expelled from The Old Shirburnian Society.

Despite setting this questionable record, Waugh went on to become the successful author of over fifty works and lived in many exotic locations throughout his life, many of which became the settings for future texts. He was also a noted wine connoisseur and campaigned to make the 'cocktail party' a regular feature of 1920s social life.

Alec Waugh was the elder brother of writer Evelyn Waugh, and son of author, critic and publisher, Arthur Waugh. He died in 1981.